Briar Hill Road

Briar Hill Road

HOLLY JACOBS

Ilex Books 2018
ISBN-13: 978-0-9992736-3-0
ISBN-10: 0-9992736-3-9

Previous Published as The House on Briar Hill Road
By: Harlequin; 1st edition (October 1, 2007)
ISBN-10: 0373654197
ISBN-13: 978-0373654192

Dear Reader,

Some books are closer to an author's heart than others. This is one of those books. We lost my mother-in-law, the heart of our family, in 2004 to breast cancer. Since then, another close friend has been touched by this disease. Writing this book is my way to honor these strong women. It's also an opportunity to remind every reader to practice breast self-examination and to have regular mammograms.

This was one of my first Romance+ Books. Books that are about a woman's journey…a journey that includes romance. I love the realism in this type of story because though a couple finds their happily-ever-after, it doesn't exempt them from pain and rocky patches. I think all relationships, no matter how loving, have tough times and are tested.

The House on Briar Hill Road deals with the ups and downs of Hayden and Brian's relationship. It explores the question of what makes a family. Is it tied together through genetics, or is there something else involved? Is it tied through love? Brian and Hayden find their answer, and the entire family learns to embrace life, love and live out loud!

I hope you enjoy *Briar Hill Road!*

And when you're finished, I hope you pick up some of my other Romance+ stories: *Just One Thing, Carry Her Heart, These Three Words, Hold Her Heart and Same Time Next Summer.*

Holly Jacobs

For every woman who's fought against breast cancer and to the families who have fought next to them.

Most especially for my amazing mother-in-law, Dorothy, who dealt with the disease with grace and dignity, but ultimately lost her battle in 2004.

And for Nancy, a wonderfully talented lady, who battled and won! I'm so proud to claim such valiant women as more than friends, but as my family.

A special thanks to everyone who works for a cure, and to Hospice, a special organization that allows people to die in the comfort of their own home, surrounded by those who love them.

Chapter One

Despite being a nurse, Hayden hated the way hospitals smelled. It had nothing to do with antiseptics and medicines—as a nurse she was used to those scents. No, it had everything to do with the odor of fear that clung to the patients.

A fear of an illness.

A fear of pain.

In some cases, a fear that came from knowing that time was short.

Hayden's fear wasn't for herself, but for the woman in the wheelchair she was pushing. Kathleen Conway. Her surrogate mother. Her mentor. Her friend.

Hayden wanted to say something reassuring. She wanted to say something that would comfort Kathleen, but she couldn't think of anything. Kathleen had always had a way of finding the right words. Hayden remembered one of her own most vulnerable moments, and Kathleen had been so eloquent. Even after all this time, the words had stuck.

"Kathleen, I've been thinking about the past."

Kathleen nodded. "Me, too. I keep seeing the little girl who knocked on my door. I'm so proud of the woman she grew into, despite all the hard times she lived through."

"You once told me *Life isn't about where you go—it's about the journey. You can live life quietly, watching the world go by too afraid to*

*take a chance and fail. Or you can throw caution to the wind and live life
to the fullest. Take chances. Sure, you'll fall on your face sometimes, but
sometimes you'll reach new heights. Either way, just trying will take you
to new, unexpected horizons.*

"Take the chance.

"Live life out loud.

"Don't just watch it from the sidelines."

The automatic doors swung open and the hospital smell
was blown away by an April spring breeze as they headed for the
ambulance bay. "Do you remember telling me that?"

Kathleen looked back over her shoulder at Hayden.

The older woman's once bright red hair had faded to a steely
gray, but her eyes still sparkled bright blue. And her smile carried
all the warmth and caring that it always had, despite her current
condition. "It was so long ago. I can't believe you remember."

"I haven't forgotten any of it. The good times and the bad. I
remember them all." Hayden leaned around the chair and tucked
the blanket tighter against Kathleen's legs.

When she stood up again she immediately spotted her husband as he came into view at the back of the van. Brian towered
over the transport driver who lowered the big steel ramp, which
was accompanied by a loud beeping noise.

Despite all the years, despite everything they'd been through
and everything Hayden knew they were going to be going
through, seeing Brian settled something inside her, filling a void
that was present whenever they were apart.

Hayden pushed the wheelchair onto the ramp. "It's time to go
home, Kathleen."

Brian leaned down and kissed Kathleen's cheek. "Hi, Mom."
The ramp lifted the chair level with the floor of the van.

"Every day, I try to look back and remember a happier time.
Today, I was thinking about Halloween," Kathleen said, more

to herself than to Brian or Hayden, who, along with the driver, pushed the chair into place, then clamped it into safety straps.

The driver went up to the front and started the van leaving the three of them in the back. Silence weighed heavily in the small space, bearing down and pressing against Hayden's heart. She felt as if all her words had now dried up, especially in Brian's presence.

The van moved from the hospital parking lot onto the busy Pittsburgh street.

Kathleen finally broke the silence. "Do you remember when Hayden came to the door that Halloween, Bri?"

October 1975

There were a few things Brian Conway was sure of. One was that he was probably too old to go trick-or-treating.

Well, no probably about it.

Twelve was too old to knock on strangers' doors and beg for candy. He should be out with his old gang of friends, running around his Upper St. Clair neighborhood, toilet papering people's houses.

But his mother had actually smiled when she started talking about trick-or-treating last month. And one of the other things Brian was sure of was that his mom hadn't smiled very much since his dad left them. Her happiness was why Brian found himself dressed like someone from a biker gang.

He looked into his bedroom mirror with disgust. This certainly wasn't his proudest moment, but his mom seemed excited about driving him into Bridgeville and watching him go from house to house. And since they'd moved from their old house after his dad left two months ago, he didn't have anyone to really go out with around here anyway.

This was all his father's fault.

Brian hated his dad. His stomach felt pinched and it burned when he thought about how much he hated his dad.

His mom told him that the divorce was between her and his dad, and she went on and on about how even if she wasn't going to be married to him anymore, his dad was still his dad.

He could tell his mom didn't like him hating his dad, so Brian stopped talking about it, but that didn't change how he felt. He still hated him. He was only twelve, but he wouldn't even call him Dad anymore. He called him Adam. *Adam* hated that and said Brian had to learn to show respect, but Brian didn't care.

Adam had never had time for him. Brian could live with that. But Adam had hurt his mom because he had a girlfriend. His mom didn't think he knew that, but he did. And it just showed how stupid Adam was, because there was no girl better than his mom.

He glanced into the mirror one more time, and pasted a smile on his face.

"Mom, you ready?" The doorbell rang before she could answer. "Hey, someone's at the door." He took off down the stairs.

"Don't you open that door until I'm there," she called, hurrying after him.

He gave her a grim look. "I'm almost thirteen."

"Yes, but we're new to the neighborhood and you need to be careful."

She paused, and gave him one of those mushy mom smiles. "Your costume is cute." She kissed his forehead.

"Mom." He wiped at the spot, hoping there was no telltale lipstick marks as his mom opened the door.

"Trick-or-treat," a small ghost cried out.

Now, he could only see a dirty sheet and sneakers, but Brian knew who it was. Cootie MacNulty. She lived down the block in an old, beat-up looking house. The school bus picked them both up at the corner, but they never talked to each other. She was several years younger than him. And she kind of hung around by a row of hedges, and only stepped out when the bus approached.

Her costume was sad. A sheet with two holes for her to look out of. She hadn't even cut the holes. There were rips where the cuts should have been.

Brian felt a funny twisting in his gut when he stared at her.

"Here, kid." Brian grabbed a Snickers bar from the bowl nearby and held it out to her. "Where's your bag?"

"I don't got one."

"How can you trick-or-treat without a bag?"

She held out her hand. "I'll just stick it in my pocket."

"But it will get mashed."

"My pants are way too big for me, so it won't, least not much."

"But what about the other houses you'll go to?"

"There's only a couple more I can walk to."

Brian felt worse. He knew the kid had it rough. Her clothes were never right and they were always dirty. No one ever sat by her on the bus. When she got on each day the sing-song taunts of Cootie MacNulty would start.

Brian was the new kid at the school, but it didn't take much to see that she was the one every kid picked on.

It had been a few weeks before he even knew she had a name other than Cootie. One of the teachers had called her Hayden.

His casual disinterest had changed that very morning.

By the time they were on the bus, most of the seats had at least one person in them. He'd found a spot midway back, but no one would let Cootie sit with them. When she got to the back of the bus, Marc Barrister, one of the cool eighth graders who always took the best, very back seat, tripped her. She fell and smacked her head pretty hard. While she was on the floor, Marc had whacked her on the head again, because he said he wanted to see if the cooties would fall out of her hair. The whole bus was laughing as Hayden got back up.

Brian knew all about the pecking order on the bus and in school. And he knew Marc was at the top, and Hayden was at the bottom. If Brian hoped to stay somewhere safely in the middle, he knew he should just shut up and let it go. But for some reason that he didn't understand, he'd not only told all the kids to lay off Hayden, but he'd punched Marc in the face. Hard.

Really hard.

After that, the other kids cleared a seat for him and Hayden.

His mom wouldn't get the detention slip until Monday. But Brian wasn't going to dwell on that. And there was no way he was going to tell her about it and ruin the weekend. He figured the detention was worth it because on the bus ride home today, the empty seat was waiting, and everyone had left Hayden alone. He just wasn't sure his mom would agree that this was a case where fighting was a good thing.

Brian still felt funny when he looked at Cootie … Hayden. Sort of guilty. It was the same sort of feeling he got knowing he had detention and wasn't about to tell his mom. It was a feeling like maybe he should have done more sooner, should do more, but he didn't really want to.

So there she stood on his porch and the feeling was only getting stronger. She had to trick-or-treat in a dirty sheet with nothing to even hold her candy in?

"Mom, that's Hayden. She lives down the block. Can I get her a bag or something?"

"Sure, honey." His mom turned to the ghost. "Hayden, if you'll wait a minute Brian will go get you a bag from the kitchen."

The kid tugged at the sheet, straightening out the eyeholes enough to see out of, but didn't budge from her spot on the porch. "That's okay. My pocket's fine."

"It's just a bag," Brian said sort of angrily.

"I'm okay," she replied in her squeaky voice.

He didn't know what else to say or what to do, so he opened the screen door and handed over the candy bar.

She grabbed it by the opposite end, as if she were afraid he was the one with cooties. "Thank you. And thanks for on the bus."

Brian didn't answer her. Instead, he allowed the screen door to slam back into place with a satisfying thwack.

"You're welcome," his mom finally said, giving him a have-you-forgotten-your-manners? sort of glance.

Brian still didn't say anything as Hayden turned and stepped off the porch, then walked down their drive. He closed the big door with far more force than necessary as his frustration bubbled over. "The other day I was in the yard working on my tree house and heard somethin'. It was her. She had a half sandwich, so I asked if she wanted a pop. I'd snuck a few from the house."

He realized what he'd admitted, but his mom didn't say anything about it. She stood waiting for him to finish. "So I asked if she wanted one. She was eating peanut butter."

His mom quickly nodded. He knew she'd understand that. His mom just got things. Well, most things. She didn't understand why he hated Adam. And he wasn't sure she would understand that he had to hit Marc on the bus. But she got most everything else, like how you needed a drink if you were eating peanut butter.

"She wouldn't take it, like she wouldn't take that bag. Guess she was right, though. She won't get much candy on our street. You think she'll try to go farther by herself?" Brian couldn't help worrying about her. "She's just a kid, you know."

He was in seventh grade, she was only in third. She was little and couldn't even take care of herself with bullies like Marc. What if someone messed with her while she trick-or-treated?

His mom ran her hand through his hair and gave him a repeat of that warm, mushy smile. He eyed her, trying to ward off the kiss that would surely follow. It must have worked because she didn't kiss him. His mom asked, "Maybe we could find out if she'd like to come with us?"

"Ya think she would?"

"We'll never know if you don't ask. Why don't you go catch up to her and see?"

"Yeah," he said, and bolted outside. Hayden was at the top of his driveway.

"Hey, kid," he started yelling before he'd gotten to her. "Want to go trick-or-treat with us? We're drivin' into Bridgeville. You'd get a lot more candy there than you will on this dead-end street."

For a minute, he thought she'd say yes, but then she shrugged and said, "I'm okay here." She looked like she was starting to walk away again.

Brian felt his anger rise. "Listen, kid, we're goin' anyway. My mom told me to ask you 'cause she thought you might like more candy, that's all."

Hayden studied him as if he were lying. "You're sure your mom says it's okay?"

"Yeah."

"But what if kids from school see you with me? They'll call you names, too."

"I'll just hit them like I did Marc."

She giggled. He'd never heard the kid laugh and kinda liked it.

"That was the best. He wasn't mean to me on the way home. Thank you."

Brian felt embarrassed. "No big deal. So will you come trick-or-treating?"

It was hard for ghosts to shrug because they had no shoulders, but this one managed it. "Sure."

"She's comin'," he yelled to his mom who was standing on the porch.

"*Ing*, Brian. *Ing*," his mom corrected. "Com*ing*. Noth*ing*. Someth*ing*. *Ings*. You keep forgetting the *g*."

His mom was picky about things like *ings* and *yas*.

"Com*ing*. She's coming—Right, kid?"

"Yes, thank you."

He led her back to his house. His mom was waiting at the door. "I'm so glad you're joining us." She knelt down and smiled at Hayden. "Why don't you phone home and make sure it's okay with your mother that you come along with us."

Hayden shrugged and looked at the wooden floor. "She won't care."

His mom touched Hayden's sheet-covered cheek. "I'd care if Brian went off with someone and didn't let me know." His mom's voice went all soft like it did when she worried about him hating his dad.

"She's not like you, Ma'am. My mom's passed out and won't even know I'm gone."

His mom looked surprised and seemed to think a minute, but then nodded and kept smiling. "Fine. If your mother is sleeping we won't disturb her, but run over with Brian and leave her a note, in case she wakes up and can't find you."

Hayden nodded, sending the eye holes slipping down to her cheeks. "Okay."

"Come on, kid," Brian said. "I'll get some paper for you."

It only took a second to write the note. He said to his mom, "We're goin' to run this over, then we can go."

"Go*ing*. You're going to run it over."

"That's what I said. You gotta watch out for my mom, kid. Soon she'll be correctin' your English, too. She's real picky."

"I heard that," his mom scolded, but she was smiling. She was almost like her old self.

"I know." Brian laughed, not because he'd been all that funny, but because his mom was smiling and he liked it. "You were supposed to. Come on, kid."

He caught Hayden's hand through the dirty sheet and pulled her toward the street. "Let's go. I want my candy."

Kathleen Conway watched as Brian ran from door to door with their little neighbor in tow.

Something about the bedraggled ghost tugged at her heart.

Kathleen's divorce had blindsided her. One day she was a happily married mom, the next, Adam was telling her he was leaving. He claimed that there wasn't another woman, but she knew there was. She'd heard through the grapevine about her.

Kathleen had felt as if she'd been moving through a fog ever since. She felt betrayed, but worse than that, she felt somehow demeaned. She'd gone through the motions, and tried to pretend everything was okay for Brian's sake, but it wasn't.

She wished she had family to call on, but it was only her and Brian and some distant relatives in Southampton, Ontario. All her friends were part of pairs, married and blissful. Some blatantly avoided her, and others made sympathetic noises, but she sensed distance, as if her divorce were somehow contagious. She hadn't kept up with any of them since her move from Upper St. Clair to Bridgeville, Pennsylvania, just outside Pittsburgh.

She'd started forging new friendships at St. Bartholomew Hospital, where she worked on the med-surg floor, but they were still new and tentative.

Maybe it was that sense of isolation that drew her to the little girl. It was clear from the few things Brian had said that she came from a hard situation at home.

Brian ran from the house to Kathleen, the small girl tripping along at his heels. "Mom, guess what, they were giving away the big Hershey bars at that house. Right, Hayden?"

The ghost nodded her agreement silently.

"We're goin' to the next one," Brian said, then they raced off before Kathleen could correct his grammar.

Hayden turned to follow Brian, but her sheet slipped off, stopping her in her tracks. As she tugged it back in place, Hayden looked over and grinned at Kathleen. Then she hurried after Brian.

It was obvious that Hayden wasn't thinking about her threadbare ghost costume, or a mother who drank too much. She was living in the moment. Happy to have found a house that gave out the big Hershey bars.

Maybe there was a lesson in that.

Kathleen realized that right now, at this very moment, she was totally content to watch the kids race from house to house.

More than content.

She was happy.

It was a good evening.

Maybe if she could figure out a way to hang on to it, to all the good moments, she'd learn to let go of the rest. She was tired of being depressed, of wondering if she could have done something different and made her marriage work. She wanted to be happy again. She wanted to enjoy what she had rather than pine for what she'd lost.

"Mom, Mom, hurry up. We've got to cross the street. That whole side's got their lights on."

Kathleen smiled. "I'm hurrying, kids. We'll go to all the houses you want. There's nothing else I'd rather do."

"See, she's comin', kid." Brian paused, looked at his mom and grinned. "Ing. She's com*ing*, kid."

Hayden pulled up her sheet and grinned at Kathleen as she parroted, "Yep, she's coming."

Kathleen laughed and took Brian's hand in one of hers and Hayden's in the other.

The world seemed brighter already.

Chapter Two

"That Halloween when you came to our house, everything changed. It was as if you'd always belonged with us." Kathleen's eyes were closed, as if she, indeed, were lost in that long-ago Halloween.

The van hit yet another pothole. Either the transport driver was aiming for every one on I-279 or the road that circled Pittsburgh was littered with them.

"Hey, take it easy," Brian yelled up at the man.

The driver mumbled some apology.

"Thanks, Brian." Hayden's hand slid across the bench seat, until it was almost touching his.

For a moment, Brian thought she was going to bridge the small gap that remained, but she didn't. And he didn't. The months of watching his mother's illness get worse had taken its toll on them both.

They'd each pulled away from the other, lost in their own misery. There didn't seem to be any emotion left as they sat on the same seat across from Kathleen's wheelchair.

Hayden kept to her own end of the bench and he kept to his. Those inches separating them seemed like miles and he didn't know how to fix it.

"I think it's going to snow," Kathleen said.

"Do you remember the snow day that first winter after you moved to Briar Hill Road?"

Brian remembered that after Hayden came trick-or-treating with them, his mom had changed. She seemed happier. Almost like her old self.

"I went to catch the bus," Hayden continued, "but Brian came out and got me. He said school was canceled and took me back to your house. You said it wasn't fair we got a day off and you didn't, so you called in sick to work."

Kathleen nodded. "When you get older, you'll have regrets, but I promise they won't be for the days you play hooky."

"It was a good day." Hayden used his mom's pet phrase. "You didn't have any sleds, so we used garbage bags and the three of us spent the afternoon out on the hill."

Hayden looked at him, waiting for him to join in. Needing him to help keep the conversation going.

"I refused to call it *sledding*. I called it *bagging*." He shrugged. "It sounds stupid now, but to a twelve-year-old it was an important difference."

His mom laughed.

"You called off work again that first winter Brian was at college when we got another big snow," Hayden continued. "We didn't go bagging, but we took that long walk down the road. Snowy days make me think of spending time with you."

"It was such a comfort having you with me when Brian left for TSU. Tennessee seemed so far away."

His mom had graduated from Tennessee State and she'd encouraged him to apply. They'd been so thrilled when he got in, until the realization hit them that he'd have to leave Pennsylvania. "It made it easier for me to leave, knowing you moved in with Mom."

Hayden chuckled. "I never really moved in. One day, I just didn't go home ... No, I take that back. The house I grew up in, the house my mother still lived in then, had never been home. I left it without a backward glance and moved in with you. My mother didn't even come looking for me. I've often wondered how long it took her to discover I was gone. She never said and I never asked. Before she went into the nursing home, we'd bump into each other on occasion, but we were strangers. That was fine with me. With you and Brian I'd found my home and my family."

Brian listened to Hayden and his mom reminisce about Hayden moving in and missing him. He'd missed them both, as well. He remembered coming home after he graduated....

May 1985

Brian pulled into the tar-and-chip driveway that led to the small white house he'd lived in since he was twelve.

He remembered leaving the big house in Upper St. Clair and moving to the much smaller one outside Bridgeville, just fifteen minutes southwest of Pittsburgh, Pennsylvania. He'd hated leaving his friends, hated the house they'd moved into. But as he sat in the car today and studied the story and a half, Cape Cod-style house with its window boxes, he felt only a sense of coming home.

Time changed things. He laughed at the less than profound thought.

The house's windows were framed by bright green shutters. They were just for show, just a decoration that couldn't be used to save the windows during a storm. But southwestern Pennsylvania was known for its occasional snowstorms and those rarely broke windows, so it didn't really matter.

He wasn't sure why he was thinking about shutters. Maybe it was easier than reflecting on the fact that the house seemed to have grown smaller since he'd left for college four years ago.

It seemed smaller now than it had over the holiday break.

Is that how it worked? When he graduated from high school everything seemed to have changed, and now that he'd graduated from Tennessee State, would everything continue to change even more?

When would it stop?

Did that diploma they'd handed him mere weeks ago alter things so drastically? He'd shifted from childhood to a quasimanhood while he was at college. He had to leave for California in three weeks, where he was starting a job working with troubled youths. He'd be the adult working with kids, which meant he'd jumped from quasi, to full-out manhood.

Grown.

Independent.

No longer relying on his mother's money, or the sporadic child-support checks Adam had sent over the last decade. The old pain no longer stabbed at him when he thought about his father. They talked on occasion, but there was no connection. Adam's focus was on his new family and he seemed eager to forget his past … forget Brian. That was okay with Brian.

He knew he should get out of the car, but he couldn't seem to move quite yet. He wanted a few more quiet moments.

He noticed that the oak tree that sat on the far side of the house was even bigger. It canopied the roof, keeping the house shaded now that the leaves were open again.

May was a beautiful time of year in Pennsylvania. He'd missed the changing seasons while he was at college. Down south in Tennessee the weather alternated between warm and hot. Things got almost as hot here, but there was more of an ebb and flow; freezing, cold, cool, warm, hot, then back down again.

Damn, it was good to be home, if only for a little while. He thought again about getting out of the car. Before he could actually move, the front door of the house flew open and Hayden rushed out, saving him from his mental meanderings.

"Kathleen, he's here," she called before she started running toward him.

He got out of the car and simply took her in.

She had on a strappy sort of wispy dress that looked totally too grown-up for the kid who'd spent her childhood dogging his heels. Her dark brown hair flew loose at her shoulders. There wasn't anything left of that girl in the young woman.

His axis tilted again with another unexpected reminder that things had changed.

But as she ran he noticed her feet were bare. And his world settled back into place. Some things might change, his perceptions might alter, but there were other things that would always be what they were.

Hayden was one of those things.

"Brian," she cried, throwing herself full-force into his arms. "You made it. I've been worried beyond belief."

"Worried about what, kid?"

She let go of him and pushed a thick piece of hair out of her eyes. "That you wouldn't make it in time."

"When have I ever let you down?"

"Never." She laughed then. That sound—more than the house, the shutters that didn't work or the tree that had grown—said *home* to him. It was the sound that had punctuated his teens.

When they were young, Hayden would follow him so stealthily he frequently forgot she was there. But then she'd laugh like that and everything else would fade.

At first the sound was sporadic, but as time went on, as their house became more and more her home, Hayden's laughter was frequent.

His mom came out of the house with a little less speed, but not a bit less pleased to see him. She smiled as she hurried to join them.

God, he'd missed them both. It seemed like an eternity since he'd been here over Christmas. He'd spent the spring break with friends down in Florida. At the time it had seemed like a great idea, but now, seeing these two women who meant so much to him, he realized he'd have probably had more fun here than he'd had there.

His mom looked more the same than Hayden did. Her hair, which had once been flaming red, had faded over the years. She was what now? In her midforties? Her hair no longer shouted red, just whispered the color it used to be under the increasing amount of soft gray. Other women might try to deny their age. But not his mom.

Kathleen Conway remained proud of what she was—who she was. She'd tried to pass that self-assurance on to both Hayden and himself. He'd like to think she'd succeeded with both of them.

"Brian." That's all she said as she reached him and stood in front of him—just his name. But he could read so much into those two syllables.

Hayden moved aside and let his mother have a turn at hugging him.

"It's good to have you home. Someone was nervous you'd be late." She glanced sideways at Hayden and smiled.

There was something between his mom and Hayden. It had been there that first night when the ghost of a girl had come trick-or-treating with them, and the connection had grown over the years. It had seemed right, knowing his mother and Hayden were together while he was so far away, busy growing up.

"If she looked out the window once, she looked a couple dozen times," his mom continued.

"You're exaggerating," Hayden said to Kathleen, before turning back to Brian. "It was only a dozen, max. And that was about eleven more times than you deserved. You're hours late."

"The traffic getting out of Nashville was horrible. It put me behind the entire trip. There was an accident on I-70 that left me standing pretty much still for an hour. But I made it." Hayden started toward the back of the car, as if she were going to help him unload. He shook his head. "Just leave it. I'll unpack what I need later."

Four years' worth of college life was stowed in his car and the trailer he'd rented. Most of his belongings were going to stay in the trailer for the few weeks he had here before driving out to California.

Tonight was Hayden's night.

With her on one side, his mother on the other, Brian headed into the house. Stepping over the threshold, he felt the last remains of tightness loosen in his chest.

Home.

"Nothing's changed." The sentence was at odds with the thoughts that had plagued him as he sat in his car and studied the house. But as he walked into the place, he couldn't remember what those differences were. All he saw was home. The hardwood floor, the light tan walls. Maybe the curtains were new, but they fit and didn't change the feel of the house. And it was that feel that he remembered most.

"Everything's changed," Hayden corrected. "I graduate from high school in just an hour and a half. That means it's all different. And I don't want to be late, so go get your shower. Your suit's hanging in the closet. I went with your mom to pick out the tie." One hand was on her hip—when did she get hips? In his mind she was still board straight from top to bottom, but somewhere along the line she'd grown hips. Hips and other new curves he didn't remember noticing at Christmas.

Her free hand was waving in front of his face. "You're in a fog, Bri. Maybe you should have some coffee before you go get that shower."

"She's bossy. Was she always this bossy?" he asked his mother with deliberate mock seriousness.

"I think she learned from the best. It was always so amusing watching the two of you trying to direct the other. There was never a definitive leader. *King of the Mountain* was always up for grabs."

"Well, since I'm graduating today, I'm grabbing. I win. I'm the boss. The top dog. The King of the Mountain. The queen of all I survey. You—" she pointed at him, wagging a finger at his chest "—coffee, shower, change."

He smiled. "Fine. I'll let you have tonight, but I don't guarantee anything for the rest of my visit."

"I'll take tonight then and we'll debate who's boss for the rest of your visit later." She glanced at her watch. "Oh, I've got to run."

Without another word, she turned and sprinted up the stairs, her bare feet slapping on the wooden treads. She stopped at the top. "I'm glad you're home. We missed you."

"Me, too, kid." he said. He watched as she turned the twist in the stairs and disappeared from sight, though they could still hear her thumping down the hall. Her bedroom door slammed and her music came on. Brian recognized REO Speedwagon.

"She never slows down," his mom said, a smile playing on her lips. "She only has one speed—mach one."

"She's all grown up now. I didn't notice that at Christmas, though there must have been some signs then. But in the last five months … Well, she ran out to the car, and there it was. The kid who spent years tormenting me is no longer a kid. It feels weird."

"It amazes me, as well, but not only her. You, too. Sometimes I look at you and can hardly remember the small, gap-toothed boy with his messy black hair who thought I hung the moon."

"He still thinks you hung the moon."

"Oh. Bri, that was an unbelievably cheesy thing to say, but it was just what I needed. Thanks."

His mom studied him a moment, as if she were truly looking for that gap-toothed boy he once was. She sighed. He wondered if that meant she'd found what she was looking for, or hadn't.

She reached out and lightly touched his cheek. "I've spent my day thinking about the past. Feeling old. The last of my kids—and she is mine, there's no mistaking that—is officially grown. Do you remember that day she decided to climb the oak tree and hang a rope swing?"

"I still have nightmares about spotting our old ladder, the one that was missing all those rungs, up against the oak, then looking up and seeing her feet dangling below the branch." He paused, remembering how scared he'd been as he held the ladder and watched her climb down. "I was doing the same kind of thing, remembering, on the drive here. The very, very long drive here."

"What sort of things were you remembering, specifically?"

"Oh, different things in different cities. I was outside Columbus and remembered her father's funeral. No one but us and her mom came. Hayden never cried. I don't know why I remembered that, but I got this mental image of her standing there in front of the casket, not shedding a tear, unlike her mother who put on a huge show for a man she hadn't seen in years. And speak of the devil, is her mom coming tonight?"

"I don't know. Hayden went down to their house last week. She wasn't gone long and didn't say a word about what happened between them."

"And you didn't press." That was the beauty of his mom. Maybe it came from being a nurse for so many years, but he suspected it was simply part of her. She had such deep patience. He knew she hadn't pushed, wouldn't push. She'd simply wait until Hayden was ready to talk. And when that time came, she'd listen, then offer whatever was needed, hugs, advice or just being there. "So, we'll see."

He was torn, part of him knowing that Hayden would want her mother there, and the bigger part knowing that if her mother came, it wouldn't turn out like Hayden wanted.

It never did.

Briar Hill Road had once been a true country road. More houses had been built between their home and Hayden's mother's over the years. The quarter mile down the street wasn't that far by county standards, but it was miles away as far as Mrs. MacNulty was concerned. She hadn't really been a part of Hayden's life in a long time. Sometimes he wondered if she ever had been at all.

"Yes, we'll see." His mom leaned over and gave him another quick hug. "Have I mentioned how glad I am you're home?"

"I don't think so. But Hayden did. And speaking of Hayden, if I don't hit the shower soon, she's likely to march down here and throw me in."

"Before you go, can I say something?"

"Anything. Anytime."

"I hate to meddle, but this once, I need to. I want you to remember that Hayden's not a little girl anymore. Although, I'm not sure if she ever had a true childhood. Sometimes life forces people to mature too fast, too soon."

He must have looked as confused as he felt over her cryptic warning, because his mom continued, "Hayden's a woman, with a woman's feelings. And she loves you. Always has."

"Like a brother."

His mom just tilted her head to one side and stared at him. Waiting in that quiet way of hers for him to think things through.

And when he did he unthought it immediately. "No, no way."

"She's dated, but she's never lit up about any of the boys the way she lights up when you call. Every comment you make, every small gesture, she holds on to and treasures. She loves you." His mom smiled. "Maybe I'm wrong. But in case I'm not, be careful.

You two haven't spent much time together in the last few years. I don't want her to be hurt. She's already lived through more heartache at eighteen than most do in a lifetime."

"I'll be careful, but I think you're wrong. She's a kid. A pain in the butt, climbing broken ladders and generally making me crazy."

At that moment, Hayden called, "Brian, if you don't get up here …" from the top of the stairs, leaving an unspoken threat hanging.

"I'm on my way." He kissed his mom's cheek. "I'll be careful."

"That's all I ask."

"Our true home isn't just a place, it's a feeling. It's knowing that this is where you belong. That these are the people you belong to. That the door will always be open to you."

Hayden had searched the rows of students and their families when she reached the podium. She felt nervous until she found Brian and Kathleen, then she calmed down.

They were sitting just behind the rows of seniors, watching her, practically radiating their pride. She'd written her valedictorian speech more for them than for her senior class. She needed them to know, wanted the world to know, how much they meant to her. But saying so in the normal course of things was too hard. This speech was her opportunity.

"Sometimes you're born into your family, into your home. But if you're not that lucky, you have to search. I didn't even know I was looking for mine until I knocked on their door when I was eight and they let me in. I never left after that, even if I spent a few more years sleeping at a different house. I'd found them and they were mine, I was theirs. Now, it's time for us all to leave home, to leave our families and our friends here at school behind. We're about to venture out into the world and spread our wings. There's so much waiting for us to discover—new ideas, new friends, new challenges."

The door at the back of the auditorium flew open and Hayden's heart sank when she saw who walked in. She wasn't sure why she'd walked down Briar Hill Road to that ramshackle house that had never been home. She wasn't sure why she'd felt the need to tell the woman who'd never really been her mother about the graduation and leave her a ticket. She'd felt it was the right thing to do at the time.…

Hayden tried to find her place in the speech and ignore her mother, ignore the fact that she hadn't even bothered to brush her black hair that had about three inches of light brown roots peppered with gray streaks showing.

"But thanks to our years here at CV High, we're prepared for whatever is waiting around this next bend. And we know that even as we leave this school, leave our houses, we'll never really leave home. We'll take those we love with us—"

"That's her," her mother cried. She was swaying as if she were on a boat and the waves were high. The left shoulder of her skimpy top slid down, revealing a stick-thin arm and a boney shoulder. "That's my girl." She waved a finger toward Hayden. "She ain't talking about me, though. Why, I don't even know—"

And no one would ever know because suddenly Brian was there at her mother's side, leading her out of the auditorium.

"But that's my daughter," her mother yelled as he hurried her through the door.

"Uh, thanks to our years at CV High we're prepared …" Hayden went on, finishing her speech, but the words which had sounded so right and rare only an hour before when she'd read through them one last time now rang hollow.

She might be valedictorian, might be heading off to college on an academic scholarship, might have shaken the dirt of her mother's house off her feet, but inside she was still Cootie MacNulty, the same girl who'd watched her parents crawl into a bottle. She'd hoped her mother would crawl out of it, if only for this one night. Her mom had sworn she would.

Though Hayden shouldn't have been surprised that her mother didn't keep that promise. Her mother had never kept any of them. But like a fool, Hayden couldn't let go, hoping that this time her mother would change.

Kathleen always said that it was only right to give her mother another chance. But tonight was the final straw. Hayden was done trying.

What Kathleen didn't realize—couldn't see because her great big heart obscured her view—was that some people would never change because they didn't really want to.

Her mother had always chosen liquor over Hayden.

"I wish you all a safe journey as you set out on this new adventure. But remember, you always have a home to come back to."

She found Brian, who'd slipped into his seat again, and Kathleen. Hayden knew that those words were so true. Her parents weren't what she'd have wished for, but she'd found her real family that Halloween so long ago. As long as she had them, she'd always be home.

A week later, Hayden pulled into the driveway and got out of her ancient Pinto with a small paper bag in her hand. She never quite knew how to express her feelings to Brian. She wanted so desperately to thank him for getting her mother out of the school last week, wanted to tell him so many deeper, more important things, but she couldn't find the words. Her simple, "Thanks," after the ceremony last week, followed by his quick nod, was as close to the subject as they'd come.

So she brought him milkshakes.

It was lame. She knew it was, but she couldn't stop herself. It was the best she could do.

She was putting in forty hours a week at Sears, then working as many hours as she could at the ice cream store, saving for college. The academic scholarship covered tuition and the cost of most of her classes, but she still had living expenses to pay for.

Kathleen had generously offered to help her with this, but Hayden was bound and determined to do it on her own. Kathleen had already given her so much and she couldn't take any more.

"Oh, Hay-den," Brian called in a sing-songy voice from the porch. His hands were hidden behind his back. He looked very happy with himself, suspiciously so.

"Brian Conway, what are you up to?"

"I've been waiting for you. Remember last night?"

"Oh, come on, it was a joke. A harmless joke."

He shook his head, smiling. "You cheated at Monopoly. You always cheat."

"It was a loan."

Slowly, he brought his hands forward. A bright red balloon sat solidly in his right one.

Not just any balloon. She could tell by the particular way it rolled on his palm that it was a water balloon. A water balloon that had been filled to its capacity. Brian had always been a pro at filling balloons until they almost reached their breaking point so that his always popped upon impact.

And Hayden knew just where he wanted to impact this one.

"Do you recall years ago when you were the one with the balloon and I promised I'd bide my time and get my revenge?"

Hayden couldn't believe he remembered her water-balloon assault four years earlier. "Bri, if you do it …"

"If I do, you'll what?" He tossed the water balloon from one hand to the other. Back and forth, back and forth, wearing that grin she knew so well.

"If you do, I'll tell Kathleen."

He just laughed.

"Fine." She stood, holding the paper bag in front of her, not that it would provide much protection. "Do your worst, but do it quick, I have a date. And be forewarned. I'll get even. Very, very even. Plus, you'll ruin this lovely chocolate shake I brought you from work."

He walked toward her and she got ready to be whacked, but he was almost up to her and the balloon still sat quietly in his hand.

"Who's the lucky fellow?" He took the bag and pulled out the shake.

"Tad. I know," she said before he could start teasing her. "His name sounds like he should be in a Gidget movie. But, despite that, he's a nice guy. More of a friend than anything, really. We're going to see a movie. You can come if you want."

"Thanks, but no." He took a long sip of his milkshake. "You do make a mean chocolate shake, kid. Thanks. You'd better go get ready."

She started toward the house, and hadn't even made the porch when he called, "Hey, Hayden?"

She turned.

Splat. The water balloon hit her chest dead center.

"You …" She didn't bother searching for the appropriate word, she immediately kicked off her shoes and took off across the lawn. He'd started to run, but he was no match for her speed. She'd lettered in track at school, even gone to States.

She knocked against him, sending them both sprawling on the lawn. He managed to hang on to his shake.

"Say *uncle,*" she cried.

She might be faster than he was, but he had sheer bulk on his side. He set his shake down and flipped her with far more ease than he had in the past. "No, you say *uncle.*"

"Never." And then—Hayden was never quite sure how it happened, but she was pretty sure she made the initial move—she was kissing him. Not like a friend. But kissing him as if she meant it. Hoping her touch told him without words all the things she felt and couldn't voice.

For a moment, a brief moment, she was more to him than a kid. She was pretty sure he was kissing her back. But she couldn't be positive because the next moment, he was standing and she was still damp on the grass looking up at him.

"I'm sorry," he said.

Not *I've been waiting for you to grow up enough to do that.*

Not *Wow.*

Not *Let's do that again.*

Just *I'm sorry.*

"For what? For getting me wet?" She smiled, as if nothing had happened. She was good at that, at pretending there was nothing wrong.

For as long as she could remember she'd loved Brian Conway. For years, it had been like a little girl who loved her hero. A devoted, puppy dog sort of love.

But when he'd come home last Christmas, there was suddenly more. She loved him in a totally new and unexpected way. She wasn't sure why or how. Maybe it was when they'd gone to the movie, and he'd slipped his arm over the back of her chair. It had almost felt as if he'd been holding her, and she'd realized how much she wished he had been. She'd just known she loved him and had hoped someday he'd realize he loved her, too.

And now she'd ruined it all by making an ass of herself.

Well, she wasn't going to let her slip of the lips change things between them. He might not feel the same way about her that she did for him, but they'd always been close. She wouldn't let their kiss change that.

"Hayden," he started in that we-should-talk-about-this sort of tone she had no problem recognizing.

But she didn't want to talk. And in fourteen days, he was heading to his new job, his new life, in California. She could *not* talk about what had happened for that long, she was sure. She was even more positive she could avoid letting him know how she really felt about him.

She glanced at her watch, then looked right at him and forced a smile. "Hey, I've got to run now. Tad will be here soon and I'm soaked."

She sprinted toward the door, then turned around and called, "Don't forget your milkshake."

She ran in the house, up the stairs and locked herself in the bathroom, knowing that something big had, indeed, happened.

She'd crushed her schoolgirl fantasies with one kiss.

That was probably a good thing, she assured herself. He was leaving to begin his career, and she was leaving for college.

It was time she grew up.

It was time to set aside the girl she had once been. It was time to become the woman she wanted to be. Strong. Independent. Capable.

She wanted to be a woman like Kathleen. A woman who could make her own way in the world.

When Kathleen's husband had left her, she'd moved to Briar Hill Road and started a life for herself on her own terms.

Hayden had made a good start. Because she'd worked hard through high school, she had her scholarship to Temple in Philadelphia. She'd been working like a maniac to save enough money to pay whatever costs were left over. It was a good start.

Yes, she'd get over this crush on Brian Conway in no time. She was ready to stand on her own two feet.

Chapter Three

The transport van no longer hit potholes, not because the driver's abilities had improved, but because they'd come to a standstill in the rush-hour traffic.

Hayden broke the silence. "Kathleen, do you remember that summer I was fifteen and tried to dye my own hair?"

"I don't remember your hair being anything but brown," Brian said.

"It was purple." Hayden cringed. "I thought it would look cool, but I ended up looking like that girl in *Willy Wonka* who'd tried his gum, which turned her into a big grape, or blueberry, or whatever it was."

"That bad?" Brian asked.

"Worse," Kathleen and Hayden said in unison.

"You didn't laugh or yell, Kathleen. You jumped on the phone and got us into that ritzy salon."

"Dorian's Day Spa."

"That was the day I learned to appreciate being a girl and getting pampered." She turned to Brian. "While we waited for their treatments to turn my hair a more normal color, your mom arranged for us to have pedicures and manicures."

Kathleen laughed and looked at Brian. "She got her finger-nails painted purple, saying if they couldn't get the dye out of her hair, at least she'd coordinate. And if they did make her hair brown again, her purple nails would be a reminder to leave the hair dyes to the professionals."

Brian studied Hayden, as if trying to imagine her with purple hair. She knew the minute he managed it, because he grimaced.

"The salon must have done the job right, because I don't remember any pictures of you with purple hair."

"There was a faint violet color left, but it was actually attractive," Kathleen said.

"We had monthly spa days after that. Your mom said it was so we could bond, but I think she just wanted to be sure I didn't try to dye my own hair again."

Kathleen grinned. "You liked going to the salon, unlike Brian, who used to act like every trip to the barbershop was torture."

"It was. Barbers and baths are the horror of every young boy." He paused a moment, and added, "Thankfully, we get over the bathing phobia about the same time we discover girls, but haircuts are still a waste of time. And I never did understand men who not only styled their hair, but used product in it. That's not natural."

Hayden laughed. "Oh, come on."

"Well, let's just say I was glad Mom had you to drag to that kind of stuff because I can assure you, Mom, as much as I love you, real men don't do pedicures."

The driver interrupted their laughter. "This is going to take a while longer."

Kathleen startled at the sound of his voice, and her quick movement sent a flicker of pain flashing across her face.

"Kathleen, can I do something?" Hayden rose.

She shooed Hayden back into her seat. "I'm fine. I missed those monthly trips when you went away to college. No more spending our Saturday mornings cleaning, so we could spend the afternoon at the mall guilt free."

"No more chick-flick Fridays," Hayden said. "With Tommy's pizza and pepperoni balls. You can't get pepperoni balls in Philadelphia. And they call Italian Ice, Water Ice. I always thought that was redundant."

Hayden's first year of college, across the state at Temple University in Philadelphia, was an adjustment. Her homesickness had almost made her decide to transfer to something closer. But then she'd hit her stride her sophomore year and remembered the last three years of college as a freeing time. "College was so different. Suddenly I wasn't the MacNulty girl. I wasn't the girl the Conways took in. I was simply Hayden MacNulty."

She'd left the baggage that was her heritage behind her in Pittsburgh. In Philadelphia, Hayden finally found herself.

She thought she'd gotten over the past, that she'd put Cootie behind her. That she'd outgrown her childhood crush on Brian. But some things you just can't forget.

There was one night in particular …

May 1989

"Brian," Hayden called, waving her hands wildly as he parallel parked his car into the small space on the street in front of her apartment.

It was May, but already hot in Philadelphia. The semester was winding down, but Temple University's Philadelphia campus was still filled with the hustle and bustle of its students, many of whom were watching Hayden perform her absurd dance, waving, jumping up and down as Brian turned off the ignition to the car.

She knew she looked like a crazy person, but she didn't care. Brian was here and she thought she'd practically burst with happiness. She'd promised herself she'd get over her crush on him, and she had. Oh, that first Christmas when they'd both come home to

Kathleen's, she'd felt awkward, but then he'd thrown a snowball at her, and suddenly, he was just Brian again.

The last four years they'd managed to see each other during the holidays at Kathleen's, but that was about it. And this year, he couldn't make it to the house on Briar Hill Road while Hayden was there, so she hadn't even seen him then. They did talk every few weeks, but that wasn't the same.

Last week, he'd called and said he was going to be in Philadelphia on business, that if she had time, he'd like to come visit her and catch up. She'd been soaring ever since.

She started to throw herself into his arms, like she once would have, but stopped short of it.

"Hey, kid." He didn't seem to notice her hesitation to hug him as he stepped back and looked her up and down. "Mom's right, you're too thin."

"You try eating at the cafeteria. That freshman twenty is a myth that was started by and perpetuated by school administrators, hoping kids would come for the good food. And I've been eating it for four years, although I've noticed that the meal quality goes way up on the days we have potential freshman on campus."

He laughed. "You can try to be a cynic, but I'm not buying it."

"Rats. I thought I'd perfected that whole senior sneer thing." She tried to look disgruntled, but couldn't quite pull it off.

Brian smiled, and she couldn't help notice how his dark hair looked good against his California tan. "Yeah, you don't have the jaded twenty-two-year-old thing down yet."

"And those extra four years you have on me mean you have the whole cynic thing down? Come on, I've heard you talk about your kids at the center. You give optimists a bad name."

"So are we going to stand in the middle of downtown Philly arguing about who's more cynical?"

"No. This way, I'll give you the tour. Bring your bag. My roommate's in Spain this semester, so the apartment's all mine, which means you even get a room with a bed, instead of the couch. She's into the color pink, but I suspect your manly ego can handle girly bubble-gum-colored sheets on the bed."

"Are you sure I'm not imposing?"

"Are you telling me you can't handle pink sheets?" He tilted his chin up and scoffed, which caused her to laugh. "I told you on the phone I was sure. You're always welcome, even if it's only to the couch. Hurry up." They walked across the street to her apartment complex. Temple had bought a number of old properties and turned them into apartments for their older students. She loved having her own space.

"Oh, I meant to tell you first thing, I got that job."

Hayden had spent the last three summers interning at a children's hospital not far from the university. They'd offered her a permanent job starting in June.

"Mom told me. She's practically bursting with pride." There was something not quite right in his tone.

She really looked at Brian and noticed fine lines around his eyes that spoke of worry, or pain. She stopped, bag in hand still and waited for him to stop walking, as well, before asking, "Hey, is everything okay?"

"Fine, just fine," he assured her, but she wasn't buying it.

She'd spent too many years watching Kathleen to try and ferret out what was wrong with him with an all-out frontal attack. She'd learned a bit of subtlety and would bide her time. But one way or another, she'd discover what was weighing on Brian before he left.

She got him settled in her apartment, then they spent the rest of that day playing tourist. She took him around Philadelphia's historic district, somewhere she rarely went herself. They went to see the Liberty Bell, to the Mutter's Museum and walked through a park.

"So, dinner at my place?" she asked outside Betsy Ross's house. "Although, I'm not sure if I'll be able to eat after seeing that freakishly huge colon at the museum. I mean, I honestly think I could have gone the rest of my life without seeing that one."

Brian laughed. "You're going to be a registered nurse in just a few weeks and have spent all your time working at a hospital, and you're telling me that a colon freaked you out?"

"Yes. That's why I have no desire to be a surgical nurse. It's good to recognize your limitations."

"As long as you don't let perceived limitations stop you from doing things you'd love."

She kept their conversation light as they picked up some Philly-cheese-steak sandwiches and a six pack, then carried it all back to her place.

She loved this little apartment so much. The chair she and Clair had bought from a secondhand store, the bright blue curtains. The pictures from magazines that they'd framed to decorate the walls. The beat up hope chest they used as a coffee table. She dropped their sandwiches on it. "Come on, dig in."

Hayden hadn't laughed so much in forever as Brian regaled her with tales from the front. He was working with Save Our Children, a grassroots operation designed to overhaul California's children's service system. Hayden knew he dealt with serious situations, but tonight he concentrated on office minutia. Who was with who, doing what and when. Funny and entertaining stories that gave her a glimpse of his life.

And though she laughed, she recognized that he was trying too hard.

"Brian, what is it?" she finally asked again, after they'd eaten their sandwiches and had a couple beers under their respective belts.

He paused a moment, looking off into space and she wondered if he was finally going to tell her what was bothering him.

"I had a new case come over my desk the week before I left. A little girl whose parents lost custody of her. She ended up in a foster family who wasn't much better. They didn't abuse her, but they neglected her. She reminded me—"

He paused.

"Of me," she filled in softly. "My parents never abused me outright, but they didn't care. Then I found you and Kathleen. But not every kid's so lucky. And on top of your job at Save Our Children, you've worked so hard to get the teen center off the ground. I'm so proud of what you do."

He looked uncomfortable with the praise. "Thanks. That means a lot. And I guess this is my chance to say ditto. Mom and I are both proud of you. And having you follow in her footsteps and become a nurse means a lot. She—" He stopped and seemed to drift away.

"What? I know you've been avoiding something, something that's tearing at you. Tell me."

"She didn't want you to know."

"What's wrong? You haven't told me exactly why you're here." He'd made vague noises about business meetings, but it didn't take a rocket scientist to figure out business wasn't his only reason for visiting her. "What's wrong?"

"She didn't want you to know," he repeated. "She's so proud of your job offer here, and wants you to take it. She was afraid you wouldn't if you knew."

"Knew what, dammit?" Acid burned in her stomach and she suddenly felt cold, bone cold, despite the warm May night.

"Hayden, Mom's got breast cancer. They found it last week. She's having a lumpectomy on Monday. She wants to be on her feet for your graduation."

"She'll have chemo and radiation then?"

"They'll have a more definitive idea of what treatments she'll go through, how much and when they'll do it, after she's had the surgery and the doctors can see if the cancer's invaded her lymph nodes."

"I—"

Hayden thought she knew what pain was, but this news cut to some previously unknown depth. She felt the tears fill her eyes, and she blinked rapidly not letting them fall but knowing she wasn't hiding anything from Brian. "What's her prognosis?"

"She said the doctor refused to even guess until after the surgery. Maybe that's it, or maybe he did tell her and it's bad, so she's not saying because she doesn't want to worry me."

"Like she didn't want to worry me."

He nodded. "She wants you to enjoy your graduation. Wants you to take this job and …" The sentence trailed off. "Hell, Hayden, she wants you to have the whole world. Just like she wants that for me. She was pissed when she found out I was interviewing for jobs here in Pennsylvania. I think I have the one in Pittsburgh, but I've got three other interviews, as well. Philly's five hours away, but it's closer than California."

"Maybe I should do the same. There are certainly enough hospitals in the Pittsburgh area that I should be able to land something." The moment Hayden said the words, she knew that's exactly what she would do. "I won't let her know you told me."

"She'll know."

"Fine, then she'll know. She'll be mad at you, not me." She tried to force a laugh, but it rang hollow to her ears. "Bri, we can't lose her."

She felt the cold deepen. It reached to her very core. Freezing. If she were this cold, she should be numb, but she wasn't. She felt every single stab of worry that pulsed through her icy bloodstream. "We can't lose her," she repeated.

"We won't. You know how strong she is." He brushed her cheek with his fingertip. "Hey, it will be okay."

"Nothing's going to be okay until I hear she's well. Until she gets an all clear. I can't lose her." If she said it often enough, with enough force and conviction, maybe it would come true. Losing Kathleen just couldn't be possible. She wouldn't let it happen.

Brian pulled Hayden close, and held her as they huddled together on the worn brown couch. She welcomed his warmth. Needed it more than she'd ever needed anything.

He kissed her forehead. She looked up and saw in his eyes as comfort turned to something more. A need that grew. There was nothing platonic about their embrace. It was something so basic and raw that it took Hayden's breath away.

They didn't say a word as the touches they exchanged became more and more intimate. It was as if words would break the magic of the moment, intrude on a union that somewhere in the back of her mind Hayden had always known had to happen.

They made their way into her room and as if by one accord, they undressed each other and crawled into her small twin bed. They held each other, and slowly they made love, learning each other's body, discovering just how to please.

Afterward, they clung to one another. Brian's gentleness quieted the fear that continued to pulse through her system. The fear of a world without Kathleen. For now she could tamp it down, the wonder of this joining overshadowing it, even if their intimacy couldn't obliterate it entirely.

She'd loved Brian in so many ways. Her champion, her mentor, her friend. But this … this was so much more.

Some time later, Brian stirred. She raised her head up and smiled, knowing that somehow they could get through anything if they had each other, had this.

"Hayden?"

"Yes?" She ran her hand over his chest.

His hand caught hers, stopping it in its track. "I'm sorry."

"Sorry?" Four years ago he'd said those words, after she'd kissed him and they'd cut her, but now it was worse.

"This … I'm not sure how we came to this, but I took advantage of you. You were in shock over Mom's news and I let things go too far. I'm sorry."

She pulled her hand from his.

Brian sat up, flipped his long legs over the side of the bed and started to dress hurriedly. As if he couldn't get away from her quick enough. "Under the circumstances, I think it would be better if I stayed at a hotel for the rest of my visit."

"Fine." There. She'd managed to say something and was amazed at how normal it sounded.

"But breakfast later, okay. We'll talk about this?"

"There's nothing to talk about. Let's just go back to what we were and forget this ever happened. But we can talk about Kathleen and how we can work together to help her through this."

"But I want—"

"Sorry. But I don't want." She pulled the sheet higher, pressing it tighter to her chin. "You can show yourself out."

"I'll pick you up for breakfast at eight, right? You'll still go?" he asked again.

"Yes."

She listened to the small noises he made as he gathered his things. Then she listened as the front door opened and closed.

He was gone.

She flopped back onto her pillow. Those two words running over and over in her mind.

I'm sorry.

I'm sorry.

Brian left Hayden's apartment, walked to Broad Street and hailed a cab. "Just drive."

He had no idea where he was going. All he knew is he had to get away from Hayden before he made more of a muck of things.

He'd made love to her.

He knew that she was as close to his mother as he was, knew how vulnerable and scared she'd be.

He should have comforted her—period.

That's what he'd started out to do. He wasn't sure how things had gotten out of hand. He'd never intended for it to happen. But that was no excuse. He was a grown man, she was graduating from college.

He realized the cab was driving through the historic district. "Let me out here."

He paid his fare, grabbed his bag and got out. He didn't know where to go, so he wandered aimlessly, wondering how he could set things right with Hayden. How he could make her understand that he did love her, and he hadn't set out to take advantage of her?

Hayden shared a connection with his mother that he'd never have. It wasn't that his mother didn't love him. She did. He'd never doubted it. But Hayden was the daughter she'd never had, a friend.

He could picture the two of them, thick as thieves, laughing over something on the television. They'd become a unit, complementing each other in so many ways. Hayden had kept his mom's music tastes current, and his mom taught Hayden to appreciate Katherine Hepburn.

His mom would need her support to get through the …

He hesitated even thinking the word.

Cancer.

Such a small word that represented such an awful disease.

He knew his mother would find him helping her awkward, but Hayden would be different. His mom needed Hayden.

And he wanted to be there for both of them.

He had to fix his relationship with Hayden.

He'd made a mistake. Taken them somewhere they never should have gone. He'd put their friendship at risk.

Brian found himself in front of a Best Western hotel on Chestnut Street and went in to get a room.

He'd figure out how to make it up to Hayden. She was part of their family, and he couldn't let one foolish mistake change anything.

Chapter Four

Brian listened to his mom and Hayden talking as the transport van lumbered toward their destination. If it had been some stranger listening, the person would never have guessed there was anything wrong as the two women laughed and reminisced.

They were talking about one of his mom's visits to Philadelphia while Hayden was at Temple. They'd taken a trip into New York City to see the musical *Les Miserables*. "And that woman with the licorice behind us." His mom smiled at the memory. "Hayden, I thought you were going to have a fit."

"It was *Les Mis,* and there's Jean Valjean, singing so beautifully and she's crinkling the licorice's cellophane."

His mom turned to him and, as if he'd never heard the story before, said, "She shushed the woman. One long, unmistakable, *shh.*"

"Did the woman shush?" he asked on cue, willing to hear any of his mom's remembrances for the umpteenth time, if only she'd continue smiling like that.

"She sure did." Kathleen laughed again, and the two of them continued talking about that trip.

He was remembering his trip to Philadelphia, and wishing he hadn't been such an ass. If he'd made Hayden talk to him, or insisted she listen while he talked to her, maybe they wouldn't have wasted all those years.

Instead, the next morning, when he'd started with, "Hayden, I took advantage of you—"

She'd cut him off. "Maybe I took advantage of you?" She'd waited, and when he didn't respond, she'd simply said, "We did what we did, now it's over. We have more important things to talk about."

On the surface, he and Hayden had seemed to be okay, but he knew they'd changed—and not for the better.

Here in the van, he noticed Hayden reach down and hold the locket she always wore around her neck, zipping it back and forth along its chain. He wasn't sure she was aware of how often she did that.

He saw his mom look at the locket, still clasped in Hayden's hand. Hayden looked at it, as well.

Brian hadn't been there when she got it, and it wasn't a story his mother usually brought up, mainly out of consideration for him. She was afraid it would hurt him, recalling what he'd missed.

He'd been offered the job in Philadelphia, but his mother had persuaded him to stay put in California. A five-hour car trip home, or a seven-hour flight? It was a horse a piece, she'd said. Why give up his job when he'd only save himself a couple hours of travel.

The doctor felt he'd got all the cancer, they hadn't found any evidence it had invaded her lymph nodes. She was on the mend.

Hayden was working at St. Bart's with his mom. She was there to help her through the chemo and radiation. There was no reason for him to uproot his life for her.

So he'd stayed, hoping the job in Pittsburgh would come through.

"The locket," his mom said.

"The locket," Hayden echoed, still clutching it.

1989

Hayden woke up to the sound of her alarm around three in the afternoon. She worked the night shift at St. Bartholomew. She'd been thrilled to get a job at the same hospital Kathleen worked at. Hayden was assigned to the pediatric floor and loved it.

What she didn't love was waking up.

She'd purposely put her alarm across the room so she had to get up to turn it off. She stumbled across the room, hit the alarm and opened the blinds, blinking against the glare of the sun.

She stared out the window. She loved this time of year. Summer was fading into fall. The leaves had lost their green glow and were fading to a darker, tired green that would soon give way to a burst of color—a final fanfare before they fell and winter set in.

It wasn't just the trees, it was the air. Crisp and cool. It still smelled of freshly mowed lawns, but beneath that Hayden always felt the early autumn air had the scent of apples. It could have something to do with the apple tree in Kathleen's backyard, or it could be that she associated early fall with apple cider and pies. Either way, fall meant apples to her.

This year, however, as much as she tried to muster her usual enthusiasm for the start of her favorite season, the coming conversation loomed so heavily over her that it was next to impossible.

It was time to be brave and get on with it. She was four months out of college, had a wonderful new job. She was an adult, and adults didn't hide from problems, they faced them.

At first she'd hesitated, not wanting to add to Kathleen's burden. Radiation was enough to deal with. But the treatments were finished and Kathleen was slowly recovering her strength.

Hayden couldn't put off the conversation any longer.

She grabbed a quick shower, dressed, then went looking for Kathleen. She found her in the front yard, planting mums in between the bushes.

"Kathleen?"

Kathleen was kneeling by a small hole, tapping the bottom of the pot to loosen the mum's roots. She looked up and smiled. "Want to pick up a shovel and help?"

She smiled as she asked because she knew Hayden's aversion to things like dirt, worms and bugs. Gardening was so not Hayden's thing. Most days, she'd have laughed at Kathleen's harmless teasing, but today, she had to really work to even force a smile.

"We have to talk." Grateful she'd finally started, still, she worried, knowing that after the words were said, things would change. The thought that Kathleen might feel anything less for her was something that made her feel physically sick.

Kathleen grew serious. She stood and wiped her hands on the front of her jeans. "It seems as if this might be a conversation that would be better inside."

She left her tools and half-planted mums, and took Hayden into the kitchen, washed her hands, and added, "Let's go into the living room."

Kathleen looked tired. "You've only been back to work for two days. Maybe you should take it easy."

"I spent the whole summer taking it easy. This is a good kind of tired. I'm accomplishing things again. Back to work at the hospital. Even planting flowers. It helps."

Kathleen sank onto the couch and closed her eyes. The movement only emphasized the dark circles underneath them. Hayden should have realized that Kathleen would be exhausted. Maybe their discussion should wait a bit longer.

"Brian called this morning, while you were asleep." Kathleen radiated happiness. "He's walking on air. That teen center he helped start? It's garnered a lot of attention and he's been asked to serve on the governor's advisory committee on child welfare."

"Oh, Kathleen, that's wonderful."

"He's so excited. This is his chance to do some real good. He hesitated accepting, saying he'd heard about the job here in Pittsburgh and he could start in October, but I told him I'd never speak to him again if he took it. I'm fine, you're here."

"So he's turning it down?"

"Turned it down. He called me again, afterward …" She paused, and smiled. "I have to thank you for that."

"Me?"

"You changed jobs in order to move back and take care of me. That's why he didn't say yes to the job in Philadelphia, and why he waited for the position in Pittsburgh to open up. That's why he was still in Los Angeles, and why he was offered this new opportunity. That's a lot of whys I have to thank you for." She wiped at her eyes. "Look at me, sentimental old woman that I am. I've been waiting for you to wake up. I stopped at Harper's Jewelry Store on the way home. I found this and couldn't resist."

She took a small black velvet box out of her pocket and handed it to Hayden. "Open it."

Hayden paused. "Kathleen, you shouldn't have. You've done so much and I—"

"Don't."

Hayden was startled by the sharp tone in Kathleen's voice. It sounded foreign.

"I mean it, don't. You've sung this song for more than a decade. I don't want your thanks. I don't need your gratitude. That's not why I invited you into my house. I invited you in because you were already in my heart. I don't know what it was, but there was something about you that pulled at me, right from the start. Maybe at first, it was simply that you were small and obviously needed someone. But later, it was more. You were, are, my daughter in every way that matters. Everything I've done, everything that you feel you have to thank me for with such frightening repetitivity was, and is, selfish. I've done those things, will continue to do them, because I love you. Because I'm proud of you."

"Kathleen—"

"And don't think I don't know why you've started your nursing career here, why you moved home. I didn't want you giving up your hospital job in Philadelphia, but a very selfish part of me is glad you did because I don't know what I'd have done without you these last few months." She wiped at her eyes again. "Now, open your gift. Then, and only then, you can tell me what you wanted to tell me."

Hayden's fingers were trembling as she opened the box. "Oh, Kathleen."

"You've never mentioned much about your family's origins, but I thought with a name like MacNulty you had to have at least a bit of the Emerald Island floating through your veins. I saw this and thought of you."

"It's beautiful." She turned the gold locket over, admiring it. The silver Celtic knot engraved on the front was exquisite. She traced the lines. "Beautiful."

"Open it."

A picture of Kathleen on one side, Brian's college graduation picture on the other.

Kathleen reached out and took Hayden's hand. "You might have other blood family, but DNA couldn't make the bond I feel, the love I feel, any greater."

It was too much. Just too much. "I hope you feel that way after I tell you what I need to say."

"Nothing can alter the way I feel about you."

Hayden didn't want to say the words, to spoil Kathleen's generous act, but she knew she couldn't wait.

"I'm pregnant."

The moment the words rolled off her tongue she felt both relief and a breathless nervousness as she waited for Kathleen's reaction.

But before Kathleen could respond, Hayden held up her hand, stopping her. "There's more."

"Twins?" Kathleen offered her a small smile.

"No. I mean, not that I've heard. I mean, God, I hope not. I don't even know if I'm ready for one."

"Do you want to tell me who the father is?"

"Now, there's where it gets tricky." Before she could spit out the name, she saw Kathleen deduce it for herself.

"Brian."

Hayden nodded. "Yes. It was just one time. One very vulnerable time. And—"

"He asked you to marry him when you told him?" Kathleen's expression shifted—her voice sounded heavy as she guessed, "You haven't told him?"

"Not yet. But there won't be a marriage."

"Hayden—"

Hayden cut her off. "You just told me about this fantastic appointment. He's got a life in California. He's making a difference … through Save Our Children, through the teen center, and now, this chance to be on the governor's advisory committee. He's got plans, and a baby was never a part of them. I'll tell him—"

"He'll want to marry you."

"I won't do it. I won't let him marry me because of a baby." Hayden had gone round and round this part of it in her head, and just couldn't find a way to make it work. A marriage forged out of obligation wasn't something she wanted for herself. And she loved Brian too much to do that to him.

Her hands drifted to her barely bulging belly, she already loved this baby too much to give her or him that kind of family. So, she shook her head as she said, "I've weighed this every which way, but I can't do it. I love him—"

"You always have," Kathleen said quietly.

There was no reason to hide it. She'd always known Kathleen knew, even if Brian seemed oblivious to the fact.

"He loves you, too. Always has," Kathleen assured her.

"Not the right way."

"There's a right way to love?"

"He's not *in love* with me," she corrected. "And I'll confess, I want it all."

"All or nothing. Compromise has always come hard to you. It's why you were such a good student, you wouldn't settle for good enough, you wanted the best. But life isn't black-and-white. Don't let your pride stand in the way of fulfilling your dreams."

"I won't. Brian should be a part of the baby's life. But I can't marry him. I can't hurt Brian, trap him in a marriage he didn't want, and would never have considered without the pregnancy. That only leads to bitterness and regret. Kathleen, I do love Brian. That night … It was just once. We were both hurting and comforted each other. It was love, but not the kind that leads to marriage."

Kathleen touched her cheek. "Oh, Hayden. I'm so sorry."

"Don't be. This might not be the ideal situation, but I already love this baby more than you can imagine. And I swear, I'll be a good mother. I know, given my family, you might be worried, but I promise you, I'll do right by her or him."

"Honey, I'm sure you'll be a great mother."

"I was going to call Brian, but maybe it would be better if I told him in person. I need to be sure he understands, that he realizes I don't want his life to change."

"His life will change."

Hayden knew Kathleen was right. "I can do what I can to mitigate that. Convince him to accept the appointment, to go on with what he's achieved so far in California. I can handle this. I want this baby," she confessed. "Want it so bad. I admit, not the best way to go about it, but …"

Kathleen squeezed Hayden's hand and smiled, hoping to reassure her. "Oh, Hayden, do you know what this means? I'm going to be a grandmother."

"Yes, yes, you are." Hayden sat rigidly next to her.

Kathleen knew things weren't going to be as easy as Hayden hoped, but she'd do what she could to help both the kids and the baby. Her grandchild. Despite everything, she couldn't quite contain her excitement over this new addition. "A grandmother. Oh, Hayden."

"Amazing, isn't it?"

"There's so much to do, to plan. Now, of course, you know that you're welcome to live here. I know you've been talking about moving out, but maybe you should wait until after the baby. I mean, don't think you have to stay with me, or that I'm trying to …" She shook her head and chuckled. "Okay, I was about to say don't think I'm being selfish, but truth is, I am. I'm not just saying that staying with me is an option, I'm asking you to. The truth is, I don't want to miss a minute. I want you to stay here, to live here for a while longer."

Hayden's shoulders relaxed, and the tension seemed to melt away. "I'd love to stay, at least until after the baby arrives."

"I'm going to be a grandmother. I swear, I'm going to spoil her, or him, rotten."

"And I swear, I'll let you."

"A grandmother." Kathleen got lost in the haze of possibilities. She'd lost her parents right after she'd married Adam. She still had some distant relatives, but no one she was close to. Now there would be a new generation in her family.

She tried to concentrate on practicalities. "As for work, if we stick to our current schedules, me on days, you on nights, then someone will be here with the baby all the time, unless you want to do daycare. I'll understand if you do, but if you don't, I'd love to keep my grandbaby. Childbirth classes? If you need a partner, I'm available …" She stopped.

"I'm railroading you." Kathleen forced herself to slow down. "I don't want you to think I'm being pushy and will take over. You decide what you want, and what I can do."

Hayden laughed. "Not railroading. Just being you. He or she is so lucky to have you as a grandmother."

"And lucky to have you and Brian as parents. No matter how this plays out between the two of you, this baby will know nothing but love from the both of you, and, of course, from me."

Though she wouldn't kid herself—she'd love to sit them down and tell them what to do, but she knew she wouldn't. She'd advise, if asked. She'd listen. But she knew they had to find their own way. All she could do was offer them her support and her love.

She smiled at Hayden, hoping it would give her peace of mind. "So, there's a huge question that should be answered immediately."

Some of that tension crept back into Hayden shoulders, and she sat up straighter, as if worried about what Kathleen was going to say.

"Am I to be Grandma, Mema, Nana or …" She continued naming every form of grandmother she could think of, and Hayden let her, laughing.

She worried about Brian and Hayden, but knew they were adults and had to work this out on their own. She'd like to tell Hayden not to be foolish and accept Brian's inevitable proposal, to have him move home. She wouldn't.

A grandmother.

She was going to be a grandmother.

Brian was riding high as he cruised down Hazeltine Avenue toward his apartment.

"Brian, dinner's on me," Lisa said. "After all, it's not every day a man has a meeting with the governor and accepts an appointment to a special advisory committee."

He wanted to say something humble, something about it not being a big deal, but it was. It was a very big deal. He couldn't help but think about all the things he could set in motion, things that could make a difference for so many of the state's children, with this position. "It is pretty cool."

"Pretty cool?" She laughed. "Oh, Brian, you are the master of understatement."

He slid his old convertible into its parking space. "Come in while I get changed." They walked through the commons of the building complex toward his studio apartment.

He'd met Lisa through some mutual friends. She was a lawyer who lived a couple blocks from him. Bright, articulate and fun. She was easy to be with, and he'd needed someone in his life who was uncomplicated.

He'd spent the summer flying back and forth to Pittsburgh, trying to juggle his work, and still support his mother and Hayden. But his mother was better, getting stronger every day, and now this appointment. Things were looking up.

"Come on. It will only take me a minute to change."

The complex was of a colonial style that would have seemed more at home in Pennsylvania than California, but maybe that's why it had attracted him. It felt like home. His first floor studio opened to the courtyard.

He noticed someone on the doorstep. "Hayden?"

She looked up, as if surprised to see him. "Brian."

"Hayden, what are you doing here?" She stood and he readied himself for her hug, but instead she smiled shyly.

"Brian." She looked past him. "Oh, I'm sorry. You have a guest. I'll just—"

"Lisa, this is Hayden, Hayden, Lisa."

"I'm sorry. I've interrupted your …" She hesitated, as if not quite sure what to say. "Anyway, I'll just go and you can call me in the morning. My flight home isn't until evening."

Lisa laughed. "So this is the famous Hayden. I've heard so much about you."

Hayden didn't seem to know what to say to that. "I'll let you two—"

Lisa cut her off. "Don't you worry about it. Brian and I can celebrate tomorrow night, after your flight. My place isn't far. I'll head home and let you two visit."

"Thanks, Leese," Brian said, at the same time Hayden said, "It can wait until tomorrow."

Lisa ignored Hayden. "I'll talk to you soon, Brian." Lisa settled the argument starting back down the sidewalk. "Nice meeting you, Hayden."

"You didn't tell me you were coming," Brian said to Hayden as he leaned past her to unlock the door.

"I came to talk to you."

He felt a rush of fear. "The doctors said the cancer was gone. That it wasn't in the lymph—"

"No, no, I didn't mean to scare you. It's not Kathleen. She's fine. She'll be monitored closely, but she's fine. I do need to talk to you though. Could we go inside?"

"Sorry. Of course."

Hayden stepped into the small foyer. He kept walking into the main room.

"Your apartment's orderly."

He looked around and noted that it would be hard for the sparsely furnished room to look anything but orderly. There was a couch, a recliner and a television in the living area. A table with two chairs in the kitchen, and he'd sectioned off his bedroom with a screen. He kept his desk behind it, as well, hiding a mess that would have led Hayden to a very different description of his place. "I keep meaning to do some decorating, but …" He shrugged.

"You're busy. Your mom's about bursting with pride over your new appointment. Congratulations."

"Thanks." He sat on the couch. "Have a seat and tell me why you're here."

Rather than sit by him, she perched on the edge of his recliner, as if ready to bolt. He'd never seen Hayden look so nervous.

"Can I get you something to drink?" he asked, hoping to calm her nerves.

"No. I just want to say this."

"Hayden, you're scaring me."

"Bri, I'm pregnant."

He didn't know what to say, how to feel. He didn't need to ask if it was his. Why else would Hayden be here?

He'd felt guilty about that night in Philadelphia, but now? That one irresponsible night had messed up all Hayden's plans. It was going to change everything for her. He didn't have to ask if she was keeping it. He didn't have to ask anything at all.

"We'll get married." The words were out before he thought about them, but the minute he said them, he knew it was the right solution and waited for Hayden to agree.

When she didn't say anything, he said it again. "We'll get married and I'll come back home. It'll be all right, Hayden."

She was silent another moment, then quietly asked, "Do you love me, Bri? Are you *in love* with me?"

"I do love you, but—"

She shook her head. "That *but* says it all. I love you, too, but I won't marry you."

That's not what he'd expected her to say. "Then I'll simply move home and convince you. I'll just keep asking until you say yes."

"No."

"Hayden." When his father had left his mom, he'd left Brian, as well. Brian couldn't have a child and not be part of his or her life. How could Hayden not see that?

"No," she repeated. "I didn't come here to bring you home, to make you marry me. Actually, it's the opposite. I came to convince you to stay here. I wanted to assure you that I'll do whatever I can so that you're a part of the baby's life."

"You're right. I will be because—"

"Brian, Kathleen told me about this governor's appointment. You can't walk away from that. I don't want you to give up what you've worked so hard for. You can do so much good here."

"I belong there. With you."

"If you move home, then I'll move out."

She said the words with such finality that Brian didn't doubt her. There was a sinking feeling in the pit of his stomach as he realized Hayden didn't want him. "Hayden, I can't leave you to go through this on your own."

"I'm not on my own. Kathleen's beyond excited."

"You told her already?" He knew it shouldn't, but knowing she hadn't come to him first hurt. She'd turned to his mother before she'd turned to him.

"Yes. And when she told me the first thing you'd do is propose, I told her I wouldn't marry you. It might be selfish, but I want it all, Brian. I want a man who's madly in love with me, who can't live without me. I don't want to be anybody's obligation. I won't do that to me, to you or to our baby."

He didn't know what to say, how to make her see that she'd never be merely an obligation to him. "Hayden."

"I'll ask again, are you in love with me?"

"I don't know how to answer that. I love you. You're my best friend. You're a big part of my life."

"I think you've answered it, and my answer is no. Everything's going to be fine, Brian. I won't marry you."

He tried to think of some assurance she'd accept, but he couldn't quite get his thoughts together.

She waited a moment, then continued. "I mean it, I don't want you moving home."

"Kathleen and I have it all sorted. I'm working nights, she'll work days. The baby won't have to go into daycare. She's on our side."

"She's on *your* side. If she were on my side, she'd be helping me figure out how to convince you to marry me." That stung, too. It felt as if suddenly he was being pushed out of the family, that he'd become an outsider.

"Bri, this baby will have both its parents. I swear, I'll never do anything to keep you from being a part of the baby's life. Stay here, serve on your committee. Help all the kids who didn't have Conways down the street to take them in. I'll do everything I possibly can to facilitate your relationship with our child. I swear it. But I can't marry you."

His confusion was clearing and in its place was anger. "*Won't* marry me. I know I can't make you, but I'm moving home and will try and make you see sense."

"Brian, don't. I mean it, I'd move."

"Hayden."

"Brian, you can do so much good here."

"You need me there." He said the words as a statement, but it was more of a question. He wanted Hayden to assure him that she did need him. That she couldn't go through this pregnancy without him.

But instead, she said, "The truth of it is, I don't. I have things in hand. I couldn't not tell you about the baby, but I didn't tell you in order to elicit your pity, or some sense of duty. Like I said, stay here. You've built a life, you have a girlfriend—"

"She's not a girlfriend. She's just a friend."

"If the way she was looking at you is any indication, a friend who could be more. I don't want you to give up someone who might be really good for you, Brian."

"Being a full-time father might be really good for me. I want to be a part of this baby's life."

"A baby you didn't know existed until a few minutes ago."

"Hayden, I want to be part of my baby's life."

"You can be as much a part as you want. If it would make you rest easier, I'll see a lawyer and have papers drawn up saying exactly that. You'll be as active in this baby's life as you want to be."

He knew he had no choice but to acquiesce. He'd known Hayden long enough that there would be no fighting her once her mind was made up. He'd keep trying to persuade her that she needed him, that she should marry him, but her expression said he wouldn't get very far. "You're sure?"

"Positive." It was as if a door had slammed shut. "Oh, and Bri, you should hear her plans. Your mom's been racing a mile-a-minute since I gave her the news. She's champing at the bit. She wants to clean out the room today, order the furniture tomorrow. I haven't seen her look so good since before the cancer."

Brian listened to Hayden recounting all his mother's plans and knew somehow he could have been there, could have been a part of it, if only he'd been able to find the right argument, the right words to convince her they should marry.

He was stung that Hayden so clearly didn't want him. She'd made plans and worked everything out without him.

He was going to be a father.

But not a husband.

Chapter Five

The driver hit the brakes and the van stopped abruptly. Kathleen winced in pain and Hayden squeezed her hands in sympathy. She was struck by how small they were. And cold.

So cold.

She adjusted the blanket on Kathleen's lap, then cupped both her hands in hers.

Brian leaned forward from his seat on the bench, and said. "We just turned onto Briar Hill Road, Mom."

Hayden glanced out the small window and saw the street unfold. It had changed so much over the years. Dirt had given way to tar and chip, and that had long since given way to paving. Houses filled what had once been empty lots. Trees that had been saplings when she was younger, had grown and now lent the neighborhood a feeling of establishment. Even though they'd long since shed their leaves, they stood sentinel, a reminder that winter would pass; that the cold would end and hotter temperatures would one day come again.

But as Hayden tried to will Kathleen's icy hands warm, she knew that spring wouldn't come for all of them and the thought brought a stab of pain. Hayden was growing accustomed to that particular sensation and almost welcomed it, because if she hurt, at least she knew she could still feel. It was better than the numbness that seemed to envelop her the rest of the time.

She watched as the transport van pulled into the driveway. The house hadn't changed nearly as much as the neighborhood had. Kathleen had put a new roof on two years ago. The black and green shingles seemed to bring a breath of freshness to the house. But other than that, and an occasional new coat of paint, it looked the same as it did the first time she'd knocked on the door.

The van came to a standstill.

Brian wordlessly started to unbuckle Kathleen's wheelchair and Hayden helped as the driver opened the door and set up the lift.

As Kathleen was lowered to the drive, it occurred to Hayden that this was it. Kathleen wouldn't be leaving the house again.

Brian's expression said he was having similar hard and painful thoughts.

"Bri—" Hayden got no further than his name because at that moment Olivia ran out to greet them. Hayden was struck by the fact her daughter was no longer a little girl. She was sixteen and on the verge of womanhood.

Brian leaned down and whispered, "Frightening how quick she's growing up, isn't it? Seems like only yesterday I was watching you run toward me from that same front door."

"Nana." Livie threw herself at her grandmother's wheelchair. Hayden made a move to restrain her, to keep Livie from possibly hurting Kathleen, who was visibly tired. At the last moment, Liv slowed and with an amazing amount of tenderness, leaned over and hugged her grandmother. Her auburn curls falling over Kathleen's shoulder, draping her.

From the house, a woman approached them. Small, squat, built like a linebacker, she waddled up to the group and knelt, so she was eye level with the wheelchair. "Hi, Kathleen."

She stood and added, "Hayden, Brian." All business, the woman took control of the wheelchair, pushing it toward the makeshift ramp that led into the house.

There was nothing left to do but thank the driver and follow. "You're sure she's who we want?" Brian asked.

Hayden could understand his concern. Marti Striver didn't look like an angel of compassion. But Hayden knew better.

1992

Hayden liked working nights. In order to attract nurses to the third shift, the hospital offered a new three-day, twelve-hour shift. That allowed Hayden four uninterrupted days with two-year-old Olivia.

It was the perfect solution.

But that wasn't the only reason for working the night-shift. Hayden liked the quiet floor, the hushed tones, the slower pace when the daytime hustle and bustle had quieted to a mere whisper of activity.

Her soft-soled shoes made no noise as she walked down the hall, ready to make her rounds. It was especially slow tonight. She only had four children that she was responsible for, which gave her an opportunity to spend time with any of her charges who had trouble sleeping. She'd read a story here, given a cuddle there.

Kathleen had always said that the comforting part was the best medicine any nurse could give and Hayden tried to remember that.

She tiptoed into Sean Martin's room. The ten-year-old was a favorite. He had aplastic anemia and needed frequent transfusions, which made him a repeat visitor to the floor. Since his initial diagnosis, his disease had progressed to leukemia, and Hayden knew there wasn't much time left for him. Children with aplastic anemia rarely lived beyond the age of seventeen. Because Sean was still so young, they'd hoped he'd have a few more good years, but that wasn't to be.

That knowledge, losing a favorite patient, was one of the hardest parts of her job. Her kids all touched her, but some more than others. Sean was one of those more-than patients. His crooked smile and eternal optimism endeared him to anyone who knew him.

She opened his door and found an unfamiliar woman in the room. The woman put a finger to her lips and walked into the hall without looking back, just assuming Hayden would follow.

She sized Hayden up, then nodded, as if she'd approved of whatever she'd seen. She held out her hand. "Marti Striver."

"Hayden MacNulty." She gave the woman a questioning look.

"I'm with hospice. Sean had a bad day and his mother was exhausted and went home for a rest. I promised to stay with him while she was gone."

"How bad a day?"

"It won't be long."

Hayden knew she should be hardened to these harsh truths. Nurses were trained to maintain their emotional distance. But she wasn't hardened, and had never mastered maintaining any kind of distance from her patients, particularly a sweetie like Sean.

"Are they taking him home?"

Marti shook her head. "They have a houseful of kids and don't think it would work. Between you and me, I don't think his mother can deal with watching him die."

"You're right, I was with her last night. She's a basket case." Hayden heard the derision in her voice and knew it sounded unsympathetic.

Before she could add anything to soften the comment, Marti said, "Everyone deals with pain in a different way. When you've been nursing a little longer, you'll recognize that. Some people shut down, some rage, some fight, some cut off everyone and some are just basket cases. His mom's doing the best she can, trying to keep it all together for him, for the other kids and for her husband. She can meltdown with us, with the medical staff, because we're safe. We don't need or demand anything from her, so she can let go of her defenses."

Hayden felt a flood of embarrassment. "I'm sorry. I didn't mean it like it sounded."

Marti laughed. "Don't apologize. I've dealt with more than my share of pain-in-the-ass families and patients, though more often than not it's the families who are the biggest pains. But I try to remember the nurse's three *c*'s. I don't always manage, but I do try."

"Three *c*'s?"

"Caring, comfort, curing. We can't always manage the cure, but the other two …" She smiled and glanced at the door. "I'd best get back in."

"I have to check the chart and then make the rest of my rounds. But afterward, can I bring you something?"

"Coffee would be nice. I'll confess, I'm addicted. My husband keeps trying to wean me onto herbal teas, but it's like drinking hot, colored water."

Hayden laughed. And though they'd only chatted about coffee and the occupation they shared, Hayden sensed something about the feisty woman … she was all heart.

Hayden watched Marti wheel Kathleen into the house, Livie trailing closely behind them.

Hayden turned and nodded at Brian. "Yes, I'm absolutely sure Marti is the one we want. She's an acquaintance of your mom's—close enough to be familiar, but not so close that intimate care will be embarrassing. You'll learn to love her. Everyone does."

For a moment, she thought he was going to reach out and take her hand. But the feeling passed. They both walked toward the porch, side by side, worlds apart.

Marti had told her so many years ago that everyone dealt with pain in their own way. Hayden had seen it for herself. Some couples came together, united in their circumstance, supporting each other, strengthening each other.

And some people cut themselves off from those they loved. She recognized that she and Brian were doing just that. Each of them pulling back from the other, struggling alone with the pain. Hayden wished she could make herself—make Brian—respond differently, but the awful truth was, she didn't know how. And she no longer had the energy to figure it out.

She followed Brian into the house, knowing that once she entered, nothing would ever be the same.

Chapter Six

Brian watched Hayden and the hospice nurse … What was her name?

Marti, that was it. Marti Stover, or Striven Something like that. She reminded him of a Volkswagen Beetle. Short, round, but dependable.

Marti and Hayden settled his mother into the hospital bed that had been delivered just yesterday. Already the room seemed foreign. The bed and other medical accouterments made it feel as if a slice of the hospital had been transplanted into their house.

Into their home.

It pissed him off, though he wasn't sure why. He knew the equipment, from the bed with the weird air mattress, to the portable toilet, would make things easier for his mom and Hayden. But simply looking at the room made him feel a sense of impotent rage.

It even had that slightly metallic smell he'd come to associate with the hospital over the last few months. He couldn't grasp how Hayden had stood working in conditions like this, night after night, year after year. Dealing with the smells and the horror of watching people suffer.

She was efficient as she worked with Marti, arranging his mom. Neither seemed bothered that they were putting his mother into a bed that, in all likelihood, she'd die in.

Die?

A world without his mother?

Brian had never thought of himself as a mama's boy. But since her illness had come back, he'd begun to realize how much he counted on her.

Even during the years when he lived on the other side of the country, he'd known his mother was only a phone call away. She'd watched over Hayden and Olivia when he wasn't there. And when he'd come home every month, she was waiting, smiling, as happy to see him as he'd been to see her.

Those times had been filled with tension and recriminations—not from his mom, Hayden or even Livie.

After Hayden had come to tell him she was pregnant, that they were going to have a baby, he'd wanted nothing more than to come home. It hurt a lot to know that Hayden didn't want or need him there.

Whenever he thought of those years, what he remembered the most was being torn. Pulled between his life in California, and his life in Pennsylvania. He'd known his position on the child-welfare committee had made a difference to the kids in California, but at the expense of the one child he wanted to be with the most—Olivia.

If that wasn't enough, he'd had to deal with Lisa....

1993

"Don't go."

The window was open, allowing a brisk Pacific wind to billow the curtains, blowing the scent of the city into the room. California was supposed to be a paradise. He tried to remember that, but sometimes it was easy to forget when he started longing for home.

His position on the governor's advisory committee had led to his paid position on the governor's staff as the Child Welfare

Director. He was having an even greater say in California's policies. But no matter how often he reminded himself of the fact, it didn't stop him from feeling as if he had let down Hayden and his daughter. He should have insisted he and Hayden marry and that he should return home, despite Hayden's threats that she'd leave.

"Brian," Lisa said again.

He kept packing his suitcase. He didn't bother looking up, didn't respond. There really was nothing left to say.

Like a broken record, they had played the same song over and over, every time he got ready to visit Pittsburgh.

"Brian." Lisa's voice was sharp and demanding of his attention.

Knowing he couldn't continue to avoid the scene, he finally looked up at his wife of a year and a half.

He knew her face intimately. The small scattering of freckles along the bridge of her nose, the scar by her right ear where her brother whacked her with a broken yardstick as they played knights.

She'd been fearless and filled with a zest for life when he'd met her. Lisa had been there after Hayden left, when he'd been so confused he didn't know which way to turn. She'd supported him, been a friend and eventually, romance bloomed. Brian had thought it would be forever, but more and more he wasn't so sure.

Lisa made it clear she wasn't happy, but Brian didn't know any other way to do things.

"Lisa, you were aware of Olivia when we married. You were there with me after I found out. You told me that you understood the situation." His voice was harder than he intended. But he was tired of doing this whenever he left.

"Yes, but—"

"You knew she was important to me, that I hate living so far from her. Hayden didn't want me there, and what I was doing here was important. That it still is important. But it doesn't alter the fact that I love my daughter and need to make these monthly trips home. Calling her every night isn't enough. Not nearly enough. You accepted all of this when we married."

"Yes."

"Then I'm not sure why every month, every trip we have to replay this conversation. It's not as if I go and don't invite you. You're always welcome. Mom said last time that she wished they saw more of you. That she'd like to know her daughter-in-law better."

Lisa's face had always shown her every emotion. Once, there had been humor. Interest. Love. Now he watched as her anger gave way to a sullen pouting. "You know it's hard for me to get away from work."

Always the same.

Did every couple find themselves reliving the same fights over and over? Did any of them find a way out of the ruts?

"You could manage it if you wanted to. But that's the point, isn't it? You don't want to."

"Brian, I'm an outsider in Pittsburgh."

"Bridgeville," he corrected automatically. "We live just outside the city in the small town of Bridgeville."

"Pennsylvania, then. I'm an outsider. You, your mom, Olivia …" She paused. "Hayden. You all have history. The stories, the inside jokes. I'm not a part of them, of any of that. They're your east-coast family. You're different there. I don't know you there. I know the west coast you. I fell in love with the west coast Brian Conway."

"I'm me, no matter what coast I'm on. If you came with me more often, we'd build our own stories and inside jokes there … ones that include you." He gently stroked her arm. "Olivia's still too young to fly across country on her own. My going there makes the most sense. It won't always be this way. She'll get older, she'll come here. But for now, I need to be with my daughter. See her on a regular basis. And I'd like you to be a part of that."

Lisa sighed and took his hand. "Well, it's too late for me to get off work now, but I'll really try next time."

He kissed her forehead. "I'd like that. We'd all like that. We want you to feel as if you're a part of the family."

"I don't. Not yet. But I'm willing to give it a chance. Now, do you have everything?"

Next time never came. Lisa put off Pennsylvania, and their fight occurred again and again, until finally she'd said he had to choose, her or Olivia.

There was no choice to make.

Brian had helped Lisa pack.

He wasn't sure why he was thinking about Lisa now. Their marriage had been a mistake from the beginning. They'd wanted different things and neither had been willing to give an inch.

He studied Hayden, who was dealing so tenderly with his mother.

During their last fight, Lisa had said that if it had been just his daughter, she'd have coped. But she could never compete with Hayden, so she was done.

He'd never thought of it as a competition. If asked, he'd have denied ever comparing Lisa to Hayden. But looking back, he had to admit that maybe his ex-wife was right.

Maybe Lisa had a point. Brian couldn't remember a time when he hadn't loved Hayden. Recently, that love had felt brittle and fragile, and he was worried. He wanted to grab on to it, hold it tightly, but was afraid that if he held too tightly, it would break.

Chapter Seven

"Are you comfortable?" Hayden asked as she fussed with the end of Kathleen's bed, straightening the covers, then restraightening them.

Kathleen hated that she was putting her family through this. "Yes. The new Fentanyl patch is working wonderfully. There's no pain."

"If you start to hurt, though, you'll tell me? Marti left medications for breakthrough pain."

Kathleen nodded. "I will. But right now, I'm okay. Sit down and catch your breath."

"I'm fine."

Kathleen knew that Hayden wasn't fine. Neither were Brian and Livie.

She hoped that the kids finally admitted they belonged together, that they were done with trials, even though she knew better. Relationships, like life, were filled with highs and lows. Brian and Hayden were going through an unprecedented low now, and she could only wish they'd find their way out of it.

Dying wasn't the hard part, leaving behind those she loved and knowing they were hurting, was.

"I know I've said it before, but I appreciate your moving back in here and putting your house on the market. I know how hard you worked for it."

"You don't have to thank me. Living together makes sense, and as much as I loved my house, this has always been home."

Kathleen groped for a happy memory, something sweet for them to focus on. There were so many to choose from, but it only took a minute for her to find the right one. "Today I've been remembering another move...."

April 1995

Hayden peeked into the living room of her small house. She'd scrimped and saved to buy it. Even after years of living here, she still sometimes felt awed that it was hers—that she'd bought it on her own.

From the doorway, she watched her daughter. Livie's auburn hair was twisted into a long ponytail that dragged along the sill as she craned her neck one way and then the other, obviously trying to see something better.

Hayden had come to check on her five-year-old because time had taught her one of life's most important mothering lessons—if a child is too quiet, something is generally wrong, or they're into something they shouldn't be.

"What's up, hon?"

Livie, a miniature Kathleen, right down to the slight sprinkling of freckles and the clear, true-blue eyes, turned, concern etching her face. "Is Nana leaving?"

Hayden joined her daughter at the front window and peered two doors down Briar Hill Road to Kathleen's house. A giant moving truck sat in the driveway.

"No, I'm sure she's not leaving. But I wonder what's up?"

"I'd like her to move in with us. I liked living with Nana when I was a baby."

Hayden was politic enough not to mention that since Olivia was only two when they moved away from Kathleen's, she was pretty sure the little girl didn't actually remember living with her grandmother. Olivia's memories were inspired by Kathleen's stories and were very real to her.

Olivia was a story collector. She listened intently to all of Kathleen's tales of when Hayden and Brian were small. Lately, Livie had been stuck on ghosts and bikers, after Kathleen told her about the first time Hayden had come to the house. Halloween was six months away, and Livie was already mulling over what she'd wear, uncertain which costume she wanted to copy.

"Can we go to Nana's and check?"

"Sure. We can go investigate, nosy Rosey, her mama's posy."

"Olivia Kathleen-Rose Conway, nosy Rosey, her mama's posy." Livie parroted the rhyme Hayden had made up years ago. The little girl tried to look miffed, because Hayden knew she felt she was too old for baby nicknames, but she couldn't quite pull it off.

As Hayden chuckled, Livie joined in.

"Let's go."

Livie hurried to the front door, threw it I open, but before she could make her escape, Hayden said, "Stop. Put a jacket on. It's cool."

It had been a cool and damp spring. Hayden reminded herself that all the rain was responsible for the lush green colors that had flooded the winter-gray landscape, but every now and again she couldn't convince herself that it was a good thing. Mainly when Livie forgot and tracked mud through the house.

Livie sighed the sigh of the truly put upon. Hayden only laughed as she pulled her own coat on.

Livie was skipping across Miss Witman's lawn before Hayden had the door shut. She hurried after her daughter, taking the sidewalk, not the lawn, not that Miss Witman would have minded. She was a sweet older lady and over the last three years had grown accustomed to the comings and goings between Hayden's and Kathleen's homes.

Kathleen's front door stood open as Hayden approached. She hurried in and shut it behind her. "Livie Conway, were you born in a barn? It's cold out and you left your Nana's door …"

The sentence faded as she spotted her daughter, Kathleen and Brian in the living room.

"Surprise." He was entangled in little girl, but he stood and walked toward Hayden, Livie holding tightly to him like a small chimp. Arms around his neck, legs around his stomach, as if she was afraid he'd disappear if she let go.

"I begged Mom to keep the secret," he offered as an explanation, although it didn't really answer anything about him arriving with a moving truck.

Kathleen was the picture of happiness as she looked from her son and granddaughter to Hayden. "It was the hardest thing he's ever asked me to do. Secrets have never been my strongest suit."

"Secret?" They all looked excited, and Hayden knew whatever the secret was, it was a good one.

"Mom, Daddy's moving home. He's staying with Nana until he can find his own house and he's going to live here in Bridgeville—"

"Well, somewhere in the Pittsburgh area," he corrected.

"From now on. Forever. I can see him all the time, and sometimes spend the night at his house, right, Daddy?"

Brian's eyes never left Hayden. He watched her as he nodded. "Right."

Hayden couldn't sort out her emotions. On one hand, Livie was obviously delighted having her father so near; on the other, it had been relatively easy dealing with Brian when there was an entire continent between them, except for one long weekend a month. Would it make things harder if he demanded more time with Livie?

The mere thought made her feel guilty and she reminded herself of her old promise that she'd do whatever she could to facilitate Brian spending as much time as he could—as he wanted to—with their daughter.

"You're moving back?" she asked just to be sure she was hearing things correctly.

He nodded again.

"For good?"

Another nod. "So, are you surprised?" He looked nervous, as if he wasn't sure what her reaction would be.

"Flabbergasted."

"Flabb … flabb … Say it again, Mommy."

Hayden dutifully obeyed. "Flabbergasted."

"Flabbergasted." Livie nodded. "Spell it."

"*F-l-a-b-b-e-r-g-a-s-t-e-d.*"

Livie parroted the letters back. Brian looked quizzically.

"We watched the last National Spelling Bee, and ever since, Livie's been planning to be the champ someday, so she spells everything."

"I didn't know." A flash of pain crossed his face.

He and Hayden had both worked so hard over the last five years to keep him and Livie connected. He'd read her a bedtime story before she was even old enough to register who the voice was coming from the receiver.

Noticing how missing so much hurt him, noticing how happy Livie was, again Hayden made a promise to herself to do whatever it took to share their daughter.

"I'm sorry," Hayden said. "I thought I'd told you about the spelling bee-itis."

"It's okay. I'm here now, and I won't miss out on things like spelling-bee champs in the making."

"Daddy, Daddy, can I help carry in your boxes? How many do you have? It looks like a lot. Maybe Mommy's friend Alex, could come help. Is Lisa in the back of the truck with the boxes? I'd like to ride in the back, but it would probably be dark." Livie's brow furrowed, then lightened. "But I could take the new flashlight Mommy bought me and then I wouldn't mind, so I could try it."

"What about a seat belt?" Hayden asked.

"Oh, yeah. I can't ride without a seat belt. But maybe you'd take me for a ride in the front? It has a seat belt, right?"

"Right. And if Mommy says, you can ride with me when I take the truck back to the store," Brian said, smiling at the mile-a-minute monologues that Livie specialized in. His smile faded abruptly. "But about Lisa."

He paused and then slowly said, "Honey, she's not in the back of the van—"

"Oh. I guess it wouldn't be fun riding with boxes if you didn't have a flashlight. But she can use mine if she wants."

He sat on the couch, and pulled Livie onto his lap, obviously as loath to release her as she was to release him. "That's very generous of you to offer to share your flashlight. But Lisa's not with me."

"When does she arrive?" Hayden asked.

Hayden and Lisa had a painfully polite relationship. Lisa didn't like her, and Hayden was all right with that. Hayden was pretty sure Lisa didn't like Olivia, either. Had she been mean to Livie, Hayden would have said something, but Brian's wife was the soul of politeness, so Hayden had let it ride, knowing it must be hard for Lisa to deal with Brian's ready-made family.

"About Lisa," Brian said again. He smoothed Livie's wild hair a moment. "You see, she's not coming. She's staying in California. Daddy and Lisa aren't going to be married anymore."

"Oh. Because she didn't like me?" Livie asked, echoing Hayden's thoughts. Thoughts she'd never voiced to her daughter.

Livie was too smart, too intuitive for her own good sometimes.

"Livie, honey," Brian said softly. Hayden could hear the emotion clogging his throat. "Lisa loved you. She still does. It's just that

Daddy and Lisa haven't been happy in a long while. Sometimes that happens to grownups. They love each other for a while, and then they stop."

"Maybe you'll stop loving me?"

Brian hugged Livie fiercely. "Never. Parents never, ever stop loving their children."

"Mommy's mommy did. She doesn't love Mommy or me. She never came to see us when she lived down the street. We met her at the grocery store one day when I was really little and she didn't even say hi. I went with Mommy later to her mommy's new home and she called Mommy a—"

"I know," Kathleen said, interrupting the painful discussion, "let's go out for ice cream and celebrate the fact my son's come home."

"Sounds good, Mom." Brian shot Kathleen a look of pure gratitude.

Hayden ached for Brian. A divorce would hit him hard. "Yes, it does sound great. Just let me run and lock up the house. After, we can help unload the van."

Hayden was glad to get away briefly and collect herself. Hearing her daughter talk about her own mother, obviously remembering the cruel words, hurt. It wasn't Hayden's fault, she knew, but still she felt guilty.

Add to that, Brian's moving home, that Lisa wasn't coming, left her feeling breathless. Her heart sped up, but she savagely tried to calm it. Brian was here to be close to his daughter, not to be close to her.

She opened her front door, grabbed her purse from the front closet and was on her way back out when the phone rang.

She didn't even think twice about answering it. She just picked it up because of some Pavlovian need to answer it. "Hello?"

"Hayden, it's Donna at the nursing home."

"Oh." Her heart sank. She had no doubt the news wouldn't be pleasant. She forced a more cheerful response. "Hi, Donna. What's up?"

"Your mother's worse than normal. Could you come over?"

Hayden glanced out the window. Brian had pulled Kathleen's car into the driveway with Livie and Kathleen in the backseat.

She so wanted to be a part of the celebration, but now that Brian was home, she'd have to get used to Livie doing things with him, without her. She'd just have to send them on their way. "Yes, I'll be over in a few minutes."

"Sorry. I would have let it be until tomorrow, but the nursing supervisor, Corrine, wants to talk to you about your mom seeing a specialist."

"Sure. I understand."

"I know you do."

Being a nurse, Hayden took a very active role in her mother's healthcare, not that her mother appreciated it. As a matter of fact, her mother resented being in a home, and blamed Hayden for it, rather than blaming her years of hard living and heavy drinking for her ill health and slipping mental status.

Part of Hayden wanted to wash her hands of the whole situation. It was no more than her mother deserved. But Hayden knew she couldn't do that. She'd never be able to live with herself if she walked away. Alex, the man she'd been casually dating for a few months, told her she was a sap, allowing herself to be used. But Hayden knew that wasn't it. She looked out for her mother because it was the right thing to do.

It's what Kathleen would have done.

And, although she couldn't walk away from her mother's needs, she did feel a twinge of resentment from time to time.

Today was one of those times.

She got her purse and went out to the car, leaning over to the driver's window. "Sorry, guys. I got a call from the nursing home. Why don't you all go for the ice cream, and I'll see about my mother."

"Problems?" Brian asked.

She'd never spoken to him of her mother and the decision last year to move her into a home. She'd never told him about the month of paperwork, getting her mother into the medicaid program in order to pay for it. She didn't talk about her mother any more than she absolutely had to.

Her mom was in the residential part of the facility, in a safe, supervised setting. All her needs were cared for. And she hated every minute of it. It had taken a third-degree burn from a small kitchen fire and a judge to get her somewhere safe.

"No new problems, just the same old, same old." At his worried expression, she added, "I can handle it."

Kathleen leaned up from the backseat. "Hayden, why don't we go with you?"

"No." Hayden had tried taking Livie there once, thinking her mother would enjoy seeing her granddaughter, and it had been a debacle. She wouldn't put anyone else through it. "I don't know how long it will take."

"We'll wait," Brian said firmly.

"But—"

"Mommy, I don't wanna go without you. Daddy was telling me about his trip 'cross the country. He was talking about the lake salt—"

"Salt Lake," Brian corrected.

Livie nodded. "And he's going to show me a map when we get back. He can just tell me more stories until you're done. Please?"

Hayden softened. She could see that it was important to Livie to have them all together and gave in like the soft touch Kathleen always accused her of being. "Fine. If you all are sure you don't mind waiting in the car. But do you mind stopping at the dough-nut store first?"

"Doughnuts and ice cream?" Brian looked puzzled.

"It's not for us," Livie said. "When Mommy's mom is mean, she takes treats in for the nurses. She says she's had patients like her mom and feels bad for the nurses. She wants them to know she app …"

"Appreciates," Hayden filled in.

"Appreciates," Livie repeated. "Spell it."

"*A-p-p-r-e-c-i-a-t-e-s*," Brian," said.

"*A-p-p-r-e-c-i-a-t-e-s*," Livie echoed, then nodded. "Mommy wants them to know she appreciates them."

Brian agreed. "Doughnuts it is, then. Let's go"

Olivia chattered during the entire ride. Telling her father about her school class, about her ballet classes … about everything. Most of the information he'd heard during their nightly conversations, but he listened again, "oohing" and "ahhing" at the appropriate moments.

They let Hayden out at the doughnut store, and after she'd bought her treats for the nursing staff, they drove the last couple minutes to the home. Hayden got out with two dozen doughnuts in hand.

"Listen, why don't you all go get your ice cream, then come back and pick me up?" she tried again.

"We'll wait." Brian looked stubborn.

"Fine. I'll hurry." To be honest, she'd have hurried regardless. Visiting her mother wasn't the highlight of any particular day. Consumed by alcoholism, Jeri MacNulty had been disinterested since day one. So after years of not having anything to do with her mother, Hayden now bore responsibility for her healthcare needs. There was no one else. And despite the fact that her mother never cared for her, Hayden couldn't bring herself to turn away.

When she was honest with herself, she admitted that she wanted to do exactly that, turn away. There were times that she felt as if she was going to boil over with hurt and anger over the situation, but she couldn't ignore someone in need. Not even her mother.

She found Donna at the second-floor nursing station. "I bring you bribes." She set down the two boxes of doughnuts.

"You don't have to keep doing this." But even as Donna said the words, the nurse opened the lid of one of the boxes. "Cream-filled. My favorite." She looked up at Hayden, doughnut in hand. "Like I said, you don't have to, but thanks."

"I do know what it's like, so it's my pleasure." Hayden wished she could stay here and talk to Donna, but she knew she had to at least make an effort to check on her mother. "Is she in her room?"

"Yes. I'll tell Corrine that you're here."

Suddenly, there was a loud scream from down the hall. "My mother?"

Donna nodded.

"I'll check on her while you find Corrine."

Hayden made her way down the hall to her mother's room.

She might be a nurse, but she couldn't help crinkling her nose at the smell. It wasn't just the ripe scent of urine, it was more. Hopelessness masked by anger. It was the smell of time running out.

Though they all had rooms, many of the residents milled about the halls. Some in chairs, some in walkers, all of them waiting. Waiting for someone to visit. Waiting for something to happen. Waiting to die.

Hayden tried to smile, stopping for a word or two of hellos to those she knew, which on the surface sounded nice, but if she was honest it was just a way to delay seeing her mother.

But she reached her mom's door and knew there was no more putting it off. Her hand on the knob, she made up her mind that this time, she was going to be sympathetic.

She opened the door.

"You." Her mother pointed a shaky, bony finger in Hayden's direction as she stepped into the room. "You put me here. You and that judge. They're trying to kill me, you know, and I'm sure that's what you're hoping for. But I stopped that girl. She tried to do me in, but I beat her off."

"No one is trying to kill you, and you can't go beating on people." Hayden moved closer to the wheelchair. "You have to try to behave."

"Oh, don't tell me what I can and can't do. I'm sure you're enjoying this. It's your revenge, having the judge say I can't make my own decisions and putting you in charge. First thing you do is stash me in this hellhole so you can steal all my money and gloat over my suffering."

Hayden didn't mention that even after selling the small brick house at the end of Briar Hill Road, there hadn't been enough money to even begin to cover her mother's debt. She didn't say that she'd had to dip into her own meager savings to clear things up. She didn't say anything at all as her mother continued raging, blaming Hayden for her current woes, for everything that had ever gone wrong in her life.

The irony that she was caring for the mother who'd never cared for her wasn't lost on Hayden. But she just knew she couldn't do anything less. Some might say that made her a doormat, but she preferred to think it showed she had strength of character, compassion even. At least, that's what she told herself when she wondered for the umpteenth time, why she bothered.

"Hayden, could you come to the office?" Donna asked from the doorway.

"And her—" her mother pointed at Donna "—she's the worst. She hates me. She wants to kill me, to keep me quiet."

Hayden told her mother, "I've got to see Corrine, but I'll come say goodbye before I leave."

"Don't bother. I'll sit here in this room and rot. That's what you want. I'll …"

Hayden and Donna exited the room, leaving her mother to continue her tirade on her own.

"I'm so sorry," Hayden told Donna. Since moving her mother into the home, she'd perfected the art of apologizing.

"And you don't have to be. You haven't done anything other than act like a concerned, caring daughter."

Hayden didn't admit it, but she knew the words were unwarranted. She wasn't taking care of her mother because she genuinely cared.

The meeting with Corrine went quickly. The staff had talked about Jeri, and wanted to bring in a geriatric psychiatrist, hoping she'd have some recommendations for keeping Hayden's mother calmer, more rational. Her mental state was deteriorating fast.

When Hayden had agreed, signed the papers and finished the short meeting, she went back down the hall to tell her mother goodbye.

"Go. Just go," Jeri hollered.

Hayden wanted nothing more than to turn and hurry out to the car where her family, her real family, was waiting for her. But her mother chose that moment to sweep her hand across a small table, sending everything on it crashing to the floor.

Knowing her family would have to wait another minute, Hayden bent to pick up the mess.

Brian shifted around in his seat so that he could see his mother and his daughter. Livie was still animatedly telling him about everything from school to her friends.

This was the right decision. For the last five years, he'd gone back and forth between the life he'd built in California, his career and friends and his family here in Pittsburgh. When he and Lisa had finally admitted their marriage wasn't working for reasons that had little to do with his family in Pittsburgh, and everything to do with the fact that they weren't suited for one another, he'd known coming back here was the correct thing to do.

As Child Welfare Director, he'd helped put policies in place that he felt had made the California's practices better, had seen to the needs of the children. There was more to be done, but he'd known it was time to leave the job to someone else.

Finally, here in the car, he felt whole rather than torn. His mom was smiling, her hand gently placed on Livie's shoulder. His daughter looked more like his mother than she did like him and Hayden. The same red hair, the same twinkle in her blue eyes. But now, her eyes weren't twinkling, they'd become concerned. "Daddy, be nice to Mama when she comes out. Visiting here makes her sad."

"Sad?"

Livie nodded. "Her mom's not a very nice lady. She yells at Mommy a lot."

He noted that Livie never referred to Hayden's mom as her grandmother. There was no more connection between Jeri MacNulty and Livie than there had ever been between the woman and Hayden.

"Why is Hayden here then?" he asked his mother. "Why take care of her? The woman never did anything for Hayden."

"You know Hayden, or at least you should," Kathleen explained softly. "She couldn't do anything but what she's doing. Hayden's all heart. Her mom's mind is getting worse every day. Physically, she's fine." She nodded toward Livie, and changed the topic, asking Livie if she wanted to go to the zoo on Saturday.

The contentment Brian felt watching his mother and daughter together was marred by his concern for Hayden. The minutes ticked by and when she still hadn't come out, he said, "Let me run in and check on her."

"I don't know if that's such a good idea." His mother's brows were knit with concern.

But Livie didn't seem to share it. "Yes, go tell her to hurry up so we can get our ice cream."

Reluctantly, his mother gave him the room information. Brian made his way through a lovely lobby to the elevators and up to the appropriate floor. This was more homey than a hospital. The floors were a fake parquet. There were paintings on the walls, and residents lining the hall, with busy looking nurses and aides weaving in and out amongst them.

He turned to the hall his mother had directed him to, and heard the screaming. He followed the numbers and found Hayden's mother's room was the one where all the noise was coming from.

The door was open, so he walked in and saw Mrs. MacNulty sitting in a wheelchair, berating her daughter. Hayden was just standing there, her hands filled with pieces of what looked to have been a lamp.

"They're going to kill me and you're worried because a little lamp broke? You're just leaving me here to die? You'll be happy when they've done me in. Then you won't have to deal with me anymore—"

"That's enough," Brian found himself saying as he faced Mrs. MacNulty. "How dare you speak to Hayden that way, after everything she's done for you? Her whole life you neglected her. And despite that, she's here, taking care of you. So don't you dare—"

Hayden was glaring at him. "That's enough, Brian." She threw the pieces into the waste-basket, then turned to her mother. "You'll be seeing a new doctor tomorrow—try to behave. I'll be back tomorrow night before work to check on you." She whirled on Brian. "And you, out in the hall!"

Not knowing what else to do, why she was obviously so upset, Brian followed. She shut the door behind her and backed him up to the wall. "Don't you ever do that again."

"What? I don't know what I did."

"Brian, I'm an adult. I'm not Cootie MacNulty who needs you to play white knight on the bus. I've coped with everything life has thrown at me, and I'll cope with this, in my own way, on my own terms. No rescuing required."

He realized his mistake. "You're right about everything you said. You're not Cootie MacNulty, and you don't need to be rescued. I just ..." He paused. "I'm sorry. Livie said to be nice to you when you came out, that coming here made you sad. I can't stand seeing you sad, seeing you hurt. I never could."

She reached out and he thought she was going to touch him, but she didn't. Her hand fell back to her side. "I know. I'm sorry I snapped like that. It was well meant, but Brian, now that you're home for a while—"

"For good. I'm home for good," he corrected.

She nodded. "Just because you're here doesn't mean you can step in and take over. I'm used to handling things on my own. Well, on my own with Kathleen's help."

"I want to help, too, if you'll let me."

"With Livie. You're entitled and Livie's going to want to spend as much time with you as possible. With Livie you can help, but with the rest of my life, my mother, my boyfriend, with all of it outside of Livie, hands off."

"Boyfriend?" That stopped him short. He remembered Livie saying something about Mommy's friend Alex. The thought of a boyfriend didn't sit well.

Oh, he knew that Hayden had to have had relationships in the past, but she'd never mentioned them and he'd never asked. A boyfriend? He wanted to ask about the man, but knew he didn't have the right.

Hayden shrugged. "I don't know, maybe *boyfriend*'s too strong a word for Alex. Friend."

"With benefits?" The look on her face told him she wasn't in the mood for joking. "Kidding. Seriously, just kidding."

At least he thought he'd been kidding. But as he dealt with a spurt of disappointment because she hadn't answered the question, he realized that maybe he hadn't been kidding. And that was absurd. He and Hayden were friends. What she did in her dating life was her own business.

Intellectually, he knew that.

"Livie and your mom are waiting," Hayden said. "Let's forget about this spat and get some ice cream." Her smile seemed forced as she started walking briskly down the hall.

Brian took off after her and grabbed her arm as he came up behind her. "Hayden, I really was kidding. I know it was inappropriate, that time and distance has taken its toll on our friendship and that kind of joking isn't appropriate. I won't do it again. But if for no other reason than our daughter, I do want to find a way for us to have a relationship. A friendship. Maybe not what we once had, but—"

"Brian, I've never stopped thinking of you as a friend."

"Me, neither."

They walked to the elevator. As they waited, Hayden asked, "So, as a friend, can I inquire if you're okay with your separation from—"

"More than that. She's pushing for a quick divorce. She'll be my ex-wife soon."

"I'm sorry."

"So am I. It's been a long time coming, and I know it's for the best, but still, I'm sorry." He shook off the deep morose that threatened to overwhelm him as he thought about the failure his marriage to Lisa had been. "Let's go get that ice cream. Tonight, we're not worrying about your mother, or my messed-up life, and we'll concentrate on our daughter. About making her happy."

"Deal. Let's go. Bet you're getting a chocolate milkshake, and I'm going to let you buy me a—"

"Banana split." At her surprised expression, he added, "I might have been gone a long time, but there are some things you don't forget."

What he didn't add was that where Hayden was concerned, there was nothing he'd forgotten.

Nothing.

Brian wasn't sure why he'd been thinking so much about when he'd first moved back home from California. Maybe he was remembering it because it had been such a happy time. He needed to cling to those memories in order to deal with everything that was happening in the here-and-now.

He peeked into the room Hayden had set up for his mother. Hayden was curled up in the recliner, staring out the window, lost in thought. His mom was sleeping and looked peaceful.

Hayden must have heard him come in. Their eyes met. She placed a finger to her lips, indicating he should be quiet. She rose and followed him from the room. "She's sleeping."

"I saw."

"I should probably get some work done and—"

"You should get some rest yourself. Whatever else needs done will wait."

"Don't tell me what to do, Bri." She bristled, just as she always had when he tried to tell her what to do—for her own good.

Hayden had never looked after herself. She'd taken care of Livie, Kathleen, him … even her own worthless mother. But never herself. It might have worked if Hayden would let him step in and care for her when it was warranted, but her stubborn pride wouldn't allow it.

And though he wouldn't admit it, that hurt. He wanted to care for Hayden, to ease the pain he knew she felt. The same pain they all felt.

"You're an emotional wreck," he said, "and it's only going to get worse. Take some time for yourself. You've been so busy with Mom, with Livie. You're ignoring your own needs and feelings in order to—"

She glared at him. "And don't tell me how I feel. How I deal with my pain is my prerogative."

"Are you two fighting again?"

Brian turned and found Livie standing just outside her bedroom door. At sixteen, his daughter was a beautiful woman. It killed him to acknowledge that fact, but she was, indeed, a woman now. A couple more years and she'd be off to college. "No, honey. Your mom and I weren't fighting."

"We're both tired," Hayden added.

"All you do since we moved in with Nana is fight."

"That's not true, Livie," Hayden said.

Livie gave them a look of contempt, as if she knew they were lying, then went back into her room and slammed the door.

"She's right," Brian admitted. "I don't want to fight with you."

"Me, neither." She sighed. "You were right, as well. I am tired. I'll try to take a nap. If Marti comes back, wake me, okay? I have to talk to her about a few things."

He nodded, leaned down and kissed her forehead. "Sweet dreams."

She gave him a look of disbelief. "Bri, there are no good dreams right now, only this nightmare. And all we can do is live with it and make it as easy on Kathleen and Livie as we can."

She turned and walked away. He wanted to stop her, wanted to pull her into his arms and tell her that everything would be okay, but he didn't say anything.

That was the biggest part of their problem. When they should, neither of them spoke. And when they should be quiet, both of them spoke up, saying things that hurt, words that left scars.

He didn't know what was going to happen when this was all over.

He didn't think Hayden knew, either.

Chapter Eight

Three days later Brian was looking for Hayden, but found Marti instead. She was leaving his mother's room with a tray in her hand.

"Do you know where Hayden went?" He felt galled, having to ask this woman he barely knew—who'd become such a fixture in the house—where his wife was.

"I sent her outside. Told her to get some fresh air. She needs to leave Kathleen's room, and *you* need to see to it that she does when I'm not here."

"I've tried. But Hayden has always done things her way."

Marti snorted. "Well, you'll have to try harder. Convince her that her way isn't the only way."

"Have you met my wife?" He smiled to let this Marti know he was teasing.

Some of her hardness faded and she grinned back. "She's a tough nut. You'll just have to be tougher."

He started toward the living room when Marti added, "She went out the back door. Maybe she's in the woods?"

It was all the help Brian needed. If Hayden had gone out back, he knew where she'd go.

She'd go to the spot she always went to when she needed privacy … his old tree house. They'd rebuilt it on one of his visits home when Livie was younger. It had been Liv's haven. Livie, who was too old for tree houses now.

He trudged through the yard noting that the grass was spongy from the past three days of rain. It smelled of the cold wet that made him remember all the times he'd made this trek behind the house to the small copse of trees.

The trees were much bigger than they'd been when he and his mother had first moved here. But the old path between the winter-dried, thorny raspberry bushes was still there and looking freshly used. A footprint clearly outlined in the mud.

He pushed through the tangle of branches and weeds until he reached the ladder. His foot on the first rung, he stopped. He could hear her inside. Crying as if her heart was breaking.

Hayden never cried. Listening to her sobs he felt more useless, more inept than he ever had. He wanted to comfort her, but he was afraid she'd rebuff the attempt. She wouldn't like that he was here, witnessing her despair.

Throughout her very hard life, Hayden's pride—her constant companion, working as armor—had kept her strong. He knew that. He'd witnessed her facing her fear time and time again.

If he went up the ladder, he'd strip her of that. He wasn't sure she'd like it.

Okay, he was positive she wouldn't like it.

But he needed to do something for her. He wanted to lend her his support, show her his love. Even at the best of times, it would be hard to get her to lean on him, but now, with the ever-growing distance between them, he was afraid it would be impossible. But he had to try.

So, Brian started up the ladder, hoping he could find some way to bridge their rift. Remembering the night he realized he was in love with Hayden.

The day after he'd moved home, Hayden invited him to come to her house at Livie's bedtime. She'd given him a key to her place. "I want you to visit Livie whenever you want to. Feel free to come and go as you please."

He'd been surprised, but he knew he shouldn't have been. Hayden had made sure he and Livie had a strong relationship.

It had been Hayden who had suggested his nightly bedtime stories. Hayden who had prompted Livie to draw Daddy pictures, from practically the time their daughter could grip a crayon.

And it had been Hayden who'd given him a camera, which she kept at her house. "I'll try and take pictures of everything you miss in between your visits."

Big packs of pictures arrived each week. There were milestones like first steps, and first teeth. But there was also the minutiae. Livie lifting a shovelful of sand from her sandbox. Livie at the zoo, at the beach, in her bath.

He shook his head. No, he shouldn't have been surprised that Hayden had given him a key and offered to keep his nightly bedtime-story tradition alive.

He unlocked her door for the first time, let himself into her house. He could hear voices, and he followed them. He paused at Livie's bedroom, unabashedly listening.

"He'll be over to tell you your bedtime story soon."

"What about when Daddy moves again?" Livie's tired, little-girl voice asked.

Hayden replied, "Silly. Daddy might move out of Nana's house, but he's staying here, in Pittsburgh, with you."

"With all of us," Livie corrected.

"Yes, with all of us."

Brian pushed the bedroom door open a bit wider. There was Livie, in pink pajamas he'd sent her a few weeks before he'd moved. They had Sleeping Beauty all over them. He'd known she'd love them. Livie was a princess fan.

She was under the covers, and Hayden was sitting on the edge of the bed, her attention so focused on their daughter that she hadn't registered his presence.

"Daddy quit his 'portant job and moved home because he missed us so much," Livie said, sounding as if she were repeating something she'd been told.

"Yes, he did."

"Daddy's heart couldn't stay away anymore, right?" He could recognize Hayden's explanations in Livie's words.

Hayden nodded. "That's just it. He loved you so much he couldn't stay in California another minute."

Livie leaned back into the pillow. "I'm glad he's home."

Her expression was one of total contentment.

"I am, too."

"Do you love Daddy?"

Hayden froze at the question, and Brian found himself leaning closer, anxious to hear her answer.

Hayden spoke slowly, as if she were trying to formulate the best answer for Livie. "Of course I love your daddy. He's my best friend. You remember the story I told you about the day I met your daddy?"

"You were on the bus and some mean boy picked on you. He hit you."

He could see Livie's indignation in her expression as she popped back up off the pillow.

Hayden stroked her wild red curls. "That's right. That boy had been mean to me for a long time, but that day, your daddy was there. He told the mean boy to sit down and leave me alone."

"My daddy's a hero."

The way Livie said the words, he knew this was the standard end to that particular story.

"Your daddy's always been my hero," Hayden said softly.

"Casey's mommy and daddy are married and live with her. Are you and Daddy getting married?"

Hayden leaned down and kissed Livie's forehead. "Hmm, I don't think that's going to happen."

"Why? Don't you love him?"

"Yes, I love him more than I can say. But your daddy and I are friends. Best friends. He's here, and he's going to try and come over most nights for your bedtime stories. And when he finds a house, you can go spend nights there. Having your daddy here will be a wonderful adventure."

"I wish he was going to live here in our house with us, though."

Hayden wrapped her arms around their daughter, holding her, stroking her back. It was such a tender, loving movement. Brian could remember the times his mother had done the same thing, wrapped him in her arms and held him tight.

Livie's arms went around Hayden's neck.

And as she hugged their daughter, Hayden finally spotted Brian in the doorway.

Her smile spread slowly, moving from her lips upward to her eyes. "Livie, turn around and look who's here."

Livie let go of Hayden and finally spied him, as well, and there was nothing slow about her response. "Daddy," she cried, springing from the bed, bounding across the room and launching herself into his arms.

She smelled of soap and shampoo … of little girl.

Hayden came up behind Livie, kissed the back of her still damp head, and said, "'Night, sweetie. Daddy will tuck you in."

Brian knew she was being kind, giving him time with Livie, but he didn't want her to leave. He wanted her to stay and be a

93

part of this new ritual they were forming. "Hayden, you could stay and we could put her to bed together."

Hayden shook her head. "I wouldn't want to intrude. This is a time for the two of you."

"It could be a time for the three of us," he said gently. "I'm home and we're going to have to find new ways to do things. I know I've always told Livie her bedtime stories over the phone. But I'm here now, and it would be nice if we could both do this together for our daughter."

"Mommy, stay."

"You're sure?" Hayden looked worried as she blatantly studied him, as if she didn't quite believe him and she was looking for some clue about his real feelings on the matter.

She stood here, willing to back out and allow him this time alone with Livie. There was no sense of jealousy. She was simply trying to reassure herself that he'd meant his invitation to stay, that he really didn't mind sharing this new ritual with her.

In that instant, realizing how unselfish she'd always been, he also realized that he loved her.

Not the love of a mentor, or friend.

But loved her in a true and everlasting sort of way.

He'd known he'd loved her when he'd asked her to marry him, but he'd mistaken the feeling for the love of a friend. Now he knew what a fool he'd been.

Knowing she'd fight against it and wouldn't be prone to believe his literal change of heart, knowing he had his work cut out for him, he didn't voice his thoughts, but savored the sensation.

Brian Conway loved Hayden MacNulty.

It was so simple. How had he missed it?

Awed by the flood of emotion, he was amazed that he sounded normal as he simply said, "Stay. Please?"

"If you're sure."

He nodded. He was sure.

Brian Conway loved Hayden MacNulty.

Now, what the hell was he going to do about it? He had no idea.

Six Months Later—October 1995

Hayden walked to Kathleen's house. It didn't matter that Hayden owned a place only two doors away, coming down this driveway, walking with the autumn leaves crunching under her feet to the four-panel front door, felt like coming home.

Kathleen hurried into the front hall, addressing Hayden in a soft conspiratorial whisper. "I need you to play along." Her smile said whatever Hayden had to play along with probably involved Livie and would more than likely become another of the family stories they'd tell for years to come.

Thinking about her daughter eased some of the sting from last night's long shift. Jason, a repeat patient, was back in the hospital. He was another favorite of hers.

Last night was a bad night. She'd sat with him as often as possible, between her other responsibilities. Worried about him, she'd even offered to play Mario Brothers knowing she'd be thoroughly trounced. She'd worried even more when he declined the game and had sat quietly, contentedly as she read him a story.

Thinking about Jason made her realize how lucky she was—Livie was such a happy, healthy little girl. Hayden would gladly go along with whatever new plan Kathleen had.

"Play along with what?" she asked Kathleen, feeling groggy and hoping she had enough wits about her to adopt whatever reaction and role her daughter demanded.

Kathleen didn't have a chance to answer as Livie practically flew into the hall. "Mommy, Mommy, Nana and I made you a

Halloween costume today." Last night, Livie had spent the night at Kathleen's while Hayden worked. Kathleen still balanced her schedule against Hayden's, just as she'd suggested the day Hayden told her she was pregnant.

Remembering that year, Kathleen's cancer, her pregnancy—it had been such a scary time, so full of uncertainty. But now, five years later, there was so much joy. Kathleen's cancer was gone, Livie was growing everyday and Brian had moved home.

Hayden had taken Livie to kindergarten before going to bed, and Kathleen had picked her up and let Hayden sleep.

It was five now, almost time for trick-or-treating and Hayden still felt half awake. "You made a costume for me?"

"You made me a *Little House on the Prairie* dress," Livie pointed out.

After months of debating what to be for Halloween, Livie had finally settled on Laura Ingalls Wilder after Brian had started the *Little House* series with her.

"So Nana and I made you one, but not a *Little House on the Prairie* one," Livie continued. Her grin was so big it was a wonder her face didn't crack. "You're going to love it, Mommy. And Daddy. We made him one, too. I'll go get yours."

She shot out of Kathleen's living room, and to the sewing room.

"She watched *The Parent Trap* today. I'm sorry—" Kathleen didn't get any further, because Livie came charging back into the room, a mass of white material in her arms.

"Here, Mommy." Livie thrust the garment into Hayden's arms. "It's just like what you wore the night you came to Nana's. I made Daddy a biker costume, too."

Hayden unfolded the white material, and sure enough, the holes in the sheet proclaimed it was either a ghost costume or Kathleen had a moth problem.

But it certainly wasn't anything like Hayden's original costume. That had been a threadworn sheet she'd taken off her own bed to use. This was a costume that had been made with love. Emotions tugged at her and she couldn't seem to form any words.

"Do you like it?" Livie sounded nervous.

Hayden nodded as she knelt down and hugged Livie, sandwiching the sheet between them. "I love it," she finally managed.

"Good. Daddy got home from his new job, and I made him put his on."

Brian's work experience in California had made finding a job in Pittsburgh so much easier. The mayor's office had jumped at the chance to hire him, and he'd been given a special appointment to a child-welfare department.

He said it was a good position and he liked it. Hayden hoped so.

"Daddy?" Livie called.

As if on cue, there was the sound of someone walking down the stairs. "Hello, Hayden."

Hayden had purposely tried to give Brian a wide berth. Not that she was avoiding him, but more because she wanted to give him time with Livie.

Now she turned around, fully knowing what she'd find.

Sure enough, gone was the suave business suit. In its place stood a Kmart biker outfit. Black jeans, a black T-shirt and faux leather vest.

"Oh, Bri," she said, trying to suppress her laughter because she didn't want to hurt Livie's feelings. "You look so tough."

"Put on yours," he commanded.

She slipped the sheet over her head and struggled for a minute, trying to find the eyeholes. Finally she twisted them into place and looked at him, waiting for him to chuckle.

Instead of laughter in his eyes, she saw something else. It was fleeting, just a blink's worth, gone so fast she wasn't sure she'd seen it at all. Brian started laughing and said, "Oh, you're so scary."

"Do you like my costume?" Livie asked. "I'm Laura."

"Ingalls," Hayden filled in.

Livie nodded, her red curls bouncing like flames around her shoulders. "Mama made it, but we bought the bonnet, right, Mama?"

"Right."

Brian knew all of that. He'd been present for a great many of the what-will-Livie-be-for-Halloween discussions. He'd been forced to sit through countless fittings. But he listened to it all again with a smile.

"Well, it's lovely." Brian looked at Kathleen. "What about you, Mom?"

"I'm sitting this one out. I work tomorrow and have a few things to finish before bed. You three go."

"Nana, you have to come, remember?" Livie, not a whiner by nature, had that hint of a squeak in her voice. She ran over to her grandmother and whispered.

"Oh, I see. Yes, I'll be coming so I can watch Livie trick-or-treat. But I'm going to forgo the costume."

"That's okay," Livie said. "You can go as my nana."

Kathleen quipped, "As far as I'm concerned, that's the best costume there is."

They set out, walking down Briar Hill Road. What had once been a barren road was now crowded with suburban houses. A trick-or-treater's paradise.

Livie ran to each neighbor's door.

"I'm here as a decoy, you understand," Kathleen said as Livie ran back.

At the next house, Hayden said, "Decoy?"

"She's planning to have to go—"

Livie was back again. And again, the group moved to the next house.

"You can just walk across Mrs. Wilkin's lawn and go right to Mr. Perry's."

With two houses to talk through, Hayden said, "Planning?"

"She's going to wait until Linda's house and have to go to the bathroom. I'm supposed to offer to take her in while you two wait across the street at the park, alone, dressed in the same costumes you wore that first night."

"The Parent Trap," they all three said in unison.

"I did try to tell her it wouldn't work. But you know Livie, once she gets an idea in her head, there's no getting it out. She's little, but she's stubborn and knows what she wants. And right now what she wants is the two of you … together. No amount of talking to her, trying to explain would sway her." Kathleen's lip twitched.

"I saw that," Hayden accused. "You think this is funny."

"Hayden, of course I don't. I mean, standing here, seeing the two of you dressed in the same costumes you wore that first time you came to my house makes me nostalgic, but I'm not laughing."

"No, you're not … but you want to." Hayden couldn't help it, she laughed, which allowed Kathleen to give up the fight and join in.

Brian just looked at the two of them as if they were nuts, but slowly he chuckled, as well.

"What's so funny?" Livie asked as she came back.

"Nothing, sweetie. We're all just overwhelmingly happy to be here with you." Hayden looked at her daughter and felt a deep sense of love.

She looked at Brian and saw that he was studying the amazing little person the two of them had created. He was clearly awed.

"Spell *overwhelmingly*."

Hayden obliged. Livie repeated it, then ran to the next house.

"When's this spelling bee?"

"I asked the teacher, and the kids don't generally participate until fifth grade."

He laughed. "I'm pretty sure she'll be ready by then."

"We did good," Hayden whispered to him.

He nodded, his eyes still on Livie standing on a front porch. "Very good."

Three houses later, on cue, Livie said, "Mommy, I have to go to the bathroom. Nana, can you take me to Miss Linda's?"

"Sure, Livie."

Hayden didn't want Livie to think her plan was going off too easily, so she asked, "Honey, do you want Mommy to take you?"

"No, I want Nana." And so saying, Livie grabbed her grandmother's hand and pulled her toward Linda's at a hurried pace.

Brian and Hayden walked across the street to the park at a leisurely gait. They took a seat on the bench.

Hayden mused, more to herself than Brian, "She's something else."

"Mom or Livie?"

She laughed. "Both. But at this moment, I was referring to Livie."

"Livie wants her parents together. A real family. I can identify with that sort of longing. After my father left …" Brian let the sentence hang there.

Hayden was surprised to hear him mention his dad. She could count on one hand the number of times they'd ever talked about him. She never asked him about it because she understood, her parents being what they were. "Do you ever speak to him?"

"Once, after Livie was born. I thought Adam might care, might be interested in the fact he was a grandfather. I guess that secretly I hoped the news would finally make him realize that he had a son. Let's just say, getting older doesn't always mean you get wiser, or that you soften and recognize what's important."

Since Livie wasn't in sight to protest, Hayden flipped her sheet up, freeing her hands. She reached out and placed one on Brian's shoulder. "I know how it hurts."

He gave himself a small shake. "I shouldn't complain. I always had Mom."

"So did I, so I guess we were both lucky. And we've done a good job with Livie. She might not have your dad in her life, but she's got us and your mom. She's surrounded by love."

"She wants more. She wants us to be together."

"I know, but she's got to accept that 'us' isn't an option."

For a few moments they sat quietly on the bench. Hayden tried to concentrate on what a beautiful night it was, on all the costumed kids who passed by them, but all she could focus on was Brian, sitting so close.

Finally, he broke the silence. "Why, Hayden? Why aren't we an option?"

"Bri, I love you, and I know you love me. But I don't think it's the kind of love meant for marriage."

He started to protest, but she held up her hand. "You would never have asked if I wasn't pregnant, if I hadn't had your daughter. I deserved then, deserve now, something more than an obligatory marriage. You had an important job that made an impact on an entire generation of children. You had a life in California. And in case you've forgotten, you're still married."

"She's pushing it through. The divorce will be final soon. And I'm working on building a life here now."

"You're on the rebound. Can you imagine what would happen if I said, yes, let's explore the possibilities between us, and it didn't work out? Livie would be crushed. We'd hurt your mother, as well."

"Hayden—"

"There's one last hurdle you're not considering. Alex."

"Hayden, my soon-to-be-divorce, our family concerns, those could be considered big hurdles, ones we might not be able to get beyond. But Alex?" He shook his head. "I've seen you and your supposed boyfriend together. Alex isn't, never could be, an issue. He's barely a crack in the sidewalk we'd have to step over."

"Hey, we've been dating for almost a year."

"On and off," he pointed out.

Hayden knew Brian was right. Alex was just a filler. Even as she thought it, she felt guilty. No one should be used as a way to fill up someone else's life.

She was going to have to break up with him. And though she might admit that to herself, there was no way she was going to admit it to Brian. She pasted her most stubborn look on her face. "Every relationship has its problems."

"When's the last time you went out with him?"

"It's been busy at work, and Livie—"

"No excuses, just the answer. When's the last time?"

She shrugged. "I'm not sure."

"I am." He looked embarrassed as he admitted, "It's been three weeks."

"You've been spying on me?"

"You forget our daughter's a font of information. She always tells me when you've gone out with 'awful Alex.' But …" He paused a moment and added, "But if she hadn't said anything, I'd still take note. At first I thought I didn't like him because he was just too slick, too …" He shrugged. "But as time has stretched out over the last few weeks, between your dates, I realized I felt relieved that you hadn't seen him. That he didn't get to kiss you good-night, or casually drape an arm over your shoulders. That's when it hit me, I've been jealous of him."

"Brian." Hayden stopped because she didn't know what else to add.

Brian obviously didn't have the same problem. "Hayden, I do understand everything you've said. You do have valid points. But I don't agree that the love we share couldn't grow into something beyond friendship. I suspect it might already be something more on my end."

Hearing those words come from Brian, she felt a jolt of … hope? Terror? She wasn't sure.

And though she wouldn't admit it to Brian, there was a possibility it was already more on her end, too. Hell, it wasn't a possibility. It was a done deal. Had been for as long as she could remember. She loved Brian. But she didn't trust that what he felt for her was anything more than friendship mixed with convenience. It would be convenient for everyone if he loved her. Livie and Kathleen would be overjoyed, and the family would be whole.

"Brian, we can't continue to go round and round about this."

"And we can't ignore it. But your concerns for Livie are valid. What if, after my divorce is final, I ask you out to dinner? A date. A real date. We won't mention it to Mom or Livie, so there won't be any pressure, any expectations."

"Just one date?" she asked, eying suspiciously. "Just one?"

"Just one. An experiment. Maybe we'd find that away from Mom and Livie we don't have anything to connect us."

"We'd have to agree up front that if it doesn't work out, we'll just let things go back to normal. Even in those moments I considered your proposals, that was probably my biggest fear, that if we tried and failed, I'd lose your friendship. I can take a lot of things, Bri, but losing you—" she shook her head "—I don't think I could handle that."

"Promise. One date. Let's see how it goes, and we'll take things one day at a time. Slowly."

Hayden noticed that during the course of their conversation, they'd both slid to the center of the bench, which meant their hips were touching. She looked up and thought that Brian might lean in and kiss her. But the mood was broken when Livie called out, "Mommy, Daddy, are you ready?"

Hayden met Brian's gaze and for a moment they held it. A moment that no one else was a part of. As if the whole world disappeared and they were the only people left.

Hayden turned back to her daughter. "Yes, we're ready."

"Sorry we took so long," Kathleen said. There was a glitter of amusement in her eyes. Or maybe it wasn't that, maybe it was simply contentment. "Linda and I got to talking, and you know how we can be."

"Let's go. Mommy, you need your costume back on."

Hayden dutifully slipped the sheet over her head.

"Good. Let's go."

Through the holes in the sheet, Hayden's eyes locked on Brian. Her face safely hidden behind the sheet, she allowed herself to smile. She was going to go out on a real date with Brian.

Happiness butted heads with nervousness as they trailed after Kathleen and Livie.

They all walked down the block, a grandmother and a *Little-House-on-the-Prairie* girl, trailed by a biker whose hand gently held a ghost's.

Chapter Nine

"Hayden?" Brian had found her. She should have known he would.

Hayden pulled a tissue from her pocket, but after a minute of wiping, realized she was a wreck and no amount of tissues would help. Of course, she hadn't planned to end up here. She did the best she could to clean up, hoping to minimize the traces of her meltdown.

"Hayden?"

She hated crying. She felt that it didn't solve anything. Couldn't make anything better. But Kathleen was getting worse, and there was nothing, absolutely nothing, Hayden could do. She felt so angry, so helpless. If she hadn't let go of some of the feelings building up inside her, she'd have exploded. But giving in, just this once, to the hurt didn't mean she wanted anyone else to witness her sobfest.

She could hear the ladder groan as Brian began climbing up to the old tree house. "Don't come up, Bri. I'm on my way down."

His head popped up into the doorway. "Too late. I thought maybe we could talk." The tone of his voice was too kind. She knew that he knew why she'd come here, why she'd sought the comfort of this place, but she didn't want to talk about it.

She was able to spout the statistics of Kathleen's condition when Marti or the doctors required them. She could quote

Kathleen's meds, their strengths. She could rattle off Kathleen's vitals. It was as easy as letting her training kick in.

But to talk about Kathleen's decline on a personal level, just Hayden to Brian? She couldn't do it. It was too close, too raw.

"I'm fine. I just needed a minute to clear my head."

"Hayden …" He paused, then nodded. "Fine." And he climbed back down the ladder.

She hurried after him, but Brian wasn't waiting. He was walking through the trees to the house.

"Bri," she called.

He stood in place as she caught up. "Did your mom need anything? Is that why you came to find me?"

"No, Hayden, my mother didn't need anything." His voice was resigned as he turned and walked away again. He hurried off toward the house.

Hayden remained where she was, frozen to the spot. The faint smell of woody dankness surrounding her in the shadow of the trees.

He'd needed her. Needed some comfort. Had come to her for it, and she'd turned him away.

She should go after him, to apologize, try and comfort him now. Try to tell him that everything would be all right, even though she knew it was a lie.

Should haves. Could haves.

Didn'ts.

Hayden didn't go. She had nothing else to offer to anyone, no reserves to draw on.

She walked back to the house, alone. So alone. Cold and isolated.

And for the moment, that bone-aching coldness was almost a comfort. It was so much better than the pain that had become as much a part of her life as breathing had.

She knew once upon a time she'd been happy, but she could hardly remember those times, and she desperately needed to.

Marti was gathering her things as Hayden came back into the room. "You okay?"

Hayden nodded. "Anything new?"

"No. Her condition is stable, so all her meds are the same. But call right away if that changes." Marti turned to Kathleen. "I'll be in first thing tomorrow."

Kathleen's eyes fluttered a moment, then opened. "I'll be here." She smiled.

Hayden showed Marti out and immediately went back into Kathleen's room, Brian at her heels.

"Hey, Mom," he said as he leaned down and kissed her forehead.

Kathleen looked at Brian and Hayden's haggard faces. She knew their concern and care for her was wearing them both out. The worry was reciprocated. Despite the fact Hayden had tried to disguise it, Kathleen could see that she'd been crying. And Brian was obviously miserable. They stood at the side of her hospital bed, not touching. Not even looking at each other.

Kathleen felt guilty and helpless. They were both holding on to their pain, not sharing it with each other.

She desperately wanted to talk some sense into them, make them see how much they needed one other. She didn't know quite how to do it.

She kept trotting out old memories, not only because they comforted her, but also as a way to remind Hayden and Brian of better times. Of when they had pulled together, rather than apart. She wasn't sure it helped, but it was all she could think of to try.

"Do you know what I was remembering today?"

"Another good day?" Hayden smiled as she used Kathleen's pet phrase.

"A very good day. Six months after Livie made you and Brian your Halloween costumes. Do you both remember that night?"

Hayden got a faraway look in her eyes, and she slowly nodded.

Brian's voice was a hoarse whisper as he said, "How could I forget."

April 1996

"Mommy, are you going out again?"

"Yes." Hayden peered into the small mirror in her room as she put a small silver hoop through her lobe. She looked over at Livie as she snapped it in place. "But Nana's going to be watching you."

"Couldn't Daddy watch me?" Livie threw herself back on Hayden's bed with enough force to bounce.

"I don't think Daddy's going to be able to tonight. It will be a special Nana and Livie night, just like old times."

"Nana said we're going to go to McDonald's for dinner, then maybe go see a movie. When we go, we get the big popcorn and split it."

Hayden could see Livie eying her, waiting for the mom-lecture on proper nutrition. She happily obliged. "Don't eat so much you make yourself sick."

Hayden loved that she fell so easily into mom-mode. Once she thought she'd never have children, for fear of turning into her parents, but she was pleased that she had turned into Kathleen instead, echoing things she used to say.

"I won't get sick," Livie muttered with a six-year-old scoff. "Daddy said I have a castor stomach."

"Castor stomach?" Hayden thought a moment, then smiled. "A cast-iron stomach?"

Livie nodded. "Yeah."

"Still, not too much junk food."

Livie just laughed as she bounced herself back off the bed and hurried out of the room, without promising. Hayden didn't have the heart to scold, or even to ask Kathleen to see to it her daughter had something nutritious for dinner. They loved these Nana and Livie dates, and Hayden realized every child deserved to feel special, and who better to spoil Livie than Kathleen?

She finished dressing and, while most of the time she hated going out and leaving Livie, she kissed her daughter goodbye with a smile and all but sprinted to her car. She was so anxious to meet Brian. There was an excited, fluttery feeling in the pit of her stomach.

She wasn't sure where things were going, but she and Brian were doing their best to shelter Livie, keeping their dates clandestine. Despite being nervous at first, Hayden had to admit, she was happy. Completely happy.

Hayden drove to the restaurant, hardly noting the first blush of spring. She normally reveled in this time of year, but tonight it barely registered, her thoughts were too centered on Brian. On being with him. On spending time with him.

Wherever this led, this time with him would be enough. She'd be content with it.

And she'd worry about any potential fallout later. Right now, she was meeting Brian.

Brian waited at the restaurant, a sense of anticipation growing stronger with every second that ticked by.

Tonight was the night.

He'd picked C'est la Vie because Lois, the mayor's personal assistant, had assured him it was dark, ritzy and full of ambiance, and he knew that women liked that kind of stuff. He was never sure exactly what it was they saw in dim rooms and fancy tablecloths. This was the kind of place that made a man worry about spilling. And he definitely didn't get the whole multiple wineglasses and enough silverware to feed a dozen people thing. But he didn't need to get it. He just needed it to impress Hayden. To show her that tonight's date was special. At least he hoped it would be special—that it would be a night they talked about for the rest of their lives.

They'd been dating for months, and things were going so well. He'd held back, not wanting to rush Hayden, but he couldn't wait any longer. He was going to ask her to marry him for the twenty-first time. Not that he was counting, or anything.

Oh, hell, who was he kidding? Of course he'd counted. Even though it had been years since he last asked her, each of her rejections had stolen a little piece of him. After the first ten, he vowed he'd stop asking at a dozen.

He'd reached fifteen when Livie was born, and swore he was done asking.

Then he told himself he wouldn't count the times she didn't let him get the question completely out.

He finally stopped when he'd come home for Livie's baptism and asked yet again. And again, Hayden had rejected him. That had been number twenty and he'd stopped.

After all, Hayden had told him that she didn't need him, that she wanted him to stay in Los Angeles because his job was important. It had been, but he recognized her real reason for not accepting his proposals. She had valued his friendship, but hadn't wanted him that way.

But things had changed.

At least, he'd hoped they'd changed.

Twenty times he'd asked, and twenty times she'd said no. He was hoping this time, the twenty-first time, broke the curse. That she'd finally come to realize that they belonged together.

Those other times he'd asked, she'd always said that she wouldn't marry because she "had to." He understood her point then. But this was different. Six years had passed by. They'd both changed, both grown. Both had relationships. His divorce was final and awful Alex had long since gone. She'd never seen the guy again after their tenuous start on Halloween.

This was their time. His and Hayden's.

He knew with an unalterable certainty that Hayden was the one for him.

He reached into his pocket, fingering the small package like a talisman.

He sensed her before he saw her.

"Brian." Just his name, that's all she said, but it was enough to make him smile.

He stood and pulled out her chair.

"You don't need to—" she started.

He cut her off with a chuckle. "I know." He sat back in his own chair and hitched it closer to hers. "I even understand why you prefer to decline. You're a competent, independent woman who's more than capable of pulling out her own chair. What can I say? I'm a caveman. A throwback. But fact is, I like pulling out your chair and opening doors for you. I like …"

He stopped, simply mesmerized by the sight of her. She'd dressed for the evening, a strappy black dress with small silver earrings and the locket she frequently wore.

She was beautiful. He must have said the words out loud, because she said, "I'm not. You're just biased."

"Not a bit."

The waiter, as he'd arranged, appeared with a bottle of Dom. Hayden glanced at the bottle, then at him. "Brian?"

The waiter poured their champagne and Brian raised his glass. "Enjoy. We're celebrating."

Hayden raised her glass and clinked it against his. "Something nice at work? Did the committee agree with your recommendations?"

Brian had dug into his new position, working with the existing children's welfare system he'd come up with a proposal to streamline things, reducing the paperwork for the social workers and adding a layer of checks and balances. His goal was to see that no child fell through the cracks.

He nodded. "They liked it and I think it's going to make a difference, but that's not what we're celebrating."

She didn't ask again. She simply waited, much like his mother would have. Waited for him to find the words and share the news.

"Hayden, I planned to do this after our meal, but I can't. Uh …" He faltered, despite the fact he'd rehearsed this in his head so many times. He took a deep breath, and started again. "We've known each other since I was twelve and you were eight. We've fought for each other, and with each other. We've been friends, best friends. We've made a beautiful daughter together. These last few months, since I came home … the two of us, together. Well, it's been special."

He ran out of steam and tried to formulate the next words. To put them together in such a way that she'd agree—that she couldn't resist.

She took his hand. "Six months, Bri. It's been six months since Halloween. They're some of the most incredible times of my life."

"I think we should tell Mom and Livie we've been dating." He braced himself for her inevitable protest and tried to prepare his strategy. He was ready for a fight.

Hayden surprised him by nodding. "I've been worried about what would happen, that they could be hurt, if we were dating and ended up falling apart, but yes, you're right. We can't keep hiding that we're together."

Well, that was one part down, next came the bigger challenge. "But I don't think we should *just* tell them we've been dating. I think we should tell them …"

He groped in his pocket, pulled out the package and pushed it toward her. "Open it."

"Bri?" She stared at the small box with a deer-in-the-headlight look—unsure what to do.

He just nudged it closer and hoped.

Her hands shook as she took the package, pulled the bow and freed the small velvet box. She opened it with agonizing slowness, stared at it a moment, then looked up at him. "Brian?"

"Mom gave me my grandmother's ring years ago and told me I could give it to my wife if I wanted, or save it. I didn't give it to Lisa. Maybe that says something about us, something I should have listened to right up front. I mean, I know she wanted something ostentatious, but …" He paused. "I guess it's bad form to bring up an ex-wife when you're proposing."

The box clattered to the table. "You're proposing?"

"That's what the ring is. A proposal. I want you to marry me."

"Bri, I've said that I wouldn't marry because I 'had' to—"

He didn't let her finish, couldn't bear to hear the word *no* again. "Dammit, Hayden, there's no have-to's here. There's you and me, and what we have … what we've always had."

"You stopped me too soon. I was going to say, all the other times you asked, I said I wouldn't marry because I had to. I wanted it all. Maybe that was selfish. I don't know. I didn't want a marriage of necessity for us, or for Livie. I wanted the real deal. The till-death-do-us-part sort of thing."

"I can give you that." It wasn't a rash promise, easily made, easily broken. It was the complete and utter truth.

She took the ring from the box and handed it to him, then extended her ring finger. "I know you can give me that, and if you ask me properly, I can give you my answer."

That horrible tightness in his chest loosened. He started to get out of his seat, so he could get down on one knee, but she laughed. "I don't think the kneeling thing is necessary. You'll wrinkle your very nice pants."

He'd kneel. He'd sit. He'd stand.

Hell, he'd juggle flaming swords.

He'd do whatever she asked, if only this time, she'd say yes.

So because she'd asked, he stayed seated, took her hand in his left one, and slid the ring toward her finger. "Hayden MacNulty, I love you and can't imagine my life without you in it. Will you marry me?"

"Brian Conway, I'd be honored." She nudged her finger forward, through the ring and nestled it in place. She admired how it looked there.

Brian was thankful she was momentarily distracted because he needed a minute to collect himself, to realize she'd said yes.

Just in case he'd misunderstood, he double checked. "Yes? You did say yes, right? You know I was asking you to marry me, asking you to spend the rest of your life with me, and you said yes and agreed, right?"

She took both of his hands in hers, then leaned across the table and kissed him, full out with no reservations.

She kissed him until he knew beyond a doubt she'd agreed.

When they broke apart, she said the words he hadn't realized he'd been waiting to hear.

"I love you, Bri. I love the way you make me feel. Love the way you look at me. You're the other half of my whole."

She laughed and looked embarrassed. "That was a bit over the top, but I guess you get the picture."

"Got it and liked it. I know it's the same for me."

She smiled.

If asked, Brian wouldn't be able to say what it was they talked about through dinner. He wasn't even sure what he was eating.

All he knew was, as he sat next to Hayden, his engagement ring flashed on her hand as she ate.

She'd said yes.

He couldn't get over the marvel of it.

As they finished their dessert he shook himself from his happy fog and put together a real thought. "Now we're really going to have to talk to Mom and Livie. It's going to be a bit of a shock."

"A good shock, I think," Hayden said. "After all Livie's machinations, she'll be thrilled. They'll both be happy for us."

Brian agreed. He thought his mother and daughter would be thrilled, but what if they weren't? Would that be enough to keep Hayden from saying yes? Would she change her mind?

The road they'd taken to get here had been filled with twists and turns. He didn't want any more. They deserved a happy ending. They deserved to live with their daughter and be a family.

They were both quiet on the short drive to his mom's house, and as they got out of the car and walked up to the front door, Hayden slipped her hand into his.

It was such a simple gesture. Brian remembered all the times Hayden had held his hand when they were younger, but after he left for college, that had stopped.

He'd missed it.

Her hand in his felt right.

How could he have not known that before?

She toyed with the locket around her neck, slipping it back and forth along its chain.

He squeezed her hand, hoping to calm her.

"Nervous?" she whispered. Before he could say anything, she added, "I am."

He didn't answer the question. He just said, "I don't expect there's going to be a problem. They'll be surprised, of course, but they'll be pleased."

"I hope so. Standing here is only prolonging things. Let's go."

"Wait. First, let's …" He leaned down and kissed her. Kissed her as he'd wanted to back in the restaurant. Deep. Hard. As if he wanted to imprint himself on her lips, make her remember, no matter what reaction his mother and their daughter gave them, that they belonged together.

As the kiss slowed, moving to something softer and more tender, Hayden snuggled into his chest, so close that it was hard to tell where he left off and she began.

"I love you." Her words were muffled against his shirt.

"Pardon me? I'm not sure I heard what you said. Could you repeat it?"

She laughed. "Ah, I forgot. You're four years older than me. Four years closer to retirement, to needing a hearing aid." Slowly, articulating carefully with a huge grin on her face. "Brian Conway, I-love-you."

"And I—"

The door popped open and Livie stood there. "Daddy, you brought Mommy home from her date with awful Alex."

Hayden looked up at him, then back at Livie. "Honey, I never said I had a date with Alex. I haven't even thought about him in months."

Livie tugged at her mother's hand. "But you were all dressed up?"

His mom came up behind Livie and gave him a questioning look, then reached down and took Livie's hand. "Livie, why don't you let your parents come in off the porch?"

They all assembled in the living room. Livie chirped about her evening with her grandmother. Something about McDonald's, ice cream and popcorn.

Normally, Brian savored these moments. Despite his nightly phone calls, he'd missed all those years in California. Tonight, all he could do was think about telling everyone he was going to marry Hayden. Once the words had been said out loud, he knew Hayden wouldn't back out.

"Mom, Livie, would you both have a seat? We have something we want to tell you."

He saw the moment his mother spotted the ring on Hayden's finger. The dawning of understanding and the quick blossoming of a smile indicated she was as pleased as he'd thought she'd be.

"Brian and I," Hayden said, taking the lead. She looked at Livie. "Your daddy and I have been dating. We didn't want to tell you both in case things didn't work out."

Both Livie and Kathleen started laughing, as if on cue.

"What?" Brian and Hayden asked in unison.

Despite her glee, his mom said, "Hayden and Brian, Livie and I are so glad that neither of you had your hearts set on being international spies because—"

Livie interrupted, bounding from her seat next to his mom and onto the couch between them. "We knew you were dating."

"But, you just asked about Alex."

"Awful Alex was a red bear. I know he's gone." Livie sounded more like an amused adult than a six-year-old.

Brian knew Hayden had to be feeling just as confused as he did. "Red bear?"

"Red herring. Something to throw you off the track," his mom clarified. "We didn't want you both to know we knew you were dating. We knew you wanted your privacy, and we understood that."

"Nana 'splained it all to me. So Nana and me pretended we didn't know, but we did. That makes us trickier than you."

"That certainly does," Brian assured his daughter. "But we're still tricky enough to know something you two don't."

Hayden reached over and took his hand. Again, he felt the rightness of the gesture. Holding her. Touching her. How had he gone so long without her?

His mom glanced again at Hayden's ring, then back at him, her eyes twinkling with delight.

He laughed. "Okay, so maybe your Nana's still trickier, but your mom and I have outgunned you, Livie."

"We hope you're as happy about our news as we are." Hayden turned to him and he nodded. "Livie, your dad and I are going to get married."

Brian wasn't the sort of man who cried. He'd learned long ago to tuck most of his feelings away and keep them to himself. He'd never shed a tear when his father left, when he moved, when his marriage failed.

But at this moment, hugging his mother, his daughter and Hayden, his emotions were closer to the surface than normal.

When his mother kissed him, she said, "I'm glad you've finally come to your senses." Then she turned to Hayden, kissed her cheek and said, "Welcome home, darling. You've always been the daughter of my heart and I'm glad you'll be my daughter-in-law finally."

At that one tender gesture, Brian brushed at his eye, telling himself it was only dust, but knowing he was lying to himself, and not really caring.

He watched the three women in his life talking, laughing, hugging each other and him. And though he could never compete with them on a conversational level—no man could—he was pretty sure he could match each and any of them in happiness.

Match them? Hell. He could win easily. Because truly, Brian couldn't remember a happier night in his life.

Chapter Ten

"Hayden, could I have a cup of tea?" Kathleen's voice was weak, barely above a whisper. Her skin was drawn taut on her thin—way too thin—frame. She looked almost skeletal.

Hayden forced a smile. It felt sharp and unnatural, as if she needed to control the volume of it, because if it got too big, too loud, it would shatter into a million little pieces. "Sure, tea sounds lovely. I'll go start the water."

In the kitchen, Hayden walked to the kitchen window while she waited for the water to a boil.

This had always been her favorite room. Large and airy, it had an old farmhouse kitchen feel to it. Bright yellow walls, checkered cushions on the chairs. She remembered sharing hot cocoa at the table with Kathleen, talking about this and that, about all minutia that seemed so important when she was young. Kathleen gave those talks all her attention, as if what Hayden had to say was the most important thing in the world.

This house, and even more specifically, this room, had always brought her a feeling of comfort.

But not today.

She stared out the window into the backyard. It was that winter sort of brown. The trees were bare. The grass was dried and looked brittle.

That's how Hayden felt. Dried out. Brittle. As if the slightest bump would cause her to break.

Kathleen was going to die soon.

The signs were there, big and bold.

Kathleen was going to die. It wasn't merely an occasional intrusion, but an in-Hayden's-face, weighing on her every second, sort of thought. She couldn't avoid facing it because each time she walked into the room and saw Kathleen, there it was.

Hayden had taken the time off work at St. Bart's by using all her vacation and ten years of accumulated sick time. She owed Kathleen nothing less and so much more. But being here and watching her spiral downhill at such an alarming rate was hard because Hayden knew that nothing she did would stop, or even slow the eventual outcome.

The teakettle whistled, shaking Hayden from her darkness. She welcomed the business of making tea. That much, at least, hadn't changed. She'd done it a thousand times. She carried two mugs down the hall and pasted yet another fake smile on her face. "Here you go. I put an ice cube in yours to cool it. It's still plenty warm, but you're not going to burn your lips on it."

Hayden set her own mug down on the nightstand and handed Kathleen hers, but Kathleen's fingers shook from the weight of the mug, so Hayden cupped her hands around Kathleen's and helped her bring the mug to her lips.

Hayden would have to find something lighter for next time. Maybe a foam cup?

Kathleen took the merest of sips, not much more than wetting her lips, then pushed the mug back, handing it off to Hayden. "That hit the spot."

With a sinking heart, Hayden knew that one sip was probably all Kathleen would drink of the tea. Her appetite hadn't been great since she had come home a week ago, but the last few days had shown a marked decline. A sip or two of a drink, a couple bites of a meal was all Kathleen could tolerate.

In the hospital, she'd be on IV fluids, at least, but part of the hospice paradigm included doing nothing that might prolong a life. IV fluids fell into that category.

Palliative, not curative.

Comfort, not cure.

Long before Kathleen's illness, Hayden had studied the hospice program. She'd taken ethics classes in nursing school. Hayden understood the theories and beliefs behind hospice's stance, and most of the time she accepted that it was important for the medical community to know when to step back for the patient's sake. Prolonging life without considering the quality, keeping someone alive only to suffer, went against the whole do-no-harm rule. But sometimes it was hard for Hayden to ignore her medical training and do nothing, when every fiber of her being longed to be more proactive than giving Kathleen a sip of tea.

She felt impotent and helpless.

Kathleen seemed to sense her unease. "Sit down, dear. Or better yet, take a nap."

"Trying to get rid of me?" Hayden teased. Well, tried to tease. She was afraid that, like everything else, it rang false.

Kathleen shook her head, moving it from side to side without lifting it off the pillow, her face looking strained, as if the merest movement was too much. "Never. But I know how much work caring for me is. I was a nurse, remember?"

Was. That word hit Hayden with the jarring realization that Kathleen was starting to refer to her life in the past tense. Not *I am a nurse,* but *I was a nurse,* as if she were already putting it all behind her.

She was still speaking. "You need to take a break now and again."

Hayden knew she'd have plenty of time when Kathleen was no longer with them. For now, she was selfish enough to want to spend every minute she could get with Kathleen. "I'll sit down for a few minutes. I know how draining it can be to watch other people flit around."

She paused and added, "Remember Marcy Finerman? Keeping her in her hospital bed at night was the biggest nursing challenge I ever faced. She—"

"How're my girls today?" Brian boomed from the doorway with far more gusto than was necessary. He walked in and kissed his mother's forehead, and then, almost as an afterthought, kissed Hayden's, as well.

Maybe that was their trouble? So much was going on that they'd become an afterthought to each other.

"You've left work early." It was a question, framed as a comment.

"I told them I'd be taking some time off." He turned his attention to his mother. "So, how was your day?"

"Fine. It was fine."

If he'd asked Hayden, she might have told him that Kathleen's day was anything *but* fine. His mother's Duragesic patch wasn't working, and Hayden had been forced to give her morphine for the advanced pain. She'd a call into Marti at Hospice to get a stronger patch so that Kathleen could keep coping. He wouldn't ask in front of his mother, but he'd probably ask Hayden later, and she'd fill him in. They'd talk about his mother, about her care, about the logistics of their lives … They'd say the words, but in the end, they wouldn't say enough.

Brian watched Hayden with Marti and he was struck again by how hard Hayden worked to keep his mother as comfortable as possible.

Hayden did so many things for his mom that he couldn't help with, from dealing with her medications to handling her personal needs.

It was wearing on her. He could see how tired she was. He knew she hadn't slept a night through since they'd brought his mom home. He did what he could, but the frustrating thing was, he knew it would never be as much as he'd like to do for his family. He wanted to find a way to make everything all right, the way it used to be, though he knew that was impossible. Their lives had altered, and nothing was going to change them back.

"Bri, is something wrong?" Hayden asked, having stopped her conversation with Marti long enough to notice he was standing there. Her question made him realize that he must have let some of his feelings show. He tried to wall them off, not wanting his mom and Hayden to see how much he was hurting. "No. No. I'm going to switch clothes and come spend some time with Mom."

"Okay. We have to get this patch on her."

"Well, I guess I should leave you to it." He leaned down and kissed his mom's cheek. It felt papery, cool and soft. Not like his mom at all. She'd always seemed warm and strong. The thought was another wound. "I'll be back in a few minutes, Mom."

She nodded. "Okay."

He was almost out the door when his mother called. "Brian?"

He turned around and she smiled, mouthing the words *I love you,* as if saying them out loud took too much energy.

He worked to get his words past the lump in his throat. "Love you, too." Then he raced out of the room and down the hall, needing to put some distance between himself and the situation.

Stopping at the bottom of the stairs, leaning back against the cold wall, he closed his eyes and gulped for breath.

"Dad?"

His eyes snapped open and he found Livie standing in front of him, studying him, her concern evident. She'd come in at some point while they were all preoccupied with his mom.

In the past, someone had always greeted her when she got home. His mom, Hayden, and later, himself. But now everyone was so busy with his mother that no one even noticed that she was here. She was sixteen, but she still needed their attention, especially now.

"Hey, Liv. How was school?" At one time that was enough to start her on a half-hour litany of the daily trials and tribulations of being a teen. But that, like everything else in their lives, was no longer the same. Rather than a litany about her day, she asked, "How's Nana?"

"The pain was worse. Marti came with a new pain patch that should help control it, they said."

Livie nodded. "How's Mom doing? She's been so down lately."

"Fine. She's fine."

Livie shook her head, red curls flying. "None of us are fine, Dad."

He was struck by how grown-up Livie was. How she'd moved beyond childish concerns.

He hoped his mother didn't realize how much her illness had matured Livie. The knowledge would hurt her. She'd feel guilty that her being sick had robbed Livie of her last bits of being young and carefree.

But because Brian did know, because it cut at him that Livie had slipped into adulthood without anyone noticing it, he reached out and pulled his daughter into a hug. Months ago, she'd have complained and tried to wiggle out of his paternal embrace, feeling she was too old for such silly needs. But he figured she needed the connection as much as he did, and rather than fighting against it, she hugged him back.

"How much longer?" she asked softly, so soft that he almost hadn't heard it.

He wished he hadn't heard it, because he didn't know how to answer her. Should he give the doctor's answer, or the one his heart prayed was closer to the truth?

In the end, he settled for, "Too soon."

Hayden walked out of Kathleen's room, Marti in tow. They came down the hall talking medical talk.

"Hi, Mom," Livie said.

As if she'd been shaken out of a stupor, Hayden started. Her eyes focused. "Oh, Livie. I'm sorry. I lost track of time." He saw panic set in. "I wasn't supposed to drive today, was I?"

"No, Mom, it was fine. Mrs. Franz said she'll drive all the time for now."

Hayden scrunched up her face, obviously not happy about the arrangement. "That's not fair to her. I won't forget again. I'll make it work. Maybe—"

"Hayden, people want to help." He understood their friends' needing to feel useful because he felt the same way, as if he couldn't feel useful enough, in fact. "It's something she can do. And it's a kindness to let her."

He knew how much Hayden chafed at asking for anything, but this time she'd have to put her pride aside and accept it. She couldn't do everything. She might not get that, but he did.

Even Livie did.

"But—"

He just looked at Hayden, waiting for her to acknowledge there wasn't much of a choice. His mother had reached a point that she couldn't be left too long, and Brian couldn't always get off work to drive Liv.

He saw when it finally sank in. Hayden smiled, but Brian knew it wasn't a real smile. That she was forcing it into place for

Livie's benefit. "That will be a huge help. Tell Mrs. Franz I said I appreciate it."

"I will, Mom."

Hayden turned back to Marti, back to the what-fors and what-nots of his mother's care, Livie's new daily ride already forgotten.

Brian felt a surge of frustration. He'd spent his life helping other people, trying to make their lives better, but here he was, unable to do anything to help those he loved the most.

"It's okay, Dad," Livie said, as if reading his mind.

He nodded. "Sure, honey."

But it wasn't okay. It wasn't okay at all that everyone forgot it was time for Livie to come home, or that she might need a ride.

Taking a page from his mother's coping strategy, he tried to remember a time when their lives had been something more than medications and temporary solutions. A time when even though there was sorrow, he and Hayden had stood together, something they seemed to have forgotten how to do.

1997

"Happy anniversary." Brian raised his glass of champagne and tapped it to Hayden's. "And to many, many more years together."

They'd driven into Pittsburgh for dinner at Johnny's, an upscale restaurant near the Monongahela incline that overlooked the city. They sat at a quiet corner table along the windows as they ate the delicious meal.

It was a romantic evening, an intimate way to celebrate their anniversary. "It's been a great first year."

She smiled and nodded. Then her expression turned more serious. "Except ..."

Hayden didn't need to spell out what the exception was. He could see her sorrow. They'd been trying since their wedding to get pregnant, with no luck.

"I saw the doctor today," she said quietly. "I had some tests done a few weeks ago."

Brian paused. "The doctor told us it was too soon to worry. We've only been trying for several months. If we could just relax—"

"Telling someone not to worry is like looking at a pot over the flame and telling it not to boil. It's not going to be able to help it, and neither could I. So I decided to address the problem head-on."

That was Hayden to a tee. She didn't beat around the bush, she forged ahead and did what was necessary. "What did the tests show?"

"Nothing. They couldn't find a reason I shouldn't be pregnant."

"So it's me?"

She shrugged. "Maybe. Maybe it's us. I've spent the day giving this a lot of thought. Maybe we're meant to be parents of an only child. I mean, think about it. Livie is seven already, going on eight. If we had another baby, it would mean starting all over. Bottles. Diapers. No sleep."

"Are you saying you don't want a baby?"

She shook her head and sighed. "No. I'm saying let's just accept that it may not happen. Let's go on from here as if we may not have any more children. If something changes, if I find myself pregnant, we'll revel in it. But let's just quit actively trying. Let's not have sex by the calendar and clock. Let's have it because we want to."

He knew she wanted a baby as much as he did. But there was merit in her suggestion. He was tired of being disappointed every month when they found themselves not pregnant. He wanted a baby, but he wanted Hayden more.

"Uh, Hayden, I always want to," he teased.

The worried tightening around her eyes loosened and she laughed. "Really? Do tell."

"Well, my love, tonight, with no thoughts of producing off-spring, we'll …" He leaned closer and proceeded to outlined his risqué plans for the evening's activities.

Hayden's laughter faded and slowly, her eyes darkened. He knew she was open to his suggestion. "Works for you?"

"Sure. But I'd like to add one or two of my own ideas to the schedule. Such as …"

Brian grinned as she added her twist to the evening's activities.

"Hey, Hayden?"

"Yes, Brian?" Her voice had that husky quality she often had while they made love.

"How quickly can we finish this dinner?"

She chuckled, raised her hand to flag down the waiter. "Check."

They sped home and made love, not because it might be a good night to make a baby, but because, baby or not, they loved each other.

Brian remembered the sweetness of that first anniversary. Despite their disappointment, they'd gotten past not having conceived another child. They'd come together and it had all been all right.

He watched as Hayden returned to his mother's room and wished he could simply take her up to their bedroom and make love to her, make the pain go away this time, as well.

But making love wasn't going to help.

Nothing would.

Chapter Eleven

It was a good day. Kathleen's pain was well under control with the new patch dosage and that, in and of itself, was enough to make it a good day.

"Where's Brian?" Kathleen asked when she woke up from her nap.

"He's run to the grocery store. Turns out the only thing left in the fridge was a tub of margarine and a bag of rather shriveled apples." She paused then added, "He even cut coupons."

Watching Brian go through a couple weeks' worth of ads, making an extensive list, had been endearing. Hayden had leaned over and kissed the top of his head without thinking. He'd looked up, surprise in his expression. She'd felt embarrassed and wasn't sure why.

"A lot of things have fallen by the wayside lately. I'm sorry about that," Kathleen said. "This isn't exactly fun, is it?"

"No one expects you to be fun."

"Oh, so you're saying I've always been a stick-in-the-mud?" Kathleen's voice was sharp.

"No, I don't think … You know I don't—" Hayden stopped midapology when she caught sight of the wicked twinkle in Kathleen's blue eyes. "That wasn't very nice."

"Sweetie, you're taking yourself far too seriously. You're taking me far too seriously."

"How can you say that? You're—" Again she stopped herself, this time because she couldn't handle saying the words out loud.

"Dying," Kathleen supplied. "When you came home after college and took care of me, I thought that maybe that was it. I prepared myself to die. But I didn't. And I've had fifteen good years since. Healthy years. I'm thankful for all of them. Seeing Olivia born, dancing at your wedding to Brian. Each and every day, every month, every year has been a gift. But we have to face the fact that I'm dying, Hayden. We're both medical professionals, and I think we both have known this would be the outcome since they found out my cancer was back."

Hayden looked out the window at the oak tree. Its bare branches were swaying in the wind. "Knowing and accepting are two very different things."

"Hayden, you've always been strong. You'll do fine. You and Brian will have each other. And Livie will have both of you. You don't know how much that thought comforts me. That you'll be here in the house. That there will be laughter again." She paused, then more to herself than Hayden, murmured, "It makes things easier knowing the family will go on, that you all will have each other."

Hayden wished those thoughts comforted her, as well, but the distance between her and Brian was becoming entrenched and marked by their silences. Just look how surprised he'd been at her small kiss this afternoon.

"Hayden." Kathleen's voice startled her from her reverie. "Today I'm remembering your wedding day." She smiled. "It was a good day.

"You both were so nervous, but Livie and I weren't. She was so young back then, and so very excited. I thought she'd just about jump out of her skin, she was so thrilled. And beautiful. Would you get me my picture? The one on the dresser?"

Hayden went to the dresser, and there in the center was the silver-framed photo. She looked at it as she carried it to Kathleen. Really studied the four smiling people in it. She couldn't find any connection to them. They felt alien, even the image of herself.

Hayden remembered being happy, but she couldn't seem to recall how that had felt.

June 25, 1996

Hayden couldn't believe they'd been so lucky. It was late enough in June that she'd feared that the weather would be too hot for an outdoor wedding, but Mother Nature had cooperated. The temperature was in the upper seventies and the only clouds in the sky were puffy white ones, ambling across the blue expanse propelled by a light breeze.

They were all gathered in Kathleen's backyard, beneath the giant oak tree. Rented chairs in rows, filled with friends. Hayden stood with Brian beneath a rented arch decorated with flowers, the minister before them. Livie stood next to her and hadn't been able to stop grinning since she woke up that morning.

"Hayden?" the minister asked.

Brian looked at her and smiled, his eyes filled with love.

Hayden felt wrapped in it, enveloped by it as she said her vows. "Brian, it took us a long time to get here. And now that we're here, I'm glad of the journey that brought us together. But I'm even gladder that the rest of our journeys will be taken together. And together, that's what I promise to you today. We're a family."

She reached and out took his hand and took Livie's, standing at her side, serving as a maid of honor. "And as a family, we can get through anything. That's what our promises create today. A family."

She glanced over at Kathleen, sitting in the front row, dabbing at her eyes. Family.

Brian shook his head. "Hayden, I hate to start our marriage by arguing with you, but you're wrong. Today doesn't make us a family. We've been that since the day you walked into our house, a crooked-eyed ghost. Today does make us partners. It cements us. There's no going back. That's my vow. I'm sticking. You can't shake me, no matter what."

"Well." Reverend Maxwell cleared his throat. "Now, that was an interesting set of vows. Brothers and sisters, if you will all rise …"

The ceremony continued with all its solemnity, but try as she might, Hayden couldn't feel the weight of the words. She was too light, too buoyant for anything to weigh her down.

She still held Brian's hand.

They'd just vowed they were family, they would stick no matter what. Like glue. Peanut butter and jelly. There was no getting around it. They were one.

"I now pronounce you husband and wife." Reverend Maxwell turned to the crowd. "May I be the first to present Brian and Hayden Conway."

Their guests stood and applauded. Livie had moved to Kathleen's side and the two of them were clapping the hardest.

"Mrs. Conway," he murmured.

Hayden was joyous, absolutely joyous.

She was now officially part of the Conway family.

"It was a good day," Hayden repeated to Kathleen as she handed her the frame.

"I'd like you to bury this picture with me. The most perfect day in a rather wonderful life. I don't want my casket cluttered with things, but knowing you're sending this picture along with me, a representation of our family, will give me comfort.

I …" Kathleen continued, talking about what music she'd like played and other details for her funeral.

The first time she'd outlined her wishes to Hayden, it was like being physically struck. But Kathleen had gone over them again since, seemingly finding comfort in organizing this one last event. Hayden had grown immune to the pain of hearing these plans. Or maybe it was her numbness that left her impervious.

"I'll make sure it's done the way you want," she promised, just the way she'd promised the other times.

"And you can bury me in that dress …"

Hayden shifted from one foot to the other. Livie and Brian would be home soon. Kathleen kept planning.

Everything kept moving forward, and all Hayden could do was let herself be carried along.

Kathleen rubbed a finger along the glass of the frame, outlining each one of them. "It was a good day," she said again.

"It was a good day," Hayden murmured, wishing things were that good now. That day, the day she and Brian were married, had felt so solid, as if nothing could ever wreck it. Rather than turn to each other, they'd turned away. Each holding on to the pain of Kathleen's illness as if it were only happening to them. She could see what was wrong, but she didn't know how to right things, and she wasn't sure if Brian knew, either.

She hoped they'd figure it out, before it was too late.

Chapter Twelve

"Hayden, I know you're a nurse and that you're trained to deal with situations like this, but sometimes it's hard to recognize the things you know when they're striking so close to home."

Marti had pulled Hayden out of Kathleen's room and into the kitchen. She motioned for Hayden to take one of the stools. Marti, in typical fashion, didn't pull any punches. "It won't be long." She took Hayden's hand, watching her, as if she expected Hayden to fall apart.

But Hayden knew she wouldn't. Couldn't.

Satisfied, Marti kept steamrolling forward. "I don't know if you want Olivia here, how she feels about it. You should talk to her and make the decision about her presence."

Hayden knew her heart was breaking, and a part of her was grateful that she couldn't feel the pain of it.

"Yes, I know I need to talk to them, to prepare them." Her voice dropped. "I know it's close, that Kathleen will d—" she hesitated on the word, then forced herself to finish "—die. Kathleen will die soon."

Marti squeezed her hand as if to force her to feel something. "When's the last time you slept?"

Hayden pulled her hand away. "I sleep."

"In a bed?" Marti's small eyes watched with a hawklike intensity.

"That recliner in the bedroom works well."

Marti shook her head. "Hayden, you need to take better care of yourself."

"Marti, I'll take care of myself later, but I've got a promise to keep first. We were so happy that day I promised …"

Six months earlier

Hayden smiled at Brian and he smiled back as they sat on Kathleen's couch.

It was a secret spouse smile. Hers she knew said, *I can't wait to be alone with you for a week.*

She could read his. It said, *I'm excited, too.*

Even after all their years together, she still marveled at the little intimacies. When he reached over and slipped his arm around her shoulder it was so casual, so without thinking on his part that she felt her heart swell.

Ten years. They'd had their tenth anniversary just two months ago. Ten years and she was as in love as she'd ever been. Brian had been so busy at work, they'd celebrated in June with a simple dinner. But they'd been talking and had decided to take a trip this fall, just the two of them.

Usually, when they vacationed they went as a family—Hayden, Brian, Livie and Kathleen, all four of them. Just last fall they'd gone to Disney World and spent a week there. It had been a blast. But this time, it was going to be her and Brian alone.

They weren't making any advance reservations. They were just going to take off and drive north. They thought they'd stop at the big peninsula in Erie. Then maybe head along the lake and go back to Put-In-Bay, an island near Cleveland, and Heritage Bay, the small town outside Port Clinton where they'd all vacationed once. Maybe they'd head even farther north to Southampton, Ontario, a lovely small community they'd visited in from time to time over the years.

It didn't matter where they went. And if they changed their minds, stopped somewhere else, went in another direction, it didn't matter. This was about a week for just the two of them, to mark a decade of challenges and triumphs. And love.

Kathleen had been on the phone as they came into the house and had waved them into the living room, gesturing that she'd be with them in a minute. She entered the room and sat on the chair across from them.

Hayden was ready to burst with excitement about the trip, so she started right in. "Kathleen, Bri and I were wondering ..." The sentence died as quickly as it had started as she looked at Kathleen's grim expression.

Something was wrong. Very wrong.

"Kathleen?"

She wasn't sure Kathleen was going to respond, but finally she sighed and said, "Brian, Hayden, we need to talk. I've tried to tell you this so many times the last few weeks, and I've decided the only way to get it done is to just say it. My cancer is back."

Hayden sat quietly, trying to absorb Kathleen's announcement, but didn't make it very far. She sort of stuck on the word *cancer* and couldn't get much further.

"I've had all the tests and waited until I had the results to tell you."

The very idea of it was so horrible, so monstrous, that it was easier to ignore the idea of Kathleen having the disease again, and immediately think about the practicalities.

Doctor appointments.

More chemo?

She and Brian would have to postpone the trip. She'd have to confirm how many sick days she had at work in order to accommodate Kathleen's treatments, which she knew from Kathleen's first bout with cancer, would be frequent and taxing especially in the initial weeks.

Hayden's thoughts were whizzing along, a mile a minute as she listed and cataloged all the things she'd have to do.

Finally, she ran out of things and glanced at Brian, who had sat equally silent. He took his arm from around her shoulder and slid a fraction of an inch away, then leaned toward his mother. "What treatments are they planning? Same as last ti—"

Kathleen shook her head, abruptly stopping his sentence.

"There won't be any chemo or radiation this time. The cancer's very aggressive—it's spreading fast and is already systemic. There's nothing to do. It's a matter of time now. All the tests have been taken, I've seen the results."

The news that Kathleen's cancer was back had been a shock, but this? Hayden didn't even begin to know how to process the words.

"I've already set up an appointment with Hospice," Kathleen continued. "My only concern now is quality of life. Whatever time I have left, I want to be as comfortable as possible."

Brian got up and knelt by his mother's chair. "But ..."

Kathleen reached out and gently touched his cheek.

Hayden wished she could cry, could walk over and hug Kathleen ... hug Brian. Do something to comfort them both, but she couldn't.

Kathleen kissed Brian's forehead. "Kids, there's nothing left to try. I'm dying."

She said it so simply. A statement of a truth that Hayden wasn't ready to hear.

Obviously, neither was Brian. "But you look fine, Mom. I know your arm's been bothering you, but other than that, you're fine."

"For now, I am fine. I'm planning to live every minute there's left out loud. Big and noisy. I want to spend time with all of you. Go up to Lake Erie as the leaves change and just enjoy the beauty of it all." She looked from Brian to Hayden. "I've promised to take advantage of every moment that's left to me. I want to spend them with the people that matter most … with the two of you and Livie."

Hayden couldn't think straight, couldn't quite make sense of what Kathleen was saying. It sounded as if she was giving up, accepting the doctors' decree and letting go. Arranging her last days.

Hayden refused to stand by and watch her die without a fight. "Let me do some research. We could find other hospitals. New, cutting-edge treatments and maybe some drug trials. We'll take you anywhere, do anything—"

"Hayden, life isn't about where you go—it's about the journey. You can live life quietly, watching the world go by, afraid to take a chance and fail. Or you can throw caution to the wind and live life to the fullest. I'm not talking about trying a new medication, a new treatment."

"You're quitting." She felt something then. A smoldering rage started to burn in her stomach. "You're not even going to try? You're going to leave us?"

"No. I'm quitting my job, but I'm not quitting on life. I plan to make the most of what time I've got left. I'm not going to spend it worrying, but rather, living. Like I said, life is all about taking a chance. Sure you'll fall on your face sometimes, but sometimes you'll reach new heights. Either way, just trying will take you to new, unexpected horizons. I don't want to watch life from the sidelines, sick from medications and treatments that aren't going to buy me much, if any, time. The quality has to count."

Hayden didn't say anything, couldn't.

"Time?" Brian asked. "How long?"

Kathleen shrugged. "Months. A year? Like I said, I've made an appointment with Hospice. I don't want to die in the hospital."

Hayden tamped down her anger. "You'll be here. Home." It was a promise.

Her voice suddenly smaller, Kathleen added, "I don't want to be alone. That's the only thing I fear in this."

"You won't be alone," Hayden vowed. "You'll be with all of us."

Brian was silent.

Pushing aside everything but Kathleen's needs, Hayden tried to decide what their priorities would have to be. First, where they would live.

"You can move in with us, we can move in here, or we'll sell both places and buy a third. You'll be with us no matter where, for as long as you have."

The look of relief that swept over Kathleen's face told Hayden that she'd been more worried than she'd let on with her bald announcement. "I'd like to stay here, but I can understand if you'd rather keep your home."

"Mom …" Brian looked helplessly at Hayden.

Hayden looked directly at Kathleen. "This was the first real home I ever knew. It's still our home. We'll sell our place and move in here."

Kathleen visibly relaxed. "Thank you."

"There's nothing to thank us for. We're here for you."

And with that major question answered, Kathleen took Hayden's hand, then Brian's. "Thank you both. I'll move down to my office and you two can take the master bedroom. Livie can keep the room she's always had here."

Hayden shook her head. "You don't have to give up your bedroom—"

Kathleen interrupted her. "The stairs have gotten to be a bit difficult, so it's for the best."

Brian knew he should say something to Hayden as they walked back to their house. But he couldn't find anything to say. She'd just agreed to throw their whole lives into upheaval for his mother. His dying mother.

He should say thank-you to Hayden.

He should say he loved her.

He should find something comforting to say.

But he couldn't say anything.

If he said any of those things, then he would be admitting his mother wasn't going to recover from this. He wasn't ready to accept that. Not yet.

Maybe not ever.

Hayden, on the other hand, obviously had no difficulty accepting the news. Why, she had them practically packed up and moved in already. She'd agreed to go to the appointment with Hospice with his mother. She was charging ahead, while he needed to stop and digest everything.

As they reached the house and opened the door, Brian hurried toward the family room hoping Hayden wouldn't follow.

But Hayden followed him. "Bri?"

"I don't want to talk about it yet, Hayden. About any of it."

He turned on the television and surfed his way over to ESPN, not caring what was on, just needing something to distract him, something to make Hayden go away and give him some space.

She didn't leave. Instead, she sat down on the other recliner, her hand on her locket, pulling back and forth along its chain. "Bri, we have to talk. We have to sort this out."

"Listen, it's not you. I'm just …" He wasn't sure what he was.

He was angry. Furious at the cancer, and he knew that was absurd. It was disease, nothing he could fight, but he wanted to do something. Hurting for himself, for Hayden and Livie, and mainly for his mom, it wasn't fair she had to go through this again. "Listen, I just need some time by myself to work this out."

"But—"

The phone rang.

"You'd better get that." Brian's voice sounded foreign to his own ears. He could tell it didn't sound right to Hayden, either. Her expressions were so vivid and he'd learned to read them so well. She was scared. Scared for his mom. Scared for him.

"Bri, whoever it is can leave a message. We need to talk about this."

"There's nothing more to say. And what if it's Livie?"

He saw her reluctance, but was relieved when she picked up the phone on the end table.

"Hello?" Her brow furrowed and her expression darkened as she listened.

"Yes. I'll be there when I can." She slammed the receiver down into the charging base. "It's my mom. She can wait."

Glad that they could put off this conversation a while longer, he said, "You don't have to wait. I'm fine."

"You're not fine," she argued. "Neither am I. We really do need to talk when I get back."

"There's nothing to say."

"Are you mad that I said we'd move in there? Her house has always felt like our real home."

"No, I'm not mad." And that was the biggest lie he'd ever told Hayden.

He was furious. Not about the move. She was right, that house had been home since he and his mom moved there. It's still where they all went to share holidays. And Livie probably spent as much time there as she did here.

No, moving to his mom's wasn't it. He was furious that his mom was sick, that there was nothing that could be done, that she was going to die.

"I just need some time, Hayden," he said again. "You go do what you need to. We'll both take tonight, then tomorrow we'll tell Livie and do everything else we need to do."

She looked unsure, but leaned over and kissed his cheek. "Okay. I'll take my cell. Call if you need me."

"I won't need you." She flinched and looked hurt by the words, so he tried to soften them. "That's not what I meant. I love you. We'll get through this."

He watched her turn and leave, concern for him still evident in her last glance.

"I love you," she said softly, leaving the room before he could respond.

Hayden remembered that day. They'd been so happy, so united. Then Kathleen broke her news.

Before she'd left for the nursing home, Hayden willed Brian to call her back, to tell her he loved her. But he didn't call her, so she kept on walking. There had been a distance between them that had never been there before. Not even during the years he'd lived in California.

She'd thought they'd bridge that distance once Brian had taken some time to adjust. But they hadn't.

She realized that was when they'd taken a first step away from each other, and it felt as if they'd been taking more steps since.

Chapter Thirteen

*B*rian sat in the too-quiet room with nothing to do but think and listen to the occasional hiss of the air mattress as his mother slept. It covered the regular mattress and blew air in and out, inflating, deflating in such a way that it helped prevent bed sores. The noise used to bother him, but he'd grown accustomed to it and found it comforting now.

He couldn't help but marvel over how things that at first seemed so shocking, gradually became everyday. Normal. Acceptable even.

But he couldn't get used to the distance between himself and Hayden. It grew wider daily, but he didn't know how to make things right.

He missed her.

He thought of the anniversary trip they'd been planning. And thought that when this was over, he'd take her somewhere special.

And that thought led to a wash of guilt. He felt as if he'd just wished his mother dead, and he didn't.

His mom awoke with a start. She looked up and smiled. "Brian?"

"I'm here, Mom."

She started to move her hand, and he instinctually reached for it, holding it. "I'm here," he repeated.

She shut her eyes, and he didn't think she was going to answer him, but finally, eyes still shut, she murmured, "It won't be long now"

Her saying that, coming on the heels of his just thinking that, made him almost queasy. "Don't talk like that."

His mother, once so vibrant, had faded, much like her bright red hair had softened to a dull gray. She was muted. She was still her, still his mother, still Kathleen Conway, but not the same. Each day she grew more quiet, pulled back from them a little. Even now, she laughed, but it was a shallow, wheezy sound, not the rich, deep filled gusto laugh she used to have.

She opened her eyes, and their once vivid blue seemed almost gray, as well. "Bri, I've always told you the truth, and the truth is, I'm ready. We had a lovely fall. That trip to the lake, Thanksgiving. We took what time I had left and we enjoyed it. But now I'm tired of fighting this. I'm tired of hurting—"

"We can get you more medicine. I'll call Hayden and she can give you something, then we'll call Marti and she can get you something even stronger."

"Shh, Bri. There's no amount of medicine to fix this. I'm just so tired. I'm ready to go. And I'm lucky I can still say what needs to be said before I leave."

"Mom." His throat constricted, cutting off any further words.

"Brian, you've been my joy. I'm so proud of you, of the man you've become."

She reached up, her face grimacing with the concentration it took to make just that one, slight move. But she did it, and caressed his face with a cold hand. So cold.

As her hand slid back to her chest, he pulled another cover up, hoping to warm her.

"Brian, you, Hayden and Olivia, you've meant the world to me. The only regret I have is leaving all of you. But I know you'll be fine, as long as you have each other. That's my comfort."

"Mom …"

"You'll be fine, Bri. I just wanted to tell you I love you. Look at the work you've done, all the children whose lives are better because of you. No mother could have asked for a better son."

Brian, who kept everything inside—his pain, his regrets—and just got on with life, felt feelings he couldn't sort out. The emotions threatened to break through his tightly held control. He waited a moment, until he'd push it all back, then said, "I love you, too, Mom. No one …"

He paused, feeling strangled and wondering how he could say the words he needed to say, knowing her time would end too soon.

"Mom, no son could have had a better mother."

She blinked as if she might cry, but she'd become so dehydrated as she stopped eating and hadn't drunk more than a sip of water at a time for days, there was no moisture to spare for tears.

"Aren't we a pair?" She laughed again, this time even softer than before.

He couldn't find anything to say to that, but he didn't need to. His mother had closed her eyes.

He began to think she'd dozed off, but then she spoke, her voice a mere whisper. "Do you remember the time you were lost in the store, and I couldn't find you? But then you called my name, Mama, over and over. Sure that I would come. Sure that I would find you."

"That security guard was trying to take me back to his office. But you'd told me to never go with a stranger."

"You're right, I did. And that's why it's okay for me to go. You won't be with strangers. You have Hayden and Livie. Family. You'll be okay." She opened her eyes then, and looked at him. "You'll be fine."

She shut her eyes again. This time her shallow breathing evened out as she fell back to sleep. This was the most she'd talked in days, and Brian knew she'd exhausted herself.

He took her cold hand in his and she smiled in her sleep.

He sat like that for a long time, just holding her hand and thinking. Wondering just what was going to happen between him and Hayden when his mother was gone.

Hayden, who'd always seemed to have the answers, didn't seem to have any this time.

Would they be able to piece themselves back together?

Hayden stood in the doorway, looking into Kathleen's room. Brian sat by the side of her bed, just holding her hand as she slept.

She turned and walked down the hall, leaving him to his goodbye.

Livie came out of her room and followed Hayden into the kitchen. "It won't be long now, will it, Mom?"

Hayden turned and saw her daughter waiting for an answer. The fact that Livie trusted her to tell the truth was evident on her face. Hayden had always tried to be honest. Sex talks, Santa-confessions … she always answered as truthfully as she could. She'd never held anything back, and couldn't do anything less this time.

So she nodded. "Not long at all. Later, when your dad is done, you can go in and say goodbye, if you want." But worrying that this was too much, she hugged her daughter. "You don't have to. You really don't need to say the words. Your grandmother knows—"

Livie hugged her. "I know, Mom. Nana knows I love her, and if I never had a chance to say it again, she'd still know. But I do have a chance, and it might hurt to say the words, but I know someday I'll be glad I did. I want her to know how much she's meant to me, how much she'll still continue to mean to me."

Hayden stroked Livie's hair, the wild red curls so like Kathleen's once were. "She's so proud of you, you know. So are your father and I. This has been so hard, and you've been so understanding. I know I haven't been there for you as much as I should have. I'll try and make it up to you when this ..." Hayden hesitated, then forced herself to finish. "When this is all over."

Livie wrapped herself around Hayden as she'd done as a child. "There's nothing to make up. You're doing fine. I'm doing fine."

Marti knocked on the kitchen's screen door once, then let herself in. "Sorry to interrupt."

Livie unwound herself from Hayden, then hugged the hospice worker. Over the last few weeks, Marti's no-nonsense ways had become a balm, soothing all of them.

"No problem, Marti. I'm going to the library for a while, but I'll have my cell. Later, when Nana's rested, I'll go talk to her. But you call if ..." Livie left the sentence hanging, but Hayden knew she meant if the time arrives.

She nodded her agreement and Livie kissed her cheek then left them.

"She'll be fine," Marti said, answering Hayden's unasked question.

"I hope so."

Marti gave her an assessing look. "To be honest, it's you I'm worried about."

"I'm fine." The answer had become so standard, that she didn't even think about it before she uttered the two words.

I'm fine.

She said it to Marti, to Livie, to Brian. She said it to Kathleen, to friends and coworkers who called.

She kept thinking that if she said it often enough, maybe she'd believe it.

Maybe she'd believe that the hole that was growing in her heart would someday heal over.

"You haven't slept for days." That was Marti, concentrating on the practical again. She knew she couldn't fix a broken heart, but sleep she could advocate.

Hayden shook her head. "I catnap."

"It's not the same. Let me stay tonight, you and Brian could both use a night off."

"We'll have plenty of nights off—too many nights off, a lifetime of them—soon enough."

"Hayden, I'm your friend."

"Then be a friend, Marti, and let me handle this in my own way. Did I ever tell you about the time Bri and I both caught the mumps?"

Marti just shook her head no.

"It was before I lived here, but Kathleen had known there would be no comfort from my mom, so she called and got permission for me to stay here. She spent days running from one of us to the other. As we felt better, she played countless games of Monopoly and Yahtzee. She made all our favorite foods. Don't you see, I wasn't her daughter, wasn't her responsibility, and she set her whole life aside to take care of me. Since that first day I came here, she's taken care of me. How can I do any less?"

"Just one night off," Marti protested. "She'd want you to."

"I can't. Like I said, there will be too many nights off soon enough." Hayden smiled at Marti. "I could use all the friendly support I have, though."

"You know you've got that."

"Thanks."

Hayden forced herself into business mode. Falling back on her nursing training had been her salvation. She knew the drill, the questions to ask, the answers to have ready. It was a balm.

"I've got all her stats from overnight." She reached into her pocket and retrieved the notebook she'd been writing everything down on. "The new Fentanyl dosage seems to be working. I only gave her three doses of morphine for breakthrough pain in the last twenty-four hours. But her urine output has gone down even more. I could use some more sponges to moisten her mouth. It's so dry it's sore. And we'll definitely need more pads. And ..."

She fell into the rhythm of her report, strangely comforted. Medicine was cold hard facts. Coping with those facts was so much easier than acknowledging what they meant—it wouldn't be long now.

Like she said to Marti, she'd sleep after. But for now, she was going to continue to do all she could to be sure that Kathleen's passing was as easy as possible. And she was going to be sure that she kept her promise ... Kathleen wouldn't die alone. She'd die at home, surrounded by her family.

That was the last gift Hayden could give her.

Chapter Fourteen

*H*ayden was dreaming. She was sleeping so lightly, that she knew it was a dream. Actually, it was more of a memory, tied lightly around a dream.

She was ten and there was a buddy lunch at school. Everyone in her class buzzed about it for a week, about what their parents, or their grandparents, their friends or relatives, were bringing for them for lunch.

Hayden hadn't bothered asking. She'd packed her own lunch just as she did every morning. She took her same seat in the cafeteria, trying not to notice how her normal tablemates had spread out over the cafeteria, their buddies next to them. But *trying* didn't guarantee success, and this was an instance where she didn't even come close. She not only noticed, but felt this queasiness in the pit of her stomach. She didn't want to eat her sandwich, but she unwrapped it and took a defiant bite anyway. She ate that sandwich because as much as she didn't want to eat it, she didn't want anyone feeling sorry for her even more.

Swallowing the bite proved difficult, and it had nothing to do with the fact that it was dry peanut butter. She took a sip from her Thermos of water. Her mother hadn't shopped in a while and the only other thing to drink in the house was beer.

"Hayden?"

She'd looked up and there had been Brian, a huge pizza box in hand. "Mom had to work, but she wrote Ms. Murray and they said I could get out of class and be your buddy. So here I am."

When she didn't say anything, Brian had continued, "Mom ordered the pizza. Lots of cheese, just the way you like it."

He'd reached into his jacket pocket and pulled out two cans of soda. "They're not cold."

Lunch unloaded, he'd taken the seat next to her. "Come on, have a slice."

She took one from him, but didn't eat it, instead just held it. "How'd you know?"

"I ride the same bus as you. I may be up in the high school now, but I still hear things." He'd looked embarrassed, but he would never admit it. "Come on, kid. It's no big deal. I got out of class to come here. And Miss Jennings said I was sweet, which means she'll give me a good grade for class participation today, even though I skipped out on most of the class."

Hayden remembered laughing then as she pushed her meager sandwich back and took a bite of her pizza. It was the best lunch she'd ever had.

Hayden snapped so quickly from dreaming to waking that she could almost taste the pizza. She'd never had a pizza that had come close to tasting that good. She lay there, lost in the past, but was pulled back to reality when she heard a rustling from the bed next to her.

Kathleen had awoken.

Kathleen had been still for so long, that the slightest movement was enough to wake Hayden up.

Hayden got out of the recliner and hurried to the side of the bed. "Hey."

Almost every day, Kathleen seemed to shrink further in on herself. Sometimes when Hayden looked down at her, it almost hurt. Waking from the sweet dream to this harsh sight was one of those times, but she wouldn't want Kathleen to know it, so she forced a smile.

Kathleen looked up and offered a weak smile, then sighed. "You're here."

"Of course I'm here. You're never alone. One of us is always with you."

Nighttime had always been her favorite hospital shift, but here, with Kathleen, the silence could hang heavily over the room. Needing to fill the quiet with something, she said, "I was dreaming about when I was little. There was a buddy lunch at school and you had to work. I knew my mom wouldn't come, but Bri did. You had a pizza delivered, and he showed up at the cafeteria with it. I loved him so much for that. You, too."

Kathleen nodded. "I've loved you since you walked into the house that first time. And I want to thank you."

Hayden hushed her. "There's nothing to thank me for. As you've pointed out so many times, we're family. This is what family does. Supports each other. You taught me that."

"I did a good job." She laughed, but it was shallow and soft, as if the effort of it hurt.

"A damned good job." Without being asked, Hayden took one of the damp sponges and moistened Kathleen's lips. "Do you think you could drink something?"

Kathleen shook her head. It was a minute movement, but it was enough. "I'm not thirsty, or hungry. Just tired. So tired."

"Then you rest, Kathleen."

Marti had talked to all of them, telling them that sometimes patients need permission from those they love to let go. Hayden had been loath to say the words, but seeing Kathleen now, so small and wasted, she found the strength for them. "It's okay to just rest, Kathleen. We're all here. We'll be with you."

Kathleen gave her hand a small squeeze. "I love you. Have always loved you like a daughter."

"I am your daughter, in every way that counts." Hayden held on to the icy hand, wishing more than anything that she could change what would be the inevitable outcome. She wished her love for Kathleen could be enough to make her better.

"You were always such a good girl. Life goes on, you know. It's a circle. Right now there's pain, but soon you'll find joy again. I want you to remember me as I was, laughing and loving all of you."

"Kathleen, we couldn't forget." She stopped, unshed tears burning in her eyes.

"Live life out loud. Make it big, make it noisy, and realize that what counts is love."

Hayden couldn't think of a reply.

Kathleen asked, "Will you hold my hand?"

She'd been holding Kathleen's hand, all along, but she reached down with her other hand, sandwiching Kathleen's between hers. "I've got it."

"Good. I can sleep now."

"You sleep. Rest. Let go. I'll be here with you."

"Hayden, promise me you'll remember."

"Remember? I'll remember everything about you."

"No. Remember what I said. Live out loud. You were such a quiet little girl. You hid in the shadows. You're hiding again. You can't do that. Live out loud. Promise?"

Hayden nodded, and that was enough for Kathleen. She shut her eyes and fell back to sleep.

Live out loud?

Hayden wasn't sure how to do that. But somehow she'd try to figure it out. She'd promised, and she'd never broken a promise to Kathleen.

Hayden sat there through the rest of the night, holding Kathleen's hand, afraid if she'd let go, Kathleen would, as well. She lost all sense of time. All she knew was the rhythmic sound of Kathleen's breathing. It was so soft, so shallow, with longer and longer moments of apnea, where Kathleen's breathing stopped altogether. Each time, Hayden thought that it was done, but each time, Kathleen drew another breath.

Brian came into the room in the wee hours, just before the sun would start to brighten the sky.

"Hayden?" With just her name, he asked a multitude of questions.

"She was awake for a few minutes. She talked about how much she loved us, asking us to remember her …" Hayden's voice broke and the tears that were always so close to the surface, welled in her eyes. "It won't be long now. She asked me to hold her hand. I think she just wants someone to be here with her."

Hayden turned and looked at Brian, grief stricken.

"Would you sit with her a while? I've got to use the bathroom, and then I'll make us some coffee."

Brian nodded. Hayden got up and he took her seat. She stayed for a moment, lingering in the doorway, watching Brian gently pick up his mother's hand. He brushed a lock of Kathleen's thin hair from her forehead, leaning down and whispering to her.

Hayden left him to it.

She had no doubt that this was Kathleen's goodbye. She knew it as a nurse, but more than that, she knew it as someone who loved Kathleen. She was saying her goodbyes because she loved them.

Problem was, Hayden wasn't ready to say goodbye.

Kathleen had said everything she needed to say. She just hoped the kids listened. She might be sick, but she could see that Brian and Hayden had left each other emotionally. She worried about them, but knew they had to find their own way back. She'd done what she could. Now it was time to let go. She was so tired.

She'd had a good life.

A very good life.

It had been filled with people she loved, who loved her in return. And in the end, no one could ask for anything more.

It didn't happen that day.

Kathleen talked to Brian, and later, when Livie came in, she opened her eyes one last time and smiled at her granddaughter then whispered, "I love you."

Hayden was so proud of her daughter at that moment as she leaned down and kissed her grandmother's sunken cheek and said, "I love you, too, Nana."

That was the last time Kathleen spoke.

Each breath was more strained than the last.

It had been days, too, since Kathleen had eaten or had anything to drink. There were times when she grimaced, as if she hurt.

Afraid that even though she couldn't voice it any longer, there was pain, Hayden talked to Marti who agreed that when it appeared Kathleen was feeling discomfort, Hayden should give her more morphine. And it seemed to work. Kathleen's sleep was peaceful after that.

It was a gray morning when Kathleen Rose Conway died.

As a nurse Hayden had witnessed death before. And knew that it was rarely the Hollywood version, with the person talking right up until the big movie climax where they'd grip themselves and fall over. Yet, the fact that Kathleen's death was so anticlimatic didn't seem right.

One moment she was alive, the next moment, she wasn't. She just stopped.

One second she was breathing, the next she sighed one last long hiss of air, and didn't inhale again.

Hayden stood at Kathleen's bedside, waiting for that next breath, confused.

Brian was standing across from her and Livie was down the hall, dressed and packing her bookbag for school.

Marti was due in an hour.

Brian said softly, "Hayden?" As if he needed some confirmation.

"I don't think she's breathing."

His voice finally roused her. On automatic pilot, she reached for her stethoscope. She pressed it to Kathleen's chest. There was one heartbeat, followed by a long silence, before there was another.

"Call Livie in." There was urgency in her voice.

But Brian didn't need to hear it to know what to do. He was already flying down the hall, and returned with their daughter. He must have already spoken to her, told her what was happening, because there were tears streaming down her face. Livie didn't bother trying to wipe them aside as she stood next to her father, his arm around her shoulder, as if he could shelter her from the reality of what was going on. Hayden stood nearby.

"It's okay, Kathleen," Hayden whispered. "You can let go."

She couldn't detect any rise-and-fall of Kathleen's chest, so she picked up her stethoscope and listened again.

She listened for a very long time.

There was no sound.

Hayden looked up at Brian and Livie, both showing their grief.

"She's gone."

Livie's silent tears gave way to full-out sobs as she buried her face in Brian's chest.

Hayden knew she should join them, grieve with them, but she couldn't seem to find her own tears, couldn't seem to move.

"Hayden?" Brian's voice was choked with emotion. He held his free arm open to her.

Part of her wanted nothing more than to be enveloped in the comfort of his arms. The other part knew she'd fall apart if she went to him, and she wasn't sure she could pick up the pieces if she did.

So she didn't.

She watched as Brian and Livie hugged. When he finally released their daughter, Livie said, "I'm going to my room."

Understanding Livie's need for solitude, Hayden nodded.

After she was gone, there was a long, uncomfortable silence.

Hayden said, "Well, I should make calls." She started to leave the room.

"Sure, it can wait …" began Brian, but as she continued to move toward the door he said, "No, damn it, it can't wait. It seems as if I've been *waiting* since Mom told us her cancer was back. You've shut me out, totally. Completely. I hate it, but I don't know what to do about it."

"You really want to have this talk now?" she asked incredulously. "Your mother's dead."

"I don't want to, but Hayden, we have to. I want to comfort you. I want you to comfort me. I want us to pull together. I need you."

"Don't you think I'd give you what you want if I could?" So many emotions coursed through her system. Anger. Sadness. Pain. Frustration. She couldn't tell where one stopped and another began. Add to that, she was exhausted to her very core. Weary both physically and mentally. She'd done all she could. And still, Brian wanted more from her?

"I don't have anything left to give you Brian. I wish I did, but I don't. I'm totally tapped out. I can't share, I can't pull together. It's taking everything I have just to keep going. There's nothing left for you." She paused and added, "I don't know if there's anything left for us."

"You don't mean that." His voice sounded as raw as she felt.

"Your mom hung on to stories of our good times. I can remember them in an academic way, but I can't feel them. I don't know if I remember how to let you in … how to love you."

"Hayden."

Words. They were only words. But she could see the damage they inflicted.

Hayden knew she should apologize. Should take them back. But she'd meant it when she said she didn't have the energy.

"I don't know what I mean, what I want. I only know there are things that need to be done. This isn't the time for this discussion."

She thought he was about to argue, to keep pushing. But finally, he nodded.

Feeling as if she had a reprieve, she sprinted into the kitchen. Its bright yellow walls seemed to mock her with happy memories. The room always seemed to reflect warmth, but today, it seemed darker and lacking the comfort it normally had.

Hayden tried to ignore the cold that seemed to seep into her bones as she called Marti, who'd promised to take care of the rest of the arrangements. Someone would be there soon to collect Kathleen's body.

Body.

At the sound of the word, Hayden started to shake. She knew that Kathleen was gone and all that was left was a shell, but hearing it was different.

"Kathleen is dead," she whispered to herself, trying the words on and not liking the way they felt.

Hayden stood for a long time at the phone, her body pins-and-needles tingly. Her mind fogged and thick. Her breath coming in shallow gasps.

"Hayden?"

Brian's voice was tight and filled with pain. It shook her from her stupor. "Everything is being taken care of."

"Where's Livie?"

"She went to her room. She didn't want to see them wheel Mom out."

"I should go check on her before the transport arrives." It seemed like just a day ago that a transport brought them home from the hospital. Today, another transport, a different kind, would come to take Kathleen away.

"We'll go together," Brian said.

They walked to their daughter's room in silence.

Brian knocked on Livie's door. "Honey, can your mom and I come in?"

"Yeah," came Livie's tear-strained response.

They went and sat, either side of their daughter on her bed. Livie couldn't seem to stop her tears, and Hayden couldn't seem to start hers.

They all sat, each lost in their own misery, until the doorbell rang.

"That's probably them," Hayden said.

Brian made some response, and Hayden left him to comfort their daughter while she took care of the next task at hand.

Keeping busy was her mantra that day and the next. There was certainly enough to do. Funeral arrangements, florists, Hospice came for their equipment. Hardest of all was finding Kathleen's outfit and taking it to the funeral home.

Kathleen had made her wishes known weeks ago. She'd asked for the dress she'd worn to Brian and Hayden's wedding, the day she'd held the wedding photo. Kathleen's words echoed in Hayden's mind. *It was a good day.*

Hayden stood in the foyer next to the coat tree that held her coat and purse, but she didn't reach for them. She simply held the plastic bag Kathleen stored the dress in and her hand shook.

"Hayden? Are you okay?" Brian had come down the stairs and she hadn't heard him.

"Are any of us?" she countered, rather than answering his question.

"I can go with you and take this to the funeral home, if you like."

"No." Her response was harsh, even to her own ears.

Brain flinched.

Hayden tried to soften it. "No, you still have people to contact. You should be the one making those phone calls. I can do this." She ran a finger over the zipper of the bag. "She was so happy at our wedding. Her and Livie. They acted as if they'd run the whole thing, they were so proud."

She hung the hanger on one of the coat-tree arms and reached for her jacket.

"Our wedding," Brian repeated. "It was a good day."

She stopped, her arm not all the way through her coat's sleeve, the phrase cutting at her.

The words she'd said earlier hung heavily between them.

Hayden didn't know how to take them back.

She didn't know how to give Brian what he needed. She wasn't even sure what it was he needed from her. But she knew he wanted her to break down and share. It wasn't that she wouldn't.

She couldn't.

"Hayden, what about us? It's not right between us. You know it and I know it."

"Why do you keep pushing? You expect me to grieve your way. I can't. It's that simple. Just back off, okay?"

"Fine. Have it your way. I'll back off." He stalked from the room.

Hayden took the bag with Kathleen's dress in it and walked out the door.

She'd fought with Brian before, but never like this. This fight had been different. Harsher. She knew she should have done things better.

She hadn't been able to save Kathleen, and now she wasn't sure she'd be able to save her relationship with Brian.

Worse, she didn't have the energy to even try.

Chapter Fifteen

*F*uneral homes always seemed muted to Hayden. Soft colors, the overpowering smell of flowers, people's whispers as they shared their grief. Platitudes, euphemisms employed to try and disguise the truth … someone was gone. In this case, it was Kathleen Conway.

Hayden stood next to Brian and Livie, to the left of the coffin. People viewed the casket, then greeted the three of them after they'd paid their respects to Kathleen. After their obligatory family condolences, they would go sit in the rows of chairs the funeral director had brought in this morning, all lined up, facing the casket that contained Kathleen.

No, not Kathleen, her remains. Kathleen was gone.

Every time Hayden reminded herself of that, the pain struck anew. But she kept saying the words to herself, needing to make them real. So far, it wasn't working. There was still some small part of herself that couldn't quite accept that Kathleen wasn't coming back.

She remembered her first trip to a funeral home. It had been sparsely populated, and there had been only one sad arrangement of flowers. It had been for her father. Her primary emotion that day was a sense of embarrassment that she didn't feel any kind of grief. She'd been to funerals since, friends and colleagues. All had been sad affairs, but she'd been there as a witness to someone else's grief.

Today, it was her grief, her family's, that was on display. And she couldn't do it.

She hung on to it, clung to it and tucked it away, making a game of hiding it. Telling herself, if she could hold on to it for another ten minutes she'd let it go, then another ten … She crept forward minute by minute. Every time she thought she'd reached the end of her rope, she pushed a bit forward, clung to her pain a bit tighter.

Everyone finally settled and the minister began his eulogy. Hayden didn't take in much.

Brian left her side and moved over, toward the center of the very crowded room, to the microphone that she realized the minister had vacated.

Brian looked good in his dark blue suit. She noticed there was more than just a hint of gray at his temples. When had he'd turned so gray? She'd missed it.

"I wanted to say something here at the funeral, something that really captured my mother. I looked through books, searching for a quote. I picked up my mother's Bible and a copy of Hayden's graduation speech fell out. Holding it, I knew I'd found the words. Hayden's words. She said, our true home isn't just a place, it's a feeling. It's knowing that this is where you belong. That these are the people you belong to. That the door will always be open to you. Sometimes you're born into your family, into your home. But if you're not that lucky, you have to search."

He set the paper down and looked out. His eyes met Hayden's. "My mother's house was not only my home, it was my wife, Hayden's, my daughter, Livie's. It was home to everyone who ever walked through the door. And to paraphrase Hayden's speech, even though my mother's moved on to a better place, she really hasn't left home because we take those we love with us. And I know my mother has all of us with her on this new journey."

He left the microphone.

Knowing she had to do this, still fighting to keep hold of her tears, Hayden rose and walked to the front of the church, passing Brian who was on his way back to their seats. She held out her hand, not sure he'd take it, but needing to touch him.

He hesitated, then reached out, their hands brushing each other lightly. That small feel of him centered and steadied her.

She stood in front of the microphone, looking at the packed room.

"Like Brian, I wanted to say something special up here, something that would commemorate and honor a terrific woman. And like Brian, the words I offer didn't come from a book, they came from Kathleen herself. She told me that life isn't about where you go—it's about the journey. Kathleen filled her journey with love. She opened her heart to her family. She opened her heart to countless patients. She opened her heart to each and every one of you here with us today. Her life mattered to so many people whose own lives were better for having known Kathleen.

"She told me, you can live life quietly, watching the world go by, afraid to take a chance and fail. Or you can throw caution to the wind and live life to the fullest. Take chances. Sure, you'll fall on your face sometimes, but sometimes you'll reach new heights. Either way, just trying will take you to new, unexpected horizons. That's what Kathleen did. She lived her life out loud and the world is quieter for her passing. It's up to us to live loud and noisy lives in her honor."

Hayden wished that she could claim to be living out loud, but right now, she was stuck in silence. Enveloped by it, tortured by it.

Pulling back from Brian again had hurt him. Though she knew it, she hadn't been able to stop herself. She wanted to fix things between them, but she didn't know where to start. She just kept hurting him.

And hurting Brain was the last thing she wanted to do.

Chapter Sixteen

There are degrees of silence. They range from the comfortable, companionable types, to the opposite end of things—to silences that hide things that need to be said, that should be said and aren't.

Brian looked across the room at Hayden, and knew that since the funeral, theirs had been the latter.

He had so much he wanted to say, but her deep silence was a wall he didn't know how to breach. Once, they could understand each other with just a look. Now, what words they did manage were incomprehensible. They said very little and it meant even less.

The day after the funeral he'd thanked her for all she'd done for his mother.

She'd looked wounded, and without response walked away.

He'd tried to stop her, but she'd ignored him.

Here, they sat in the same room, next to each other, but not quite touching. That had been the way of things for them. Close, but not touching. And Brian wanted to touch her, to feel her … to have her feel him.

"Hayden."

She looked up, but simply sighed and said, "Please, not now, Bri." Her voice was heavy with exhaustion and sadness.

He wasn't sure what she thought he was going to say, but he was pretty certain it would come out wrong, so he gave up. "Okay."

He picked up his paper.

It was easier to hide behind it than confront the fact that he was losing his wife, and he didn't know why.

Two weeks.

It had been two weeks since Kathleen had died.

Hayden stood in what once had been an office, then became Kathleen's room. Now, it was just an empty space.

Hospice had come and taken their equipment away, and all that was left in the room were the personal items Kathleen had brought in to hopefully make it feel homey.

Hayden had never asked Kathleen if it had worked.

And now she never could.

All the things she should have said and didn't clicked like a catalog of items in her mind. She worried that she hadn't thanked Kathleen enough, that though she'd told her that she loved her, Kathleen hadn't understood how much. Kathleen had been her mother, her friend, her teacher, her mentor, her biggest cheerleader …

How could you be sure someone understood that they impacted your life on so many levels?

"Hayden?" Brian was standing in the doorway.

It bothered her that her inclination was to say, not again.

Brian had spent the days since Kathleen's passing hovering. Watching Hayden. She wasn't sure what he was watching for, but the questioning looks, the furrowed brow … it was all making her decidedly uncomfortable.

"Yes?" She tried to force a smile, but didn't think it was all that convincing.

He took a step into the room, barely over the threshold. "I got a call from the Realtor. They have an offer on our house."

She'd forgotten all about their house being on the market. They'd only moved the bare essentials over from the house two doors down. They'd thought Kathleen's illness would move more slowly, that they'd all have longer. It had moved too fast, and things Hayden had thought would be done by now weren't. "That's good, I guess."

"We'll have to go through both houses and decide what we're keeping, how we're going to combine both households into one."

"Yes, I suppose we will."

She leaned back against the window sill, almost sitting on the wide ledge, and looked at the former office, trying to imagine it as anything but Kathleen's. They would probably use it for an office again.

Hayden tried to picture her desk in here, along with her computer and some books lining the walls, but she couldn't quite manage it. All she could see was the hospital bed and Kathleen's ill body.

"It's a good offer," Brian said.

Hayden nodded, not knowing what to say.

"We'll have enough to pay off the mortgage we took on Mom's."

"Okay." Forcing herself to be practical, she tried to feign some interest. "How long do we have to clean everything out?"

"A month easy by the time they get everything ready and set a closing date."

"A month." She nodded. "That's doable."

"We can decide what we're keeping, then do a big house sale there, getting rid of whatever we're not bringing here."

"That makes sense."

It did make sense, and it was good news, but Hayden couldn't feel any sense of anticipation. Couldn't imagine this house being anything but Kathleen's.

Try as she might, she couldn't imagine living here with Brian as husband and wife. She knew that was ridiculous, that they'd both lived here as children, that this had always been home. But without Kathleen, it didn't feel like it anymore.

She realized Brian was still standing there in the doorway, looking at her. "Hayden, talk to me."

"About what, Bri?" She got up and started pacing, feeling caged, though she didn't know why. Truth is, she didn't know much of anything right now. "Just what is it you want from me? I sure as hell don't know. I've done everything I was supposed to. And now I'm lost."

"Hayden, I'm just as lost as you."

"I guess in the past, if one of us was sinking, the other was there to pull us up. But we're both sinking this time. So, who's going to rescue us?"

He didn't have an answer, but then, neither did she.

"Let's give each other more time." She hoped that this would one day feel like home, despite the fact Kathleen was gone. And she hoped, given enough time, she'd figure out how to repair the relationship between her and Brian.

He said, "I feel as if every passing minute we drift further and further apart. Maybe we'll be so far apart we won't be able to get back to each other?"

"If that's the case, maybe we shouldn't be together."

She heard herself say the words and wished she could suck them back in. Brian looked as if she'd struck him and she knew she'd hurt him. She hadn't meant to.

"Is that how you really feel?" His voice was soft and almost vacant.

She wanted to close the distance that separated them, him in the doorway, her opposite, next to the window. But she didn't, and he didn't. All she could do was say, "I don't know how I feel. I'm numb." That at least was the truth.

"You wouldn't have said it if you didn't mean it on some level."

"Maybe I do. Is that what you want to hear? Maybe we made a mistake when we married. Maybe I still think that you did it because it was convenient. Your marriage to Lisa had broken up. You'd moved home. It was easy to be with me, because we share a daughter, because we both loved Kathleen."

She'd never put the feelings into words before, but as they tumbled out, she realized there was a truth to them all. It would be easy to blame the distance between herself and Brian on Kathleen's death, but that was just an excuse. Maybe the distance had been there since the beginning? Despite the fact they'd had ten good years, maybe on some level she'd held a part of herself back from Brian, afraid to give him everything because she needed to protect some piece of herself for the inevitable day he left her.

"Maybe, Brian, I wonder if now that Kathleen's gone and Livie's a junior and graduating next year, then going to college, what we'll have left? Maybe I'm wondering just what will hold us together?"

She waited, hoping Brian would say something about their love being enough to hold them together. Needing him to say that she'd never been just a convenience.

But he didn't say anything. He merely walked out of the room.

Hayden, wanting to go after him, but unsure what to say if she did, sank to the floor and cried.

Livie was almost grown, almost ready to start a life on her own. She'd lost Kathleen, and now it looked as if Hayden might lose Brian.

What would she be without them?

2004

"What would I be without you? Lost, always searching …"

Livie continued, flawlessly going through her lines for the school play, Hayden reading the other parts.

As her daughter finished, sounds of applause startled them both. Kathleen and Brian were standing in the doorway, clapping.

"Oh, gee," Livie moaned, ducking her head into a couch pillow.

"Come on," Hayden coaxed. "If you can't do the lines in front of the three of us, how on earth are you going to manage in front of the whole school?"

"I don't know. I'll probably forget every word, trip and stumble and make a huge fool of myself," Livie announced.

"Was I this dramatic at fourteen?" Hayden asked Kathleen.

"You were worse," Brian assured her.

"How do you know? You were away at school."

"I heard things."

Hayden looked at Kathleen, who laughed. "Not from me, I swear."

She looked questioningly at Brian. "Hey, I'm not going to give up informants. I just know that you were more dramatic than Liv has ever managed."

"Lies, all lies," Hayden told Livie. "I was the soul of easygoingness."

As they bickered back and forth, Hayden laughed, and finally asked, "What would I do without all of you?"

"You'd fade away," Livie said with effect.

Hayden had laughed. "Oh, no. I'd probably get daily massages and a new car every year. I'd only watch PBS and …" She continued to tease them with more and more outrageous plans, but deep inside she knew Livie was right—without them, she'd just fade away.

Brian was right, too—she was as dramatic as Livie, she laughed for no reason except it was silly to imagine her life without them. They were a family and nothing could ever take that away.

That night a few years ago had seemed like nothing overly important at the time. Hayden had just been studying lines with Livie. But now, looking back, she wished she'd paid more attention. She tried to remember what they'd done after Brian and Kathleen had come in on their rehearsal.

Had they gone out to dinner? Maybe gone into the kitchen and all worked together cooking?

Tacos? Maybe spaghetti?

She couldn't remember and it bothered her. She should have stored away every detail. They'd all been there. They'd all been happy.

How on earth had she not seen what she had when she had it?

Now that she didn't, she recognized her loss, but didn't know how to get it back.

What would she be without them?

The question nagged at her, but no answer came.

She wanted to go after Brian and ask him if he remembered that night.

She might not remember what they'd eaten, but she did recall thinking that if she'd lost her family, she'd lose herself. But Brian and Livie were both still here. It was Hayden who felt lost.

Would she lose her family because of it?

Chapter Seventeen

*L*ivie's junior year ended as summer arrived, warm and beautiful. Hayden recognized the season, but couldn't seem to find the joy in it she normally would have.

The house down the street had sold to a young couple and as she pulled into her own drive, she spotted Cathy crossing Miss Witman's lawn. She waved, but scooted into the house, before the terminally chipper young mother-to-be could come over and spread her happiness all over Hayden.

Watching someone so in love only made her situation harder to bear. The harsh words she'd exchanged months ago with Brian had driven a wedge so deep that they'd simply learned to go through their days without talking. They might still be together, but they'd never been so isolated.

Two months after Kathleen died, Brian had come in late and spent the night in the guestroom, claiming he didn't want to come in their room in the wee hours of the morning and wake Hayden.

Slowly, his sleeping there became more and more frequent. He would arrive late from work, then sleep in the guestroom. Oh, his clothes were still in the master bedroom, but Brian wasn't, except on nights Hayden was on duty at the hospital. To be honest, he might have still used the guestroom then, as well. She had no way of knowing. He'd always taken care to make the bed when he got up.

Hayden came home from work and made her way sleepily to their room. As always, the bed was made and any evidence of where Brian had slept was erased.

Normally, after a long shift, going to bed was inviting, but today, she wasn't sure she could face that king-sized bed on her own. She felt as if her troubles with Brian were coming to a head, and she was afraid of what she'd be left with when the smoke cleared.

Brian was in the master bathroom, so she showered down in Livie's, then put on pajama pants and a T-shirt.

She went to see Livie before she tried to get some sleep. Liv was spending her summer working at a local bakery. "Hey, kiddo."

Livie looked up from her breakfast, obviously surprised. "What are you doing up?"

Hayden took the stool next to her. "Hi, Mom. Nice to see you. What's new in your world?"

Livie grinned. "Sorry. Hi, Mom. Nice to see you. What's new in your world, and why aren't you in bed?"

"Maybe I just wanted to see you before you left for work. You've been so busy lately." Despite the fact she knew it would probably keep her awake, Hayden reached over to the coffee-maker, an easy reach from her stool, and poured a mug.

Livie swallowed a bite of her toast. "It's a good busy, though. I like the job, and the money will be nice for college."

Livie was so responsible, but occasionally she was too responsible. "Honey, you don't need to work yourself to death. We want you to leave time for some fun. Your dad and I started an account for you when you were little, and Nana left you money for college. You don't have to worry about college costs, or even living expenses."

She shrugged. "Yeah, I know. But like I said, I like keeping busy."

"You have to slow down and deal with things some time. I worry. How are you doing, really? I don't think I ask you that question often enough." She felt a stab of guilt. She'd been so preoccupied with her own pain and worrying about her faltering relationship with Brian, that she'd neglected Livie's feelings, Livie's needs.

"I'm okay, Mom. It still hurts, but Nana and I said everything that we needed to say. You don't need to worry about me. You've taken good care of me. You took care of Nana, too." Hayden knew, of course, that Livie was almost an adult, but hearing these very insightful comments from her daughter choked her up. Words deserted her.

"Mom?" Livie reached out and hugged her.

Hayden pulled herself together. "I was asking about you, hoping to comfort you, and here you are comforting me."

She accepted the truth of it, Livie wasn't just growing up, she had grown up. Looking back, it seemed fast. Too fast. One more year, then she'd be off to college. And that would leave Hayden and Brian here on their own. A house filled with silence and no Livie to break it up.

Hayden felt more morose than she had coming home, but she tried to cover it, not wanting Livie to worry. "You keep saying you're okay, but how are you, really?"

"Really?" Livie paused, appearing to give the question some consideration before answering. "I miss Nana. We all do. And though it's getting easier, I still think about her every day. Something happens, and I think, I can't wait to tell her, then I realize I can't … I won't ever be able to tell her again and it hurts as bad as it did right after. But I am fine, and I know that these feelings are part of the grieving process. It's normal to think about her and miss her."

"When did you get so smart?"

Livie smiled, which had been Hayden's intent. "Rumor has it that it's genetic."

"Oh, that's swee—"

With a twinkle in her eye, Livie interrupted, "So I probably should thank Dad."

Hayden laughed out loud. "Cold, that was so cold."

Livie grinned. And took the last bite of her toast. "Mom, I'm coping and I know that day by day it will get better, but we do need to talk."

There was a sudden seriousness in Livie's expression. Hayden's momentary relief gave way to a new surge of anxiety. "Honey, you can always talk to me about any of your problems."

"That's just it, Mom, it's not my problem. It's yours. Yours and Dad's. I'm worried about the two of you. I have been for a long time, since before Nana—" she hesitated, then managed to get the word out "—died. I thought maybe it was just stress and that you two would work things out after, but it's been a while and things are worse."

Hayden lied automatically. "We're fine—"

Livie's expression was one of exasperation.

"I know Dad is sleeping in the other room."

"It's not like that. We're both on different schedules and there was so much to do, with selling the old house, clearing it out and settling everything here that … We didn't just decide to sleep in separate rooms—it's merely been convenient."

"It was never convenient before."

"Livie, I—" Hayden's realization that her daughter had grown up came back to her. "You're right. Things haven't been right between your dad and I for a long time."

"So, what are you going to do about it?"

"I've been thinking maybe we should take some time apart. We've talked about it."

Well, *talked about it* may be putting too fine a spin on it. Hayden had asked if he wanted to be somewhere else, live somewhere else, and he'd just looked at her and told her it might be for the best. Those few sentences didn't really qualify as a talk, but considering how little they'd said to each other the last few months, it was as close to talking as they came anymore.

"You two have spent months apart, even though you're still living in the same house. So maybe you two should spend some time together, remember what it was like before?"

"Livie, it's not that we don't remember, it's ..." She stopped. Kathleen's illness had put a strain on them, but Hayden feared it was her harsh words after Kathleen's death that had driven their relationship beyond the point of repair.

"You two were planning a trip before we found out Nana's cancer was back. To celebrate your anniversary. Maybe you should take it."

"Livie ..."

Looking desperate, her daughter kept going. "Maybe we all should take it. I mean, if you two will be splitting up, if I'm going to be from a broken home, then I think I deserve one last family vacation. And maybe some time together will remind you what you had, what you could have."

"Things have changed. We both have changed."

"That's a cop-out."

"Morning." Brian walked into the room and smiled at Livie, but avoided eye contact with Hayden, as if she'd become invisible.

For a moment, she was Cootie MacNulty again, sitting on the bus, wishing she was invisible so that no one would pick on her. But those days were long gone, and Hayden MacNulty Conway had grown into someone who not only expected to be seen, but deserved it.

"Morning, Brian," she said loudly and clearly, throwing down the gauntlet, daring him to try and sidestep her. She'd spent so many years invisible to her parents, she wouldn't step back into that role, not for anyone, not even for Brian.

He looked up and their eyes met and held. He dropped his gaze first, but he'd seen her and acknowledged her. And right now, that was enough.

But it wouldn't be enough for long.

He kissed Livie's cheek, then walked over to the coffeemaker and poured himself a cup, before sitting opposite Hayden and Livie at the counter.

He took a sip, then slowly lowered the cup, studying them both. "What's up?"

"Livie was just telling me that she knows you're sleeping in the other bedroom, knows that we're having a problem—"

Livie interrupted. "And before the two of you break up and leave me a child of divorce, I want a family vacation. One last trip to remember when I'm trying to divide my holidays between the two of you."

"And I was about to tell her that she can't blackmail us back into our old relationship, since that's her ultimate goal. Not just a last vacation, but rather us reconciling." Hayden tried to keep her tone gentle, but she wanted Livie to understand that this wasn't like when she was young and watched *The Parent Trap,* planning her parents' Halloween costumes.

Coercing them into a trip wouldn't mend her and Brian.

Hayden didn't know if anything could. She knew they were broken, but until she could figure out how it happened, why it happened, she didn't think any amount of planning would heal what was wrong between them.

She looked from Brian to Livie. Her daughter's eyes were filled with tears, her voice hoarse and brimming with emotion. "I don't want you two to lose what you've worked so hard for." Her voice lowered as she added, "Nana wouldn't want it. She'd hate it if she thought she'd somehow driven a wedge between the two of you."

"Livie, she didn't ..." Hayden started, then not knowing what else to say, how to convince Livie, she turned, where she'd always turned, to Brian.

He took their daughter's hand. "Honey, it was us, not Mom and certainly not you."

"I don't believe it, and I'm sure she wouldn't, either."

"That's not fair," Hayden said, feeling angry, where just minutes before she'd felt guilt. "You can't just manipulate us both like this. Our relationship, for better or worse, is ours."

Livie mirrored Hayden's anger as she stood, pushing her stool back with enough force to send it toppling. The crash reverberated through the kitchen, and Was a loud prelude to the heat of Livie's retort. "No, Mom, you're wrong. Dead wrong. Your relationship with Dad, for better or worse, affects me. It's not about just the two of you. I'm here, as well."

"Livie," she and Brian said in unison.

"One last vacation. Just the three of us for a week. I'm not looking for miracles, I'm looking for one last memory, one last time it's the three of us. That's not too much to ask, is it? Next year I'll be getting ready to go away to college, so this is really our last chance."

Brian shook his head. "Livie, you know we'd do anything for you, but—"

"There's no *buts* in this. None at all." She reached into her back pocket and pulled out a well-worn piece of paper. She slapped it on the counter. "I've carried this around for a week and a half, waiting for the right time to show it to you both. I've already paid for the cottage. There's no refund. I'm going in two weeks and I'll be gone for a week. You're both welcome to join me, or not."

Hayden picked it up, studying the reservation receipt. It was the cottage Kathleen had rented from time to time. "How did you …" She left the question hanging as she read the part on the receipt that said *paid in full, non-refundable*.

"Mom, you're right. My college is all paid for, I didn't need to work this much this summer. But I called Mr. Durkie and he let me make payments on the cottage while he held my reservation. He sent me that last week. I've paid off the entire thing. If we don't go, then all my work this summer will be for nothing."

"We can pay you back the money," Brian said.

Hayden hadn't bothered to offer. She knew her daughter. She knew the stubborn look that was on Livie's face.

Olivia Kathleen-Rose Conway was a force to be reckoned with when she had that look on her face. She turned to her father and said, with far more maturity than a seventeen-year-old should possess. "I wouldn't take your money. You'll either come and accept my gift, or you won't."

She picked up the stool, set it back in place and with a deceptively soft voice said, "You both decide. But I'm going. And I'd really like my parents to come with me. One last week, just the three of us. It's not that much to ask, is it?"

She walked out of the room, and Hayden found herself sitting opposite Brian, who was once again not looking at her.

"So now what?"

Brian stared at his coffee, sighed and looked up. "How do you want to handle it?"

"I'm going."

"Can you get the time off from work? I know you took a lot of time off when Mom …" He let the sentence just hang there.

"When your mom was sick. Yes. But everyone at the hospital knew her. They understand how hard this has been. They'll give me a week off. Unpaid, of course, but we'll handle it."

He nodded, back to staring at the coffee.

"Can you get the time off?" she countered.

"Probably. But—"

"Bri, no matter how rocky our relationship is, we've never stopped putting Livie first. And Livie obviously needs this. She's worked all summer to do this."

She slid the receipt across the counter.

"Look. It's not just any cottage. It's *the* cottage. Our cottage."

He studied the receipt. "Shit."

"Can you say no? I can't."

He sighed again, then nodded. "I'll make it work somehow."

She could sense he felt he was being backed into a corner.

She reached out and touched his hand. Once, she'd have done so without thinking about it, it would have been so natural. Now she thought about it and did so with a sense of purpose.

His gaze snapped from the coffee to her.

"Bri, we were friends for years before we got married. No matter what happens, I don't want to lose that, lose you. It's only a week and it matters to our daughter. That's enough for me. Can it be enough for you?"

He didn't answer, just pointed out, "It seems like forever since we spent time together."

"Well, I remember it took us about eight hours to get from here to Southampton, so we'll have all that time in the car to start us off."

Southampton, Ontario, sat on the shore of Lake Huron. Kathleen used to have family in the area and had taken Brian there often when he was young, but Hayden had only been there twice. Once when she was in her teens, then a second time when Livie was five.

It was beautiful up there. She still remembered that first trip.

1981

Captain and Tennille's "Do That to Me One More Time" played its last notes and the radio host started talking again. Brian knew what was coming, but hoped against all hope she'd fallen asleep, or fallen out of the car.

Or maybe she found the radio host's patter engrossing enough to forget to ask—

As if on cue, Hayden piped up. "Are we there yet?"

Brian glanced in the rearview mirror. She was sprawled across the seat, looking bored beyond belief. "It's only been twenty minutes since you asked that the last time."

"So, we're twenty minutes closer … is that close enough?"

"No. We'll let you know when we get there, kid. Just be glad we've got a radio station again." For about a hundred miles there had been nothing but static on the radio. Hayden had filled the silence with humming.

Terrible off-key humming.

Hayden was many wonderful things, but she was no singer. He'd been thrilled he scanned the static yet again and found the station.

"Stop bickering, both of you," Kathleen scolded, laughter in her voice. "I thought that because you're starting college and high school, you could handle a trip."

"A trip, yes," Hayden said, "an epic journey, no. I mean, this has Homer's *Odyssey* written all over it. 'Tell me, O muse, of that ingenious hero who traveled far and wide after he had sacked the famous town of Troy.' Of course, I wouldn't mind sacking Troy … it would be more adventurous than this trip."

"Show-off," Brian muttered.

"Me? You're the one who's been all *I'm a man, let me drive* to Kathleen. As if suddenly, you turn eighteen and we little-womenfolk need your input to accomplish anything, when all along you're just covering the fact you can't read a map. 'See now, how men lay blame upon us gods for what is after all nothing but their own folly.'"

Brian groaned, which he knew to Hayden was a white flag of defeat. The kid had a memory like nobody's business. If she read something once, she could quote it forever. And she would, or at least it would feel like forever on this—the car trip that wouldn't die.

"We'll be there in less than an hour now, Hayden," Kathleen, the voice of patience and reason said. "We used to come up here almost every summer when I was little. My mother was Canadian, and her family lived in Port Elgin. We'd stay at her aunt's lakeshore cottage, and visit with them. And we'd take day trips. There's this one store that has a stuffed polar bear—"

Brian knew that Hayden had heard variations of this story before, ever since his mother had started planning the trip.

Hayden's loud exclamation was right on time, interrupting his mother. "That's so gross."

"Maybe it is, if you think about it. But when I was little, we'd go to the store every visit and my mother would tell us stories about Nanook of the North, a polar bear that pretended to be stuffed by day, and did marvelous things at night after the store had closed."

Brian glanced over at his mom, who was smiling, lost in her memories.

"There's none of your family left at all?" Hayden asked, though she'd asked it before. She seemed to love to hear his mom's stories of her family. Maybe it was because the poor kid had no family to speak of.

"No. My mom's dad died when she was young, and her mother died when I was twelve. There are probably distant relatives, but no one I really know. When Bri was little, we used to come up every year, but it's been a long time."

Brian remembered exactly when they stopped coming. It was after his dad left. There hadn't been much money after that, and vacations were a luxury they did without.

"I'm sorry your family's all gone. I'll bet they were wonderful."

He glanced in the rearview mirror and saw that wistful expression on Hayden's face. She loved his mom and spent an increasing amount of time at their place. It wasn't unusual to come down in the morning and find her on the couch. And it wasn't surprising.

Hayden's mother spent most nights at the bar, which left Hayden all alone in the ramshackle house down the street.

Some guys might have minded a kid like her creeping into their families, but Brian knew that his mom would be lonely when he left for school in a few short weeks. Hayden would keep her company. He liked knowing they'd have each other.

"My family was pretty special," his mom said with cheer. Then she sat up and pointed out the window, giving a little squeal. "Oh, look there's the sign. We're almost there."

Brian couldn't remember ever seeing his mother like this. She pointed out things the entire drive through the small, sleepy town of Southampton. And she was little-kid excited as they finally pulled into the cottage drive.

The cottage sat on the edge of the beach, no grassy lot around it, just sand.

They quickly settled in. His mom and Hayden shared one room, he had the other to himself. After they'd unpacked, they all got back in the car and headed into town to the grocery market to stock the kitchen, then they had a quick lunch and went out to explore.

It was cool here along the lakeshore. Much cooler than it had been in Pittsburgh. The sand was coarse, and the water lapped at its edge.

That first night, they all stood on the beach, watching as the sun set. His mom had mentioned the sky as it turned orange-pink, outlining the small lighthouse.

That's what Brian remembered most about Hayden's first trip to Southampton. That first sunset on the beach.

All three of them had sat barefoot in the sand, but with their sweatshirts on to fight the northern chill as they watched as the sun sank down onto the lake. The sky illuminating the lighthouse his mother had told Hayden all about.

And his mom, reminiscing the whole time, recounting stories of her childhood, of her family.

He remembered her happiness.

"You were such a pain on that first trip. Every ten minutes asking if we were there," Brian said, the force of his memory so strong, he still could remember his teenaged annoyance with Hayden.

"I was furious with you. I knew every time I asked the question it annoyed you, so I kept it up on purpose."

"Why were you furious?" He'd never heard her mention that before.

"You were going to college. Kathleen organized the trip, and told me she knew you'd get busy, that you'd go away a boy but come back a grown-up. She wanted one last vacation with you while you were still just her son, her boy."

"I didn't know." His throat felt tight and his eyes felt dry thinking about his mom knowing he was leaving. He remembered being happy she'd have Hayden around, and he remembered being excited about going to school. Had he had any bouts of homesickness? He couldn't remember.

"She didn't want you to know she was dreading letting you go. I hadn't planned on coming along on that trip, I thought it should be just the two of you. But she said—" Hayden paused and blinked hard, as if trying to hold back tears "—but she said it was a family vacation and that meant I had to come."

"So why were you mad?" Brian might have been raised by a single mother, might have grown up with Hayden acting as his shadow, might even be the father of a teenaged girl, but none of that had helped him understand the workings of a female mind.

"I was furious because I knew she was right, that you were going to leave us. I was mad that I'd finally had a family, and you were splitting it up. I was so pissed. It burned in my gut that entire trip. Kathleen knew it, just like she always knew things. That final night at the cottage, she hugged me and asked if I'd like to consider moving in with her fulltime. She claimed I'd be doing her a favor, that she couldn't stand the idea of an empty house."

Hayden brushed the tears out of her eyes. "I miss her so much, Bri. She was my stability. I could count on her, no matter what. You can't know what that felt like after so many years of having no one. She gave me a family. I hate to think what would have happened to me if she hadn't taken me under her wing."

"You were and are a survivor. You'd have survived and overcome your family, with or without us."

"I'm glad I got to do it with you both. I don't think I ever thanked you for sharing your mom with me like that."

"She loved you …" He wanted to add, I loved you, but didn't.

"Bri, I just want to say—"

The phone rang, interrupting whatever Hayden had been about to tell him. She answered the call.

"Hello?"

Whoever it was, the news wasn't pleasant. He watched her expression turn dark.

"Okay, I'll be right there."

"Your mom?" he guessed.

She nodded. "I have to go."

"If Livie comes back, I'll tell her we're in."

Hayden nodded and left. Brian wished the phone call had been held off a few more minutes, wondering what she'd been about to say.

Chapter Eighteen

Hayden stood outside the nursing home with a feeling of déjà vu.

In all the years she'd been coming here, nothing had really changed. From the shrubs planted along the brick exterior, to the flowers they planted each spring and summer, to the benches and picnic tables in the yard.

Her mother's condition had meant she'd been there for years. Jeri MacNulty had wasted away, bit by bit, year by year. Dying by increments. She used to come out to the small courtyard by the entrance when she'd been in an independent-living section. But as her dementia worsened, she'd been moved to the long-term-care unit and the only time she left the building was if Hayden took her out.

Knowing she couldn't put off the inevitable, Hayden walked into the lobby area. When she'd first begun coming to the home, she'd been impressed with the cheerfulness of both the decor and the staff.

Year after long year, she'd walked through the perky lobby, to the elevator, up three floors to the nursing unit. Here, the appearance was more hospital-like. Carpet gave way to tile, the reception desk into nursing stations. But the walls were a cheery rose color, and the staff was as nice and likeable as the rest of the home's employees.

And her mother still had the same bitterness, the same anger as she'd always had, but now it was marked by more confusion. The doctors diagnosed her with multi-infarct dementia brought on by blood clots on the brain. It was a disease that predominantly struck people older than her mother, but being outside the norm didn't soften the blow. Piece by piece her mother lost memories and time became blurred. Aphasia had wreaked havoc on her speech.

Yet, through all of it, her mother's rage remained intact, and she targeted it on Hayden with as much accuracy as ever.

The elevator doors opened, and her mother sat in a wheelchair, screaming at the staff. Not screaming words or obscenities as she once would have, but a wordless, ire-filled primal scream.

"Mom?" Sometimes if she could distract her, her mother forgot the anger. "Mom, I came to see you."

"You." Hayden had heard that tirade so many times, she knew the script.

"Would you like to go for a walk outside? Get out of here for a while?"

Her mother nodded. "Yes, take me in."

Hayden knew that by *in,* her mother meant *out.* She mixed up her words, when she could find them at all. "Fine, Mom. Just let me tell the nurses and we'll go outside for a while."

Kim was standing at the desk and had obviously heard the exchange, but Hayden walked over to her anyway. "How long?"

"Two hours. We have a call into Dr. Shelton, but—"

"But she's taking forever to get back to you, and you could use a break."

"I'd take her outside myself, or get one of the aides to, but it's been one thing after another today and we're short staffed, so …"

"I do understand. It's no problem. I'll take her for a walk. Maybe a change of scenery will help."

"Thanks, Hayden. This is as hard on her as on the rest of us. I think she's aware enough that she knows what she's doing, she just doesn't have any way to control herself anymore."

"Even if she could, my mother wasn't someone who ever tried to control herself. I don't know how you deal with it every day."

"Like anything else, there are good days and bad."

Her mother screamed again, a piercing, blood-curdling sound.

"And there's an example of a bad one." She quickly got her mother organized and wheeled the chair into the elevator and pressed the lobby button.

"Hate it there," her mother mumbled. "Hate it. I want to go for ice cream."

Hayden questioned, "Ice cream, or did you mean, home?"

"Home. I want to go home."

"I'm sorry, Mom. You can't do that."

"I want to go home." The small brick house at the bottom of Briar Hill Road had sold the year after her mother had moved into the assisted-living facility. The Wilkosz family had brought the run-down place back to its former glory. Repaired, landscaped … the house screamed happiness, something it had never known when the MacNultys had lived there.

Hayden hoped that whatever karma was left from her family had been wiped out by the Wilkoszes. Hayden would occasionally catch little Eric or Amy playing on the lawn. Of course, that was years ago, and the Wilkosz children were too old to spend much time playing, but it still seemed a happy home.

"Let's go outside and sit under the trees. We'll talk there."

"Home, home, home, home …" her mother screamed as Hayden wheeled her through the lobby. Thankfully, Lori, the receptionist, and only two other people were there to witness the outburst.

Hayden didn't try to reason with her mother, didn't try to quiet her—she knew better. She just hurried onto the path that led to the grove of trees at the back of the building. She pushed the wheelchair up next to the picnic table and sat down, facing her mother.

"Now, take it slowly and tell me what's wrong."

"You did this." Her mother pointed a finger that wobbled as it hung midair. "You."

"Mom, you have a disease, do you remember?" She didn't bother naming it, but just explained, "Blood clots in your brain. It's why it's sometimes hard to find your words. Take your time and tell me."

"You put me here."

"Yes, I did. You couldn't stay at home. You weren't thinking clearly and were a danger to yourself and others."

"You hate me. You took away all my chances."

Hayden knew the story of how, even before her birth, she was to blame for all her mother's woes. "I know. You were going to make it big, be a dancer, then you got pregnant with me and had to get married to Dad. Dad with his lofty dreams, but no follow through. Dad and his drinking. I know, Mom. I ruined your life."

She nodded. "You're getting even."

"That's not true."

For an hour she sat listening to her mother spew her hate and frustration. Hayden hoped that by letting her mother vent, she'd be calmer for the staff tonight.

Time slipped by. She glanced at her watch. "We have to go in, Mom."

"Throw away the bee."

"No, Mom, I won't throw away the key." Though it was tempting. And just thinking it made her feel horrible.

Hayden couldn't leave her mother alone and uncared for. Too many residents had families who put them in the home and then forgot about them. People who only were visited on the holidays … if then.

No one, not even her mother, deserved that.

As she wheeled her mother back into her room, then checked in with Kim at the nurses' station, she kept thinking about her mother's life, how she held on to her pain, took pleasure in it even.

As Hayden waited for the elevator, she glanced in the mirror and almost didn't recognize her own reflection. She looked washed out, pale … and angry.

She realized for the first time that she looked like her mother. A younger version, but there it was. She'd never noticed the similarities in their looks until now. Maybe it wasn't just the physical likeness, maybe it was something else. The bitterness.

She went outside, but rather than getting into the car, she went back to the picnic table. Thoughts tumbling over each other.

After years of doing everything she could to be as different from her mother as possible, to be as much like Kathleen as possible, maybe genetics won out in the end. She was more like her mom than she wanted to admit. Her mother had spent her life mourning the things she felt fate, or rather Hayden, had robbed her of.

Hayden thought back over the last six months. About her rocky relationship with Brian. She'd pulled away from him. He'd pulled away from her, but that was no excuse. They'd both just stopped trying, lost in their own muddled feelings. Even now, she'd been toying with the idea of a separation.

She'd loved Brian for as long as she could remember, and yet she was willing to let that go because it was too hard, would take too much to repair what they had.

What did that say about her? About her love for her family?

She tried to be honest with herself … why was she willing to walk away rather than fight?

Because if she fought and lost, it would be worse. If she let herself fall back in love with him, tried to hold on to Brian and their relationship, and he still slipped through her fingers, she might not ever recover. It was easier to just let go now, while she was used to the distance between them.

Kathleen's words came back to her … *live life out loud.*

Her mother had never done that. She'd lost what she felt was her one chance and slunk into the shadows, preferring to stay there than risk trying again.

Hayden was slinking, rather than risk trying again.

When did that happen?

When had she become the kind of person who would prefer living quietly on the sidelines rather than living life out loud?

The last six months—before that even, if she was being honest—she'd pulled back when she should have stepped up. She hadn't said anything when there was so much that needed to be said.

Maybe it was time for taking a step forward, saying something, at least one thing that needed to be said.

I'm sorry.

It wasn't much. Just two words, but maybe it was a start. It was more than she'd ever had from her parents. It didn't make up for closing herself off from Brian and Livie, but maybe it was a start at opening herself back up to them.

Suddenly the trip to Southampton looked brighter.

Brian walked into the kitchen and was hit by a wave of smells. Spicy, sweet. There was a humidity in the air that said water had been boiled. The overall feel was warm and inviting. He thought all this, but in the most casual sort of way, noted there was something different. And then it really hit him—someone was cooking.

It had been months since someone had cooked. The three of them had collectively lived off salads and take-out. But tonight, someone had cooked.

He took another step into the kitchen and saw Hayden at the stove. She turned and smiled. It was a tentative expression that said she expected to be rebuffed. That expectation reminded him of what a failure he was. When Hayden had needed him most, he hadn't been there for her. He'd let her down.

She'd shouldered the burden of caring for not only his mother, but for him, for Livie, for her own ungrateful mother. And he hadn't been able to do enough to help her.

Now she smiled at him, and waited for him to walk away. He offered her a tentative smile and was rewarded by a look of relief passing over her face, followed by a more natural smile.

She stirred whatever was in the big pot. "I thought I'd cook."

"I see that."

She glanced back at him. "Livie just got in and went to clean up."

"Let me wash my hands and I'll help you set the table."

He hurried to the sink and watched Hayden bustle around the kitchen. Something was up. He couldn't quite put his finger on what, but it was there.

He went to the cupboard and pulled out four plates, then stopped. Hoping Hayden didn't see, he put one back, then turned. As he did, Hayden gave him a wry smile. She understood. "I do it all the time," she admitted, stirring.

He'd just finished putting the silverware on the table when Livie walked in.

"I see I timed that right," she teased, gesturing to the table.

"Not right enough," Hayden assured her. "You can slice the bread while your father pours the wine," she looked at Brian and added, "If you don't mind?"

"No."

After months of not meeting his eyes, of avoiding talking to him, Hayden's openness was encouraging.

She brought a huge pan of lasagna to the table and extra tomato sauce, then went back and brought three salad bowls.

"Sit, everyone."

Livie caught his eye as they did and raised a brow, silently asking him what was up. He shrugged. He had no clue.

"Before we eat, there's something I have to say, and I might as well just get it over with. I went to the nursing home today and looked in a mirror. It sounds stupid, but what I saw in my reflection was my mom, both in my features and my actions. She's bitter, blaming life, blaming me, for everything that's gone wrong. She shut everyone out years ago, and never opened up to let anyone else in."

"Mom, you're not bitter, you're just—" Livie groped for a word "—sad."

"Maybe. Maybe bitterness comes from holding on to a sadness too long. Letting it eat away at you. I don't know. But what I do know is, like my mom, I shut out everyone. I held on to my pain, rather than share it. The more I held on to it, the higher I had to build the walls to keep it in. Finally, the wall was so high, I couldn't scale it to get to the two of you. I left you both during a time you needed me most. I'm sorry."

"Hayden—" Brian stared.

She shook her head. "I don't need either of you to say anything. I just wanted to apologize and tell you that I'll try to do better. To be here … really be here."

Livie reached across the table and took her mother's hand. Hayden smiled at their daughter, genuinely smiled. He couldn't remember the last time he'd seen that expression on her face.

He wanted to take her other hand, but was afraid she'd pull back, and if she still pulled away from him after making her apology, he'd know for sure it was over between them. He wasn't ready to know that yet.

So, rather than take the chance and risk yet another rejection, he didn't reach for her. But he did say, "I won't say it now. I'll wait a while longer, but I get to have my turn sometime soon."

She looked worried, but nodded. "Soon. Right now, there's a real dinner on the table for the first time in I don't know how long. Let's dig in."

She'd taken a step back to him. He was going to be satisfied with that for now, so he obliged. He dished up his plate and joined in the purposefully light conversation.

He'd bide his time.

Hayden liked having the last word, and he'd let her have it, for now. He could wait.

He'd done it in the past.

November 1981

"Go on, say it, college boy." Hayden had him cornered, but he wasn't about to admit defeat.

He'd left for college in Tennessee in August, and here it was, almost Thanksgiving. His first visit home. He'd expected a teary reunion with his mom and Hayden. Instead …

He looked up at the bedroom window. She was still there, water balloon in hand, poised, daring him to try to get in the house without saying the words.

"Hayden, this is childish."

"Hey, I'm a freshman in high school, not in college, so I can afford to be as childish as I want." She shook her hand, making the balloon wiggle within it. "Come on, college boy, say it."

"I'll get you back if you do," he warned.

"Oh, now who's being childish, Mr. Delta Delta Dork?"

The red balloon in her hand was huge, straining from the pressure of the water it contained. She shook it a bit. "Say it."

"Fine. I'll humor your childish ways."

"I'm waiting."

"Hayden is queen of the mountain, empress of all she surveys."

"Glad you remember, college boy." She whipped the balloon out the window, and it hit his car rather than him. "You may enter."

"I'll remember that balloon, Hayden. One day, when you've all but forgotten, I'll get even."

"The oh, so mature, college boy speaks," she hollered before she slammed her window shut, making sure she had the last word.

Brian sat at the table not sure why he was remembering water-balloon fights. Hayden had started it with that Thanksgiving one when he was a college freshman. He'd waited until he was a senior in college to get even. He'd hit her with one and the resulting battle had ended in their first kiss. But he'd had his say.

Of course, he hadn't said anything very wise. He'd apologized for kissing her when what he should have done was simply kissed her again.

He wouldn't make that mistake again.

When the time came, he'd get the last word in … and hopefully the first kiss of a new beginning.

It was odd that a pan of lasagna and an apology made him this hopeful, but then when had anything between him and Hayden been normal?

Feeling better than he had in months, Brian ate his dinner and smiled at his wife, who had the good sense to look a bit nervous.

Chapter Nineteen

"The trip is taking just as long as I remember, and that's saying something because I remember it lasting forever," Hayden joked, knowing she sounded as whiney as she had that first time to the cottage.

That first time, Brian had teased her mercilessly. Their second trip with Kathleen and Livie had been filled with family chatter.

Now Brian drove in silence, just casting her more of the odd looks he'd been shooting her for days, ever since she'd made her apology. She couldn't figure out what those looks meant, but they were making her curious.

"I remember when we all came," Livie said from the back. "Well, mainly I remember images, the lighthouse, this one piece of wood that washed up a few houses down from ours. I remember stringing a blanket over a branch and making it my tent. That's really about it."

"You were so little." Hayden was struck by the thought of Livie at that age. She'd been all legs. Her hair, uncontainable, red tendrils going every which way. Missing front teeth. And freckles … oh, what a week on a beach will do to freckles. There were millions. She smiled at the memory. "It was such a lovely vacation. Every night we walked into town. There's a little variety store, and we'd each pick a treat. I always got—"

H O L L Y   J A C O B S

"Cream soda," Brian interjected. "And. Livie, you liked the rootbeer."

Hayden smiled at him, pleased he'd joined in, then turned back to Livie. "You weren't allowed to have sodas very often, so getting one every evening was quite the treat."

"What did Nana like?" Livie leaned forward.

"Rootbeer. She's the one who got you hooked on it."

Before they rhapsodized any further about the wonders of root beer, Brian pointed. "There's our exit off Route 21. That wasn't too bad, now, was it?"

Livie and Hayden groaned in unison. "Dad, that was the longest eight hours of my life."

"Oh, come on, it wasn't that bad." Brian suddenly seemed cheery.

Hayden started to relax, but then he shot her another of those odd looks and punctuated it with a smile she couldn't quite read.

"If I'd remembered the trip was this long, I'd have maybe made reservations somewhere closer to home," Livie maintained.

"It wouldn't have been the same," Hayden assured her. "We're so glad you thought of it. Thank you again, honey."

Brian wended his way through the small town, taking a left at the end of the main street, driving past summer cottages that were mixed in with the year-long residences. Between the houses Hayden could catch a glimpse of the beach, the water or just the horizon.

She opened her window and the scent that said you're here flooded the car. The lake smelled differently than an ocean, fresher, crisper.

Brian finally eased the car into a driveway by the small weathered cottage. The shingles had faded from the brown Hayden remembered to a faint tan. Rather than looking worn, the weathering added to the cottage's charm. The building seemed to be part of the landscape, blending in perfectly.

"We're here." Livie already had her door open and was hurrying to the side door. "Mr. Durkie said he'd leave the key in the—" She didn't finish the sentence because she'd already opened the mailbox and retrieved a solitary key on a chain.

Hayden and Brian were barely out of the car, and Livie already had the door opened and had sprinted into what Hayden remembered was the kitchen.

"She might be almost grown up, but there are times, like this, that she's still our little girl." He reached out, took Hayden's hand and gave it a squeeze, then obviously realized what he'd done. His head snapped up and he studied her, looking as if he was trying to decide if she minded or not, if she was going to withdraw as she had so often lately.

She smiled what she hoped was a reassuring smile, and squeezed his hand back, not letting go. "Yes, she'll always be our little girl."

They walked into the kitchen and nothing had changed. The same butcher block table sat in the center of the room, with twice as many chairs as they needed. The counter was still a circa nineteen sixty Formica, the appliances white enamel with black showing through where they had been nicked over the years. The same wagon-wheel lighting fixture hung heavy over the table.

Hayden took it all in, standing in the doorway. There was a comfort in the fact that everything here stayed the same, as if time hadn't touched it.

"Mom, Mom, look, it's all the same." Livie's words echoed her thoughts. She couldn't help remembering the last time they'd been here. Livie was just seven. The day before they left Southampton to go home, she'd come prancing into the room with Kathleen on her heels and said …

HOLLY JACOBS

1997

"Mom, Mom…." Livie was dancing from one foot to the other on the cottage's linoleum floor, obviously excited about something. "Come on, Nana, tell her."

Kathleen smiled indulgently at Livie and took her hand, which soothed her spastic hopping. "Hayden, Bri, if it's all right with you, Livie and I are going on a day trip. We'll be back sometime after dinner tonight."

"It's an all-about-me day." Livie's excitement was evident as she started bouncing again.

Kathleen had started all-about-me days years ago. A whole day where the "me" in question got to do whatever he or she wanted. Kathleen had gifted Hayden with more than one all-about-me day, although Hayden's had become much quieter days than Livie's.

"And then we're going to the movies, and having ice cream for lunch and stopping at the store so I can say goodbye to Nanook of the North and Nana will tell me all his stories, then—"

"Do you think you can do all that in one day?" Brian asked. He messed Livie's hair, which never needed any assistance looking wild.

Hayden smoothed the silky strands as Livie nodded.

Kathleen grinned. "Maybe we can't get it all done, but we sure can try, right, Liv?"

"Yep. Me and Nana are interrupted."

"Intrepid," Kathleen supplied.

Hayden carefully schooled her expression. It wouldn't do to let Livie see she was amused. She turned and saw Brian was valiantly trying to suppress a grin, as well.

Livie obviously decided permission had been granted and squealed, then kissed Hayden and Brian, and was out the door on the way to the car before any of the adults said anything.

"Well, I guess we said yes." Hayden watched out the window. Livie climbed into the car and laid on the horn.

Kathleen started for the door, then turned back. "You two will be okay without the car?"

"We'll be fine," Brian assured her. "Hope you can say the same after what looks to be a very busy day."

"We'll be more than fine. I look forward to days like these with Livie. Soon she'll be too old to want to spend a day bumming around with her doddering grandmother."

Hayden laughed. "I can't imagine you ever doddering."

Kathleen grinned. "I'll do my best to avoid it. Oh, and we absolutely won't be back until after dinner. The cottage is all yours." She winked, turned back toward the door and hurried out.

"Oh, she's subtle." Hayden laughed.

"Very." Brian pulled her into his arms. "So, what should we do with a whole day to ourselves?"

"We still have the Sunday crossword puzzle to do."

He kissed her neck.

"Or, we take a walk into town and check out that antique shop Livie never wants to let us stop in." Her voice much higher, she mimicked their daughter. "I don't wanna go, Mommy. It's so boring and dusty. I think it might make me sick." She coughed for emphasis.

His lips moved lower, caressing the curve between her neck and her shoulder.

"Or, I guess we could go out on the beach for a bit." Teasing was getting harder as Brian kept up his gentle persuasion.

"Mmm," he murmured, his lips now on her shoulder, tasting, reminding her how hard it sometimes was to find time for this with both their daughter and Kathleen in the house.

"Or maybe …" She paused as her fingers slid down his chest and rested on the waistband of his jeans. "Maybe the two of us should stay in the cottage. It's cool today. Cool enough that we could probably use the fireplace and pull that quilt out in front of it."

He looked up, grinning. "Do tell. So what would we do with that quilt in front of a small fire?"

"Well, let me see if I can outline a few possibilities." She stood on tiptoe and whispered her ideas in his ear. His hands traced small circles on her back, distracting her from her planning.

She gave up the game and simply changed her attention from his ear to his lips and kissed him. They were married, and still, touching him like this, holding him, being with him sometimes struck her with a sense of wonder.

He was hers.

She was his.

And as the thought occurred to her now, it only intensified the feelings of longing.

When they finally broke off the kiss, he took her hand and silently led her toward the living room.

"A whole day to ourselves," he said, a smile on his face.

"A whole day …"

Hayden stood in the doorway of the cottage a decade later, looking at the kitchen, the sweetness of the memory making her smile. But remembering how close they were then only reminded her how distant they were now. Things had been better since that night she'd apologized, but they were still nowhere close to where they'd been that day so long ago.

She wanted it all back, but wasn't sure how to go about getting it.

"Mom, come on, let's see what the rest of the place is like." Livie sped out of the room.

Hayden followed after her, Brian, too.

The great room was the same, as well. Hardwood floor, clean, but not shiny new. They bore evidence of years of families vacationing here. To the left was the fireplace. For another moment, that afternoon they'd spent in front of it on the quilt flitted across her mind.

She forced herself to look away. There were couches and a huge stone coffee table. To the right, a bar, another couch and a couple overstuffed chairs. And straight ahead, a sliding-glass door that let out to a patio. Beyond the patio, the beach, the lake.

Hayden walked to the sliding-glass door and looked out, knowing what she'd see … the island with the lighthouse.

Livie came up beside her and hugged her. "It's all the same, isn't it, Mom?"

"Just the same, honey." She slid the door open and stepped out onto the cement patio.

Livie shouted, "I'm going to go claim my bedroom."

Hayden stood, looking out over the small beach to the lake. Lake Huron stretched in front of her, wide, deep and if she remembered correctly, cold. She loved the water, the sand … just loved it here.

Brian followed her and stood behind her. "Why didn't we come up here more often?" His question was a whisper against her breath.

She realized how close he was standing, and took a step to give herself room to breathe, before she turned and shrugged. "We got busy. After my first trip, you were in college, me in high school, both too busy. And after that second trip with Livie, she got active in school activities and—" she shrugged again "—life just got in the way."

"Life shouldn't get in the way of the pleasures. We should have made time."

"We did … now. Thanks to Livie." Their daughter was a force to be reckoned with.

The force appeared in the doorway, just as Brian said, "She's a stubborn little thing."

Livie snuck up behind him. "Yoo hoo, Dad. The stubborn little thing is right here."

He turned. "Busted."

"Yep, you are. In all fairness, I'd like to point out that I wouldn't have to be stubborn if my parents weren't so stubborn themselves."

"So, what you're saying, Livie, my love," Brian asked, "is this is a case of the apple not falling far from the tree?"

"The trees," she corrected, pointing from one of them to the other. "This apple didn't fall far from her trees."

Hayden couldn't help but laugh. It was strange. For months she'd mourned Kathleen, worried about her relationship with Brian, but coming here seemed to have given her some distance from all that. Maybe it wasn't just this trip, maybe it was her apology, her finally admitting there was a problem and deciding she wanted to try to fix it.

It didn't matter what the reason was. For the first time in a long time she felt she could breathe. "Listen, let's get our suits and go down to the water."

"You know it'll be too cold for you." Brian turned to Livie. "Both times we've been up here, your mother's put on her suit every day and tried the water, and every single time, she's declared it's too cold for people, but just right for polar bears."

"Hey" Hayden protested, "one of these times it might be warm enough."

"Always the optimist." He laughed. "Let's go find our suits, then."

Optimist? Hayden was pretty sure that wasn't an apt description. She'd been a realist. And these last few months she'd been a pessimist. Maybe it was time to give optimism a try?

That first swim—and Brian had been right, the water was too cold—set the tone for the rest of the week. They played on the beach most of the day, and in the evening, after supper, they walked into town. The first night. Hayden reached for a cream soda and it felt as if the last ten years had never happened.

Livie reached for a rootbeer. "Nana would like to know I've kept the tradition."

"She would at that," Hayden agreed with her.

All three of them sipped at their sodas as they strolled along the waterfront back toward the cottage. Hayden felt that sense of optimism bloom. Maybe she and Brian could find their way through this.

She stole a glance at her husband—he was laughing at something Livie had said—and desperately hoped they could.

Chapter Twenty

The thing Brian loved about the Southampton cottage they'd always rented was its sense of togetherness and simplicity.

There were no friends for Livie to run off with, no jobs or distraction calling him or Hayden away from the family.

His mom had implemented a no-television policy here when he was a child, and they'd maintained it on Hayden's two visits. That meant finding ways to entertain themselves as a family. They'd spent the last three days doing just that.

Trips to the beach. The local sites. Board games that simply gathered dust in a closet at home became entire evenings worth of entertainment. Scrabble, Monopoly, card games. Hayden, despite her normal easygoing nature, was highly competitive, and Livie was a chip off the mom block. He watched the two of them finish a particularly long game of Scrabble.

"Disease," Livie crowed, laying *D-I-S* on top of a previously played *EASE*. "Ah, all those spelling bees pay off. I've got a great vocabulary, if I do say so myself. And that's it. I used all my letters. Game's over. How many do you have left, Mom?"

"The stupid *Q*. If you'd left any of the *U's* open, I'd be the one gloating right now."

"Unfortunately, this game allows for only one winning gloater. Although, when you started the game off using all your letters, I seem to recall a bit of crowing then."

Hayden turned to Brian for a show of support. "Do you see the type of child we've raised?"

"Dad, don't listen to her. She's just a sore loser."

He laughed. "I suggest we proclaim Livie the winner, and go out to the beach."

"Oh, we haven't done iron ore yet." Livie hurried to the closet, pulled out a bucket and chose three large magnets.

Watching Hayden grin as widely as Livie, he hastened to agree. He'd do anything to see both of them look so relaxed.

They each took a magnet—he'd used them all as a boy—then walked down the beach, looking for a dark patch of sand.

When they found some, they dragged their magnets along the sand, picking up the iron ore that was mixed into it.

He never could figure out what was so fun about the process. After all, the only thing they'd ever done was fill up small glass bottles with the ore, then cap them. He still had a couple of the bottles tucked around the house somewhere. But while he didn't understand the whats and whys of the enjoyment of it, he couldn't deny that it was fun.

As Livie talked about starting her senior year of high school, about her classes, about anything, he realized that maybe the fun of it came from the company. The three of them had nothing to do but chat and visit.

He stopped dragging his magnet and simply watched Hayden and Livie, trying to freeze the moment and store it away for the future.

His mom would have said, *this is a good day.* The thought made him smile.

"Dad," Livie said, pulling him from his reverie, "I asked …" Her sentence faded away as her attention was drawn somewhere beyond where he sat.

He turned around and saw a small group, probably a family by the looks of it … a family that contained a boy who appeared to be the same age as Livie.

Brian turned and faced his daughter. "You were saying?" he prompted.

She blushed as she brought her attention back to him. "Uh …" she shrugged "… I have no idea."

"Cute boys can do that to you," Hayden teased.

"Mom …"

Brian and Hayden looked at each other and burst into chuckles. For that moment, they were connected. It felt like old times.

"You two need to grow up," Livie grumbled, which only made them both laugh harder.

Livie picked up her magnet and started raking it through the sand again. "I thought we were hunting iron ore, not ganging up on me."

"We can do both," Hayden assured her.

"Multitasking. We're good at it." Brian wiped a bunch of iron ore into the bucket to prove the point.

Livie shot them eye daggers.

He held up his hands in surrender. "Okay, okay. We're done now, I promise."

Livie snorted. "That's what you say, but we all know that you love picking on me."

"What can I say? When you're good at something, you should—" He stopped as Hayden abruptly elbowed him playfully.

"Seriously, we're done," she promised their daughter.

Livie peeked up and over Brian's shoulder. "He is cute," she said, which set Brian and Hayden off again. This time Livie joined in.

As they sat laughing, teasing and sifting for iron ore, Brian considered what was going to happen between him and Hayden. He hadn't pressed the issue because, truth be told, even after her apology, he wasn't sure where they stood. So, he hoarded all the moments of this vacation and prepared to save them against that possible future. Moments he'd be able to recall and savor, ones he could look at and remember what it had been like when they were all together.

After about fifteen minutes, the boy in question came over. Brian started to rise, but Hayden took his hand and kept him seated.

"Hey," said the kid.

He was tall, lanky and looked young. Very young. Had Brian ever been that young?

Livie stood as she answered with an equally articulate, "Hey."

Brian wanted to get up and toss a towel over Livie, or better yet, a turtleneck and pants, but Hayden maintained her grip, keeping him from doing either. All he could do was study the boy in question.

"Wanna swim?" the kid asked.

"Sure." Livie started with the kid toward the water, then suddenly remembered her parents. "I'll be back, okay?"

Brian had just been reflecting on how nice it was that Livie didn't have any friends to hang out with. The irony of her meeting someone within a couple hours of that thought wasn't lost on him.

But he could sense the futility of mentioning so now, so he settled for, "Sure."

Hayden released his hand and grinned at him.

"Did you notice that it was too cold earlier when I went in?"

"It was. But maybe it warmed up in the last few hours." Hayden stared after their daughter, who was squealing as she followed the boy into the water. "It seems like a long time since we were that age."

She and Brian sat alone on the sand, a half-filled sand bucket of iron ore between them.

Brian wished she hadn't let go of his hand. He wanted nothing more than to reach out and take hers, then pull her into his arms.

They'd started growing closer, but they weren't quite at that point yet. Then Hayden smiled at him, and as Brian smiled back, he acknowledged that he was willing to wait, to work at getting his wife back even more. She was worth it. They were worth it.

Somehow they'd do it.

Again, Brian had hopes that maybe they could figure a way out of this.

The next day Hayden stood washing dishes by hand. The cottage didn't have a dishwasher, and normally she'd balk at the lack, but it was strangely comforting here, being at the sink, looking out the window at the wild sand-filled yard with its strange patches of flowers and weeds. To be honest, it was hard to tell which was which.

They only had a few days left, a few days left for her talk with Brian.

As if on cue, he came into the kitchen. "Want me to dry?"

"Sure."

She waited, afraid he was going to start the talk, but instead, he simply picked up one of the glasses, stood next to her and dried it.

Hayden could smell Brian's cologne. It was a spicy scent that over the years she'd become accustomed to, so much so that she rarely noted it anymore. It was just a part of Brian. But after their long emotional separation, it hit her as if for the first time.

She breathed deeply, remembering all the occasions he'd held her and she'd been enveloped by the scent. Brian took the cup from her hand, jolting her from her thoughts.

"This is such a pretty view." He dried the cup, set it down and took another.

Hayden released a long breath. She hadn't known she'd been holding it until that moment. She was so relieved that his choice of topic was the view not anything deeper.

"I was thinking the same thing. I—"

"Mom, Dad." Livie burst into the kitchen from outside. "I ran into Tim, that boy on the beach yesterday. His family's going to go up to Port Elgin and wanted to know if I could come along. Can I?"

Part of Hayden wanted to say no—she wanted to keep their daughter as her buffer zone from Brian. But looking at the excitement on Livie's face and considering Brian's choice of conversation topics, like the view from the window, maybe it wouldn't be so bad.

"Sure, honey," she finally said, and was rewarded by a quick hug. "Did they have any idea when they'd be back?"

"Mr. Johnson said probably not until after nine."

"Okay. If it's going to be later than that, call, okay?"

"Sure. I will. Thanks, Mom." Livie ran upstairs and came back with a sweatshirt and her purse. She hurried to the door, but paused before opening it. "You're sure the two of you don't mind spending the day alone together? I mean, I could stay if you need me to."

"We'll be fine," Brian assured Liv.

Hayden nodded her agreement, touched that Livie would change her plans to stay, and yet sad that their daughter felt the strain between Hayden and Brian so acutely that she'd feel as if she had to. "Go have fun."

For a moment, Livie still hesitated.

"Go," Hayden prompted.

And with another wave, Livie was gone.

Brian helped Hayden finish the dishes, but there was no more conversation between them. Immediately, the cottage seemed silent.

As they put away the last of the dishes, Hayden looked at Brian, who was looking back at her.

The day stretched before them. Just the two of them. It had been a long time since they'd been alone for a whole day. "So, what did you want to do?" She hoped he had some idea.

211

Brian hesitated. "I don't know. Maybe just a quiet day. We could take a walk into town and get lunch there, rather than cook. Uh … We could do some reading and …" He shrugged.

"A walk a little later, then lunch sounds nice." But that meant they had to fill the hours until lunch.

They both puttered around the house. Hayden could tell that Brian was trying to avoid her, but she couldn't take offense because she was trying equally hard to avoid him.

They both finally settled, books in hand. Hayden was on the couch on one side of the big stone coffee table, Brian on the other in the recliner.

She picked up her book for the umpteenth time, trying to get lost in the words, but instead, getting lost in her thoughts as she toyed with her locket—the one Kathleen had given her so many years ago—running it back and forth along its chain.

Every time she sneaked a peek at Brian he seemed as fidgety as she felt. It was almost a contest … who would break first.

Brian did.

He set his book down with a thud on the stone coffee table and leaned forward, toward her. "Hayden, this is ridiculous. We have the house to ourselves for the day and a conversation that's been hanging there between us, both of us know things need to be said, to be settled, but both of us are avoiding it."

She followed suit, setting her book down and leaning toward him. "You're right. If we're going to do it, let's just do it. It's been months since things between us were right. We don't talk, we don't even sleep in the same bed."

There were twin beds in the room they were using at the cottage. The last time they'd come, they'd pushed them together so they could sleep next to each other. This time they let them alone.

"I know." He raked his fingers through his hair, looking frustrated. "Hayden, I just don't know how it happened. How did we get here?"

Hayden knew she had to come clean, to own up. The knowledge had been weighing on her. "I could say it was me, that when Kathleen got sick, I shut myself off. All I could think of was my pain, my loss. That one day, in the tree house, I cried alone. You came and tried to help, but I wouldn't let you in. I blew it."

"I did try that day, but you tried, too." Brian got up off the recliner and walked around the table, taking a seat next to her on the couch. "Hayden, look at me."

Reluctantly, she did.

"Hayden, you were there for my mother when it counted. You comforted Livie. Helped her through the whole ordeal, both as it happened, and after. I hate to call you a liar, so I'll settle for calling you confused. You thought of everyone and everything *but* yourself."

She shook her head. It was a mark of Brian's kindness that he tried to salve her conscience for her, but she knew better. "Bri, I didn't comfort you. That day at the tree house, I didn't let you comfort me. That's what couples should do, comfort each other. Instead, I cut you off. That day, I was crying, but I couldn't let you see it, I couldn't let you cry with me."

"Why?"

His question was so gentle it hurt, knowing that this was what she'd thrown away. She could have had his caring, his support, throughout Kathleen's illness, and after. These last few months, she could have had this … him. But she shut him out. She didn't know how to answer his question because she wasn't really sure herself.

"Why? I don't know. Maybe I was afraid if I cried with you I'd really let myself go. I'd fall apart and if I did that, I wasn't sure I could put myself back together. And I had to be together to give Kathleen what she needed. Maybe that's it, or maybe I just reverted to what I know, standing on my own two feet. Alone." She reached out and took his hand. "It doesn't matter why. What matters is that I'm sorry."

Olympics Jacobs

She waited, knowing that he was going to agree that she should apologize. She'd pushed him away for so long, let the distance between them grow so great, they'd never get back to where they were.

After a long silence, Brian finally said, "Do you remember our first kiss, out in the yard? You'd brought me a chocolate milkshake?"

"And you threw a water balloon at me—"

"I'd promised you I'd get even that Thanksgiving my freshman year."

She laughed. "You do know how to bide your time. And after that I kissed you. I didn't plan it, didn't mean to, but I did. And for a minute, I thought you kissed me back. But then, you broke it off and apologized."

"Remember the first time we made love?"

"Brian, I remember all of it. You comforted me that night, and I thought it might be something more, but then you—"

"I apologized. That first kiss, the first time we made love … both times, I wanted you. Hayden, I can't remember a time I didn't want you. But back then, I pushed you away. I tried to tell myself that you were too young, that I was being noble. But, Hayden, I don't know if you were ever really young. Given how you grew up, I don't think so. Honestly, I was afraid that if I let myself truly fall for you, I'd lose myself in you. My mother loved my father like that, totally head-over-heels. When Adam left, it nearly killed her. I was afraid that if I truly fell, then you left, it would be like that for me. So I pushed you away."

"Bri—"

He squeezed her hand. Slowly he said, "I pushed you away both of those times. I blew those opportunities to have sooner what we ended up having so much later."

"Bri, but you came back, we found each other. So there's no point—"

214

"Maybe loving someone means sometimes you blow it, but because they love you, they give you another chance."

"Are you saying you'll give me another chance?"

She waited, holding her breath for him to answer the question.

"No. I won't give you another chance."

Her heart sank at the finality in his voice. She blinked hard, determined not to cry. She'd known this was coming, actually knew it back when they married. She'd known Brian couldn't stay in love with someone like her.

"Hayden." He reached out, took her chin and gently forced her to look up and meet his eyes. "Hayden, you don't need another chance, but I'm hoping you'll give me another one. A third one. I know I don't deserve it."

"Bri, you didn't do anything."

"You're wrong. You didn't mess things up between us, I did. I heard you crying in that tree house. Hell, I could see your pain every single day. I could have reached out to you, could have beaten down your wall and made you share. I could have told you that if you fell to pieces, I'd help you pick them up. But I didn't push, didn't hold you. I just walked away and let my own pain consume me. I let you take care of everything, of everybody. I blew it, Hayden. And though this is the third time I've pushed you away when I should have held you close, I hope you'll give me another chance. I swear, I'll get it right. I'll be there for you "

"Brian, you've always been there for me. When you beat that kid on the bus for calling me Cootie. When you took me into your house and then invited me trick-or-treating. You shared your home and your mom. You're my constant. Maybe I felt I could push you away because deep inside I believed you'd always come back. That's not fair. It's taking advantage. But I didn't do it on purpose. And, Brian, you're the first one in my entire life I've ever trusted enough to push."

She laughed then, through her tears. "I don't know if that's truly a compliment, you know. But maybe that's a good definition for what love is ... knowing you can push the person you love and they'll always come back."

"New rule ... if you push, I'll pull. Like this ..." He reached over, finally bridging the distance as he pulled her into his arms, pulling her tight and hugging her.

Hayden went willingly. Oh, so willingly. Coming into his arms was coming home. She'd missed this. Missed holding him, kissing him. Feeling as if she had the right.

She shifted, moving back, not to draw away, but to get closer. Their lips met and suddenly the tenderness of the hug deepened and intensified. They simply held each other and kissed, for how long Hayden couldn't guess.

Brian was the one to break it off. "Hayden? You're crying."

She reached up and felt her cheek, wiping her eyes. She was. She hadn't realized it. She knew they weren't tears of sorrow, they were tears of joy. Tears of relief. "I'm happy. It feels like forever since I've been happy like this. You know, your mom told us to live out loud, but maybe she should have said, love out loud. I'm going to do just that. I want to tell you every day, I love you. I want to show you."

"I love you, too."

Those words seemed to settle everything. All the doubt, all the anxiety, all the pain.

They took their walk on the beach. The northerly wind kicked up, blowing over the lake, chilling them both as it picked up sand and sent it skittering. Waves crashed into the shore.

Brian's arm was around her shoulder so Hayden scarcely noticed the chill.

When they were almost back to the cottage, Brian said, "We should probably go in."

"Probably." Despite the low temperature, she could stay out here forever, simply wrapped in Brian's arms.

But then he grinned. "Livie's not going to be home for a long time yet. I bet we could think of some way to warm up real quick."

"Oh?"

"Well, we could start by moving our beds together, like last time and then we could …" He wiggled his eyebrow and grinned.

Hayden laughed a happy-to-the-center-of-her-being laugh. "We could …" She wiggled her brows. "I think that sounds like a perfect plan."

Holding hands they bolted into the house. Hayden's heart was light. Lighter than she could remember it.

And after they'd moved their beds together, it was lighter yet.

This. This was living out loud—loving Brian, being loved by him. How could she have ever doubted that?

He slipped under the covers and patted the bed next to him. "Come to bed, Hayden."

But she knew what he was really saying was: come home to where you belong.

Hayden was happy to oblige.

Chapter Twenty-One

*H*ours later, still in each other's arms, they heard Livie arrive at the cottage.

They'd spent the day in bed. They'd skipped going to town for lunch and made do with sandwiches. They'd gone all out and ordered a pizza for dinner, then eaten it in bed … cold.

It was almost nine o'clock as Livie came up the stairs. She knocked on the bedroom door and called out in a stage whisper, "I'm home."

"Okay, sweetie. I'll see you in the morning. Don't wake your mom."

"Okay. 'Night."

They heard her footsteps retreat down the hall.

Hayden giggled. "Why is it I feel like a teenager who almost got caught?"

"I know how else I can make you feel like a teenager …"

She laughed simply because there was so much elation bubbling inside her that she had to let it free or simply bust with it. "Do tell."

"Why don't I show you instead?"

He did.

And he was right. She did still feel like a teenager. Being back here with Brian like this felt like the first time all over again.

The next morning, Brian coaxed Hayden into the shower with him. What started off as a purely functional event turned into something much more entertaining. By the time they finished, the hot water had been exhausted, and so was he.

"Maybe we should go back to bed and take a nap?" he asked as they scurried into their room.

"Bri, Livie will be getting up soon. We should tell her …"

"That I'm amazing? That we still have it? While I do agree, I might suggest our seventeen-year-old probably won't want to hear it."

Hayden took a pillow and tossed it at him.

"We should tell her that we've reconciled.

That was her plan with this trip. She'll be thrilled."

He grinned. "Hayden, are you blushing?"

"No."

"Come on, I'm pretty sure your cheeks are pink."

"They are not. Now, stop that. Let's go start breakfast."

"First things first." He leaped onto the floor at her side.

Hayden laughed, which had been his intent. He'd missed the sound. He pulled her into his arms and kissed her soundly. "Along with all our other resolutions, I'm adding this. We start every morning with a kiss and go to bed every night with another."

"I think I can agree to those terms." They stood, arms around each other.

"I love you," Hayden mumbled into his chest.

"Did you say something?"

"I love you."

"Sorry, I don't think I heard you."

"You're such a dork, but despite that, I love you."

"I love you, too. Let's make breakfast. Then maybe later, we can tell Livie we're taking a nap."

As they made pancakes and bacon, he teased her and she teased him right back. How could he ever, for even the briefest second, have entertained the idea of ending his relationship with Hayden? To do so would have been amputating the best part of himself. How could he have missed that?

"Mom, Dad. Tim wanted to know if I could…" The sentence faded as Livie stood in the doorway, studying them. "What is it?"

"Your mom and I … we're okay now."

She looked from him to Hayden and a grin started to spread across her face. "Just like that?"

"Not just like that, but we made it to the other side," Hayden said. "And we want to thank you."

"You do?"

"You planned this vacation, pushed us together when we'd both been thinking about just walking away. You helped us more than you can know."

Livie hugged them both, pulling the three of them close. Brian found his arms filled with Conway women, and couldn't imagine anything better.

"So, what you're saying," Livie said as they broke apart, "is I'm brilliant and you want to think about getting me a car, right?"

Livie had been lobbying for a car since she'd gotten her permit. "Well, your mom and I will have to talk, but since all your money this summer went into paying for this vacation, and since we have Mom's car just sitting in the garage, it seems to me you might be able to call it your own. Maybe."

Livie likely missed the *maybe* part due to the loud shriek as she rushed over and hugged them both.

"I don't want you to think I did this for a car, but …" She hugged him again.

"I didn't think that, and don't get too excited until your mom and I have talked." He saw Hayden over Livie's shoulder, nodding her approval so he added, "But I think you can consider it a done deal."

Through breakfast they talked and laughed about cars and boys and the start of the school year. There was nothing huge or profound, and yet, Brian felt as if this breakfast, this morning was a new beginning. From the amount of smiling his wife and daughter did, he was pretty sure they felt it, as well.

They'd weathered the storm.

He realized there would be others, other moments that tested their relationship, but after this, he was pretty sure they could make it through anything.

"I'm going to town with Tim. He said he'd buy me lunch and we could go see a movie, if that's okay with you two?"

They'd barely nodded yes before Livie was tearing through the house to get ready.

"Another afternoon to ourselves. What will we do?" Hayden asked.

Brian grinned. He couldn't seem to stop grinning and laughing. To be honest, he didn't want to. "I seem to remember last time we were here Mom and Livie took off, and we stayed in front of the fireplace all afternoon."

He'd mentioned his mom, and though he still missed her, the memory was a sweet one. There was some pain, but it was muted when compared to the pleasure of thinking about Kathleen. From the smile on Hayden's face, he knew it was the same for her, too.

He took her hand and swore to himself he'd never let go again.

Hayden was right. His mom had talked about living out loud, and that was important. But as Hayden had said, so was loving out loud.

Chapter Twenty-Two

*H*ayden hurried down the quiet corridor of the hospital at one o'clock in the morning. It was almost a full-out run. The smell of the antiseptic cleaner that the nighttime housekeeping crew was using filled her nostrils, making her already queasy stomach tighten. She'd never cared for the smell, but her reaction to it had never been like this. This was a whole new level of not liking it.

She rushed into the restroom just in time.

Five minutes later, still feeling weak from throwing up, she was back in the hallway.

"Hayden?"

She smiled as she spotted the short, squat lady with the most amazing smile. "Marti." Hayden hugged her. "What are you doing here? One of ours?"

"No. I was here for someone on another floor and thought I'd pop up and see if you were working tonight."

"I am." Seeing Marti brought back the most painful time in her life, but rather than feeling crushed by the memories, she felt … she searched for a word … *relieved* that those days were behind her. But that wasn't quite it.

Ever since the trip to Southampton they'd known happiness, and an appreciation for how good things were between her and Brian.

"So how are you, all of you?"

"I'm fine. We're all fine," Hayden said, meaning it.

Marti didn't question the statement, just quirked her eyebrows.

"Really. I am now. If you'd asked months ago, the answer might have been a different one, but I am fine now. Bri and I are both fine," she added. "Livie, too. She's loving school."

"Good. I worried about you all. Every family copes with loss differently."

"That's a tactful way of saying we didn't cope well. But we eventually figured things out."

Marti nodded. "I thought you would. But if you don't mind me saying it, you're looking a little green around the gills."

"I am. I'm not sure what kind of bug I've got, but it sucks."

"Nurses make the worst patients. Why don't we go sit in the lounge for a few minutes. I'll make you some herbal tea that might help settle your stomach."

Marti got Hayden settled on the couch and busied herself at the microwave. While she worked, she asked, "How's your mom?"

"The same as ever. They have a new combination of drugs that seem to be helping stabilize her mood swings. It wasn't just that she was a problem for the nurses, it was that she was miserable. No one should have to live like that."

"She's lucky to have you."

Marti brought a cup of steaming tea to Hayden. One sniff was all it took. She set the cup down, bounded off the couch and sprinted to the restroom again.

When she got back, sure that she'd purged her stomach, Marti was waiting, smiling. "So when are you due?"

"What?"

"The baby," Marti said slowly, "when's it due?"

"Baby." Hayden's hand dropped to her stomach. "Baby?"

223

She tried to remember when she'd had her last period. She'd always been irregular to the point that she no longer watched the calendar.

The realization sank in. "Oh."

"Oh. I take it a test is in order?"

Hayden nodded, lost in the enormity of the what-ifs. After trying for so long, and finally admitting defeat, could they have gotten pregnant? It was too much to hope.

"Let me know when you find out for sure," Marti said as she left.

Hayden made it through the shift, still nauseated, but feeling a growing sense of excitement. It had been a while since her period, and she'd been feeling sick, off and on for days. She was only forty. Women had babies when they were much older than that.

She stopped at the drugstore on the way home and picked up a pregnancy test. She went straight into the bathroom, not wanting to raise Brian's hopes and just minutes later dash them.

She'd never used an at-home pregnancy test before. When she suspected she was pregnant with Livie, she'd gone straight to the doctor. But now she couldn't wait. She read the instructions, which if they were to be believed, said the test was accurate. Very accurate. Accurate enough that whatever it decreed, she could pretty much rely on.

Stomach flu, pregnancy.

Stomach flu, pregnancy.

She waited for the test results, the two options going back and forth in her head.

Stomach flu, pregnancy.

She checked her watch, and with hands shaking, looked at the small stick.

Stomach flu, pregnancy.

Tears in her eyes, she hurried into the bedroom and stood a moment, watching Brian asleep in their bed. After months of separation—both physical, which was bad, and mental, which was worse—it looked so good having him back here. The thought came to her whenever she saw him there.

She walked to the side of the bed, and sat. "Bri?" She ran a hand through his hair. "Wake up."

His eyes fluttered open.

"Hey, you. Come over here." He pulled back the sheet and patted the bed next to him.

"I have a surprise for you. A big surprise."

"A surprise on a Saturday morning? Does it have anything to do with you being naked under these sheets with me?"

She grinned. "I'd like it if it ended that way. But it starts with me showing you this." She pulled the small white stick out from behind her back.

Brian looked at it, his sleep-fuzzed brain obviously not quite comprehending.

"We're pregnant."

He sat up and took the stick. "How?"

"Well, first the girl's body releases an egg ..." She laughed. "I think it was Southampton. Okay, so it could have happened almost any of the nights after that, but I choose to think it was that first night together again in Southampton."

"Pregnant? Pregnant?" he repeated, looking dazed. Then slowly a smile spread across his face. "Pregnant." He opened his arms to her. "Come here."

Hayden went and he pulled her in tight. "Pregnant," she whispered against his bare chest.

"After all these years, I'd totally given up hope. Livie leaves for college next September. That's what—" he did the math in his head "—eight months? I was planning to take you on a trip to Europe. Something wildly romantic. Paris maybe."

"Instead, we can stay home and change diapers." She laughed, then touched his cheek. "I don't mind the change of plans. Do you?" She needed to hear it from him.

"How can you even ask?" He hugged her again. "A baby. We're going to have a baby. I missed so much of Livie when she was born." He paused. "Do you think she blames me?"

The question had come out of the blue, flooring Hayden. "Blames you?"

"Livie, for not being here? For missing all those moments?"

After all this time, he still harbored guilt?

"Bri," she said gently, taking his hand in hers, trying to reassure him without words. When his expression didn't register relief, she tried again. "I don't think I've ever seen a girl who was so loved. When I used to hold the phone to her ear and you'd speak, she'd go crazy, her hands and feet going a mile a minute. She loved you, and never doubted you loved her. That's all any child needs."

"But I'll be here for this baby … for you. God, Hayden, I plan to pamper you and take care of you. I …" Words failed him.

"I never doubted it, Brian. I never doubted you."

It was good that she hadn't. Unfortunately, Brian had. Even during their first decade as a happily married couple, he'd occasionally worried that somehow he'd screw up. Then, after his mother had died and his relationship with Hayden floundered, he'd been sure he'd screwed up.

Since then, he realized that if they'd talked about it, if they'd shared their own personal self-doubts, their marital problems might not have deteriorated to the point they had. So rather than hold on to his feelings, he expressed them to her.

"I know we've talked over our problems, and I don't want to beat a dead horse, and hearing you say that you know I'll be there means a lot, but I need you to really know, to understand, I won't mess this up. I'm here for you. Whatever you need. Whatever

Livie or this baby needs. I won't let the words we don't say come between us again."

Hayden took his hand again. "I mean it, I know. No matter what happened between us I never doubted that you'd be there for me, for Livie."

She was smiling, so was he. He pulled her into his arms and simply held on tight.

"I love you." During the bad times those were the words they'd needed to say the most.

"Me, too," Hayden assured him. "I love you, Brian Conway."

Six months later

Time.

Hayden had read somewhere that quantum physics had proven that time wasn't finite. That it expanded and contracted.

The last six months had sped along at an astonishing rate, and now she found herself here, in this place. A year ago she wouldn't have believed it.

She knew she was waxing philosophical, but as she glanced over at Brian, sound asleep in the recliner, then down at the baby in her arms, she couldn't seem to stop herself.

"Mom?" Livie cried as she flew through the birthing-room door. "I saw the note when I got home."

Hayden pulled the blanket down to give her daughter a better look at her brother.

Brian woke up and joined them, running his left hand tenderly along Hayden's cheek, his right touching the baby's small fist. "Becker. We're going to name him Becker."

"Nana's maiden name," Livie said.

Hayden nodded. She looked at the three of them and marveled. This was her family. She loved them all so much. She'd gone through so much to get here.

As much as Hayden still cared for her mother's needs, her mother had never been her family. She was the woman who'd given birth to her.

For the longest time Hayden had credited Kathleen with giving her a family, but as Hayden looked at her husband, she knew it was Brian who'd rescued Cootie MacNulty that day on the bus; it was Brian who'd given her a home. Brian who'd given her a family. First, by sharing his mother, then by giving Hayden two beautiful children.

She raised her hand and covered his. "Thank you," she said.

"For what?"

"For this. For them. For us." Her eyes filled with tears, which she valiantly tried not to shed. Finally, she gave up the battle and let them fall freely. "Hormones," she said, but she knew that wasn't it. She was simply overwhelmed with feelings of love, of gratitude … of being exactly where she wanted to be.

Brian came down and hugged her, murmuring small I-love-yous in her ear, and she reached out with her unfettered hand and eased his head to her and kissed him. In that one kiss she tried to imbue all her feelings, the largest of which was love.

"Oh, geez, you guys. I mean, I'm happy you two are back together, but really, a little less showing it in front of me and the baby." Livie laughed, and leaned over to her brother. "Beck, honey, you're really in for it. These two are going to drive you nuts with all the kissing and stuff, but believe me, even when they drive you crazy, you're a lucky kid."

The baby started to wiggle and make noises. "I think he wants to nurse," Hayden said.

"After that kiss, I can't take much more. I think I'll roam the halls and look for cute interns." She grinned. "I figure you two could use a bit of alone time."

She leaned over, kissed Hayden and left.

"She's some kid," Brian said. "And if Beck's anything like his older sister, I suspect we're going to have our hands full. But I'll confess, I'm looking forward to it."

"Me, too." Those two little words didn't seem to go far enough to express how she felt about their future. Of watching Livie graduate, go to college, get a job, get married. At watching Beck start from scratch, learn to crawl, to walk … And at having a chance to be with Brian, to grow old with him, to have him at her side. No, those two words didn't go nearly far enough, so she added three more that did. "I love you."

"Love you, too," he replied.

Hayden was sure their relationship would have its ups and downs, but she was also sure they'd find their way through them. She planned to live out loud, love out loud and treasure every good day.

She looked at her family and knew it was a good day.

Epilogue

Hayden and Brian held hands as they sat in their chairs, watching Livie walk up onto the stage.

Over the last twenty-five years, Hayden had grown so accustomed to the way her hand felt in Brian's that frequently she didn't even think about it. But tonight … tonight was a night for not only remembering, but acknowledging the importance of the small things.

Holding Brian's hand was one of those things.

Livie stood at the microphone at the center of the ballroom. "I'd like to thank you all for coming tonight to honor my mother and father's twenty-fifth wedding anniversary. It's such a milestone, one that deserves this kind of occasion. I'd like to ask Mom and Dad come up and say a few words, but before that, although most of you know us, I'd like to introduce us. I'm Olivia, their daughter, and …" She waited as Becker joined her. He was slowly leaving that awkward teen stage and beginning to grow into his body. Tall, lanky and in need of a few pounds, his hair wild and in desperate need of a trim, he smiled. "And I'm Becker."

Livie leaned over and gave him a hug, but with typical teen-boy reaction, he ducked out of it. His fair complexion turned a subtle shade of pink.

Hayden's hand tightened around Brian's.

"And the family's grown. I'd like to introduce my husband, Lou, and our daughter, Kathleen, and our son, Sammy."

Hayden watched as her family gathered center stage. Lou was a lovely man who'd joined their family six years ago. A pediatrician, Hayden had met him at the hospital, a new doctor in a strange city. She'd brought him home for dinner, and there'd been something immediately there between him and Livie.

Livie had told Hayden then, that he was the first man she'd met who came close to living up to her father. That was when she knew that Livie was going marry Lou.

Three years ago, they'd made her a grandmother for the first time. Little Kathleen was the spitting image of a woman she'd never meet, but would be a part of her life through the many family stories. She held her father's hand as they walked onto the stage. Lou carried Sammy, who was just a year old now, and quite the hellion. He reminded her a lot of Becker at that age.

There they all stood. Their family … Kathleen's legacy.

Livie continued, "We wanted to do something to honor Mom and Dad on this very special day. Two people who've spent their lives doing for others, not only through their careers in medicine and social work, but through the way they've cared for their family. Becker and I are probably the most fortunate kids ever. Our parents loved us and always put us first. And my kids are so blessed to have such a special pair of grandparents. So, please join us in honoring my parents' twenty-five years of marriage. But more than that, their lifetime of love."

The crowd clapped.

"Mom and Dad?" Livie called, beckoning them onto the stage.

Brian didn't let go of Hayden's hand as they stood and walked up to the microphone.

Hayden let him go first, willing to let him speak for both of them because the tremendous lump in her throat made her wonder if she'd be able to.

She looked out at the crowd. Colleagues, friends. Then back at her kids, her family and the lump only got bigger.

Brian cleared his throat, then squeezed her hand. "Before I turn the mic over to my better half, let me just say…" The crowd laughed and he quickly added, "Not that I'm saying Hayden talks too much …"

The laughter got harder.

"Let me just say, the last twenty-five years have been wonderful, but my journey with Hayden started a long time before that. I was twelve and dressed as a biker, she was eight and a sorry-looking ghost. She knocked on our door and my life was never the same." He kissed her.

He moved over, and because they were still holding hands, practically dragged her in front of the microphone.

She was silent, not sure she'd find the words she wanted. Glancing at all of them, her family, she remembered that little girl who'd knocked on the Conway door. She'd been so alone. Despite the fact she had parents, she'd been so much an orphan.

"That day I walked down Briar Hill Road and I knocked on Brian's door, I was coming home, even if I didn't know it then. That one Halloween, my whole life changed. It was a turning point. Our lives, Brian's and mine, have been filled with other moments like that, times when something happened and everything changed."

She leaned closer, their arms touching. Even after all these years, just touching him could give her such comfort. "Some might say that a life is defined by the big moments, ones that alter a person's direction. I'd say, those are the times that punctuate a life, but don't truly tell the story. My story with Brian is told in the little things. Like in the water-balloon fights, the roadtrips, teasing each other and later with our children. All those small moments with Livie and Becker, and now with Kathleen and Sammy. Bedtime stories, school plays. All those moments of love.

That's where our life is written, in a lifetime of them with each other, with our children, with our grandchildren and with Brian's mother, Kathleen. Some of you never met her, and though Brian's mom has been gone for many years, she's still alive in our family. We share memories of the amazing woman who gave us so much, taught us not to be afraid and to live every precious moment of our lives out loud—to risk ourselves for what matters. A woman who showed us what matters most is love."

Hayden stopped, tried to harness the emotions that were welling up inside of her. "I want to thank you all for being a part of our story … a part of our family. Thank you for celebrating this day, celebrating love, with us."

Dear Reader:

Thank you so much for picking up Briar Hill Road. I hope you enjoyed this story that's so near and dear to my heart. If you did, please consider leaving a review to help others find it.

Bio:

Award-winning author Holly Jacobs has three million books in print. The first novel in her Everything But ... series, *Everything But a Groom*, was named one of 2008's Best Romances by Booklist, and her books have been honored with many other accolades. She lives in Erie, Pennsylvania, with her husband and four children and two dogs, Ethel Merman and Ella Fitzgerald. You can visit her at http://www.HollyJacobs.com.

If you enjoyed Briar Hill Road, read

Same Time Next Summer

Prologue

"CARO. CARO, COME ON."

Twelve-year-old Carolyn Kendal threw open the
cottage door and ran out onto the porch. The
force of the wind took her breath away.

She looked out at Lake Erie. The wind had whipped it
into a frenzy, pounding wave after wave onto the shore.

Stephan Foster, her best friend each summer, was on his family's porch, waving at her.

Caro tugged at the leg of her swimsuit. The suit didn't fit as well
as it had when she'd arrived with her mom and dad at their
Heritage Bay, Ohio, summer-home last month. She smiled as
she continued pulling it into place. Normally, she didn't like
things to change but she was pleased that she'd finally started
growing. For two years she'd been lamenting her lack of
height, certain she'd never get any taller than four feet eleven.

She glanced down at her chest and hoped that
if she was growing taller, she'd also start growing out, but truly, she didn't feel very optimistic.

Optimistic was her word of the week. She liked
the way it felt as it rolled off her tongue.

Optimistic.

It seemed like such a happy word. And on days like
this, when the beach was this perfect, it was the right
word to describe herself. She was optimistic.

"Caro." Stephan's voice was laced with exasperation.
"Come on. We haven't had a day like this all summer."

He was now down on the beach, waiting for her.

"Caro," he called again, louder, more impatient.

And though she knew they were getting too old for
this game, there was a comfort in it. She might be starting seventh grade in September, but this was familiar
and hadn't changed. She stopped pulling at her yellow
suit, quit playing with words and ran to him. Her bare
feet made a slapping noise on the cement walkway
then quieted as soon as she reached the rocky sand.

"Here comes one." Stephan stood poised, ready to run.

Caro got ready, too. She extended her right leg, bend-
ing at the knee, waiting for just the right moment. She
knew from years of experience, it was all about the right
moment. Too soon, too late … either would ruin the run.

"Go." Stephan sprinted forward and
she followed on his heels.

The wind whipped the marshmallow-puffy clouds
across the sky. Pushing. Pushing. The clouds
bumped into the sun high over head. That was
the moment that signaled they could start

They ran between the rocky cliff and Lake Erie, on the small
swatch of pebbly sand, chasing the edge of the sun's shadow.

Sometimes, if the breeze was lazy enough, they would catch
it. But on days like today, when the wind really kicked up,
they never did. But it didn't matter. The joy was in the chase.

"We lost it." Caro stopped, panting for air.

"There will be another shadow in a few minutes." Stephan,
a year older than she was, had the weight of that extra
twelve-month's wisdom. This time he nodded sagely, his
summer-long hair flopping onto his forehead, and added,
"Yep, everything always changes. We just have to wait,
catch our breath, 'cause there's always another shadow."

Everything always changes. There's always
another shadow, she thought.

Other Holly Jacobs Books

Romance and Romantic Comedy Single Titles
Just One Thing
Same Time Next Summer
Not Precisely Pregnant
Can't Find NoBODY
Hung Up On You
I Waxed My Legs for This?
Her Second-Chance Family

PTA Moms Trilogy
Book 1 Once Upon a Thanksgiving
Books 2 Once Upon a Christmas
Book 3 Once Upon a Valentine's

Words of the Heart series
Book 1 Carry Her Heart
Book 2 These Three Words
Book 3 Hold Her Heart

Cupid Falls series
Book 1 Christmas in Cupid Falls
Book 2 A Simple Heart: A Cupid Falls Novella

Dear Fairy Godmother … series
Book 1 Mad About Max
Book 2 Magic for Joy
Book 3 Miracles for Nick
Book 4 Fairly Human

Everything But … series
Book 1 Everything But a Groom

Book 2 Everything But a Bride
Book 3 Everything But a Wedding
Book 4 Everything But a Christmas Eve
Book 5 Everything But a Mother
Book 6 Everything But a Dog

Maid in L.A. Mystery series
Book 1 Steamed
Book 2 Dusted
Book 3 Spruced Up
Book 4 Swept Up

Perry Square series (A Holly Jacobs Classic)
Book 1 Do You Hear What I Hear?
Book 2 A Day Late and a Bride Short
Book 3 Dad Today, Groom Tomorrow
Book 4 Be My Baby
Book 5 Once Upon a Princess
Book 6 Once Upon a Prince
Book 7 Once Upon a King
Book 8 Here With Me

WLVH Series:
Book 1 Pickup Lines
Book 2 Lovehandles
Book 2 Night Calls
Book 3 Laugh Lines

Whedon Series
Book 1 Unexpected Gifts
Book 2 A One-of-a-Kind Family
Book 3 Homecoming Day
Book 4 A Father's Name

Valley Ridge Series
Book 1 You Are Invited …
Book 2 April Showers
Book 3 A Walk Down the Aisle
Book 4 A Valley Ridge Christmas

Short Stories and Novellas
Able to Love Again
The Book
Labor Day
There He Was
13 Weeks
Bosom Buddies
Cinderella Wore Tennis Shoes

Nothing But … Short Story Series:
Book 1 Nothing But Love
Book 2 Nothing But Heart
Book 3 Nothing But Luck

Love all the books? Try a bundle or boxset!
Short Stories for the Overworked and Under-Read Anthology
Maid in L.A. Mysteries Bundle

www.ingramcontent.com/pod-product-compliance
Lightning Source LLC
Chambersburg PA
CBHW060150180626
46813CB00007B/2690